HAUNTED

A LEXIE STARR MYSTERY NOVEL

HAUNTED

JEANNE GLIDEWELL

FIVE STAR
A part of Gale, Cengage Learning

Detroit • New York • San Francisco • New Haven, Conn • Waterville, Maine • London

GALE
CENGAGE Learning

LIBRARY OF CONGRESS CATALOGING-IN-PUBLICATION DATA

Glidewell, Jeanne
    Haunted : a Lexie Starr mystery novel / Jeanne Glidewell. —
1st ed.
    p. cm.
    ISBN-13: 978-1-4328-2594-2 (hardcover)
    ISBN-10: 1-4328-2594-1 (hardcover)
    1. Starr, Lexie (Fictitious character)—Fiction. 2. Haunted
houses—Fiction. I. Title.
PS3607.L57H38 2012
813'.6—dc23   2012003820

First Edition. First Printing: July 2012.
Published in conjunction with Tekno Books and Ed Gorman.
Find us on Facebook– https://www.facebook.com/FiveStarCengage
Visit our Web site– http://www.gale.cengage.com/fivestar/
Contact Five Star™ Publishing at FiveStar@cengage.com

Printed in Mexico
1 2 3 4 5 6 7 16 15 14 13 12

ADDITIONAL COPYRIGHT INFORMATION

The recipes contained at the back of this book are supplied by the author. The Publisher is not responsible for your specific health or allergy needs that may require medical supervision. The Publisher is not responsible for any adverse reactions to the recipes contained in this book.

Dedicated to my husband, Bob, who has stood by me through thick and thin, even during my darkest hours while I was experiencing several serious health crises. And also to my two stepdaughters, Roxanne Zarda and Stacey Glidewell, for all the joy they have brought to my life, and the beautiful grandchildren they have provided.

ACKNOWLEDGMENTS

I'd like to thank my editor, and wonderful and prolific author, Alice Duncan, of Roswell, New Mexico, and Five Star Publishing for their roles in continuing the Lexie Starr Mystery Series. I'd also like to express my gratitude to all my family and friends for their support of my writing career.

ONE

"Somebody killed the dead guy!" I heard my daughter, Wendy, shout from the parlor, as something large made a loud thud on the floor. "Come quickly, Mom!"

"What? What did you say?" I shouted back. Surely I was suffering from temporary deafness. I removed the earbuds of my iPod so I could hear more clearly. I'd been listening to George Strait and pinning up a graphic of a ghost in the library, when I'd heard the noise.

"Come into the parlor! The young man, Walter I think is his name, is dead. Really dead!" Wendy yelled. "And I mean really, really dead. Stiff-as-a-board dead! I just spoke to him a little over an hour ago, and he seemed fine at the time. Now he's dead."

I really didn't want to hear my daughter say the word "dead" one more time. She had to be mistaken. Walter Sneed was a college kid from here in Rockdale, Missouri. He'd been going door to door last week, looking for part-time work to make a little extra cash to help with college expenses. He'd shoveled snow out of the driveway before, and I knew he was a hard worker, and a good, polite young man.

So we hired him to lie in a makeshift coffin and jump up occasionally to scare young customers as they traipsed through the Alexandria Inn. He wore a vampire costume, complete with fake fanged teeth. He had drops of fake blood all over his shirt, and a part of a wooden stake stitched into his costume to appear as if he'd been stabbed in the heart with it. It was a very realistic-looking, gruesome costume, and I was proud of it.

My boyfriend, Stone Van Patten, had recently purchased the old turn-of-the-century home, and restored it as a bed and breakfast. It had been my idea to turn it into a haunted house during the Halloween season, primarily to promote business at the inn and familiarize the town with the establishment. Ours was the only free haunted house in town. I thought it would be a lot of fun, and the young kids in Rockdale would really enjoy it. But this was certainly not what I had in mind, not by a long shot!

I hurried to the parlor, nearly tripping over a hard plastic tombstone in the process. Wendy must have dropped it when she noticed Walter was not moving, or even breathing. Walter was indeed stiff-as-a-board dead. I'd hoped Wendy was just being melodramatic, even though she wasn't prone to lying, and she was not that great an actress either. At twenty-eight, she was working as a deputy coroner, or assistant to the county coroner in St. Joseph. St. Joseph was just a few miles from our location in Rockdale. Anything we couldn't find in Rockdale, we could find in St. Joseph.

Wendy was scrutinizing Walter's body as it lay prostrate in the coffin. Wendy had a tendency to find death fascinating, particularly if foul play was involved. I hadn't raised her to be so morbid, but then again, I couldn't force her to become a pediatrician as I would have preferred. She'd told me that although she really loved children, she wasn't so wild about them when they were ill. She didn't think there was anything lovable about a child with a nose dripping down into its socks, or a cough that was nearly always directed right at someone's face. Still, I'd dreamed she would save young lives, not cut up ones that couldn't be saved.

"What happened to him?" I asked. After all, finding the cause of death was Wendy's forte, not mine. Surely she could tell by just looking at him what had caused his death.

"Somebody must have killed him."

"How do you know he was killed, Wendy?"

"Well, actually, I don't," she conceded, as disappointment flashed across her face. "But he's awfully young to just up and die like this, don't you think? He didn't seem to be having any pain or discomfort when I last talked to him, which wasn't all that long ago. I asked him if he wanted to take a break for lunch, and he told me he'd already eaten so would just rest while he waited for the haunted house to open back up for business."

"Uh-huh. So what happened to him?" I asked again.

"I'm not sure yet. Nothing obvious stands out. There doesn't seem to be any stabbing or gunshot wounds, and no signs of strangulation," she said, as she looked for ligature marks around his neck. I was a little taken aback at how excited, almost giddy, Wendy sounded.

"Rigor mortis hasn't set in yet, though, so he hasn't been dead very long, Mom. This is unbelievable." Wendy sounded as if she'd just discovered a treasure chest full of gold doubloons, instead of a corpse in the parlor. "Have you got your phone, Mom? We need to call nine-one-one, even though it's too late for him to be resuscitated."

I shook my head, as I had left my phone in the kitchen. I could hear Stone's footsteps coming down the hall and knew he always carried his cell phone in his front pants pocket. He'd no doubt contact the authorities once he was made aware of the situation.

I noticed now Walter's lips looked pale; his skin had a bluish, waxy appearance. He was a tall, thin guy with strawberry-blond hair and a very light complexion. He suddenly looked older than his twenty years. But then, death can do that to a person.

"What's going on in here?" I heard behind me.

I turned to see Stone standing in the doorway, a look of apprehension on his face. His almost translucent light blue eyes looked into mine as he ran his fingers lightly through his silver hair. It took him a little while to speak as he observed us leaning over the coffin.

"Is something wrong with Walter?" he asked. "Is he sick?"

I thought carefully for a few seconds. What was the best way to break this to him? He had already had one man, a guest named Horatio Prescott, killed on the premises not awfully long ago. That untimely murder had occurred on the first night the inn was open for business, which wasn't the best way to celebrate a grand opening. It took a while for the establishment to get over the stigma of being the scene of a violent murder, an extremely rare event in Rockdale. It then took months to begin to build up a clientele. News of another death here at the inn would not sit lightly with Stone, because it would surely cause a stir in this small community.

"He's dead!" Wendy blurted out. Subtlety was not one of her assets.

"Oh, my God! Not again," Stone gasped. "Why do people keep dying in the Alexandria Inn? Is the inn cursed? Poor Walter! He's so young. Was he ill? Wendy, please tell me he was asthmatic and suffered a sudden asthma attack. I've known of people younger than Walter who've died suddenly of aneurysms."

"I wish I could tell you it was probably an aneurysm, Stone," she said, "but I don't think it's very likely he had an aneurysm, asthma, or any other chronic illness. But then again, anything is possible. Professional athletes die suddenly on occasion from a wide variety of causes. Walter seemed like the picture of health to me. He was on the college basketball team, and ran cross-country in high school. He told me that just this morning. He also mentioned he was a strict vegetarian."

"I sure hope some freak ailment killed Walter. Is there any reason to think otherwise? Is there any sign of foul play, Wendy?" Stone asked. He obviously was not interested in the young man's eating habits. As things stood, avoiding meat had not prolonged his life.

"Not as far as I can tell," she said. "There's no apparent reason to suspect there was foul play involved, yet I do suspect it, for some reason."

"Should I try CPR? How long ago did he stop breathing?" Stone asked Wendy. He was still hoping Walter could be saved, could somehow come back from the dead, and the crisis averted.

"I don't know, but it's too late for CPR. He's gone and has been for a while, or I would have already started CPR. We practiced it on dummies in one of my college courses. Feel his skin. His skin is blue, and he's cold as a fish."

"Shouldn't we call nine-one-one?" Stone asked, shock still apparent on his face. Not waiting for a response, he pulled his cell phone out of the pocket of his trousers, and punched in the number. As he dialed, he said to me, "Close down the haunted house. Quickly! Get everyone out of the inn. And don't let any kids into the parlor. Something like this could traumatize them for life. It's traumatic enough for me."

"There are no kids in the house right now, Stone," I assured him. "We're closed for lunch. But we'll put up 'closed' signs and tell any waiting guests we've had to shut down because of an emergency."

"Don't tell them why we had to close down. Just say something important has come up. Be vague if anybody asks. We don't want the news of Walter's death to leak out before the next-of-kin are notified," Stone said.

Wendy and I sprang into action. The Alexandria Haunted

House, which had just opened the previous day, was officially closed for business.

Two

My name is Alexandria Starr, or Lexie for short. I'm a forty-nine-year-old widow, soon to be at the over-the-hill, ripe old age of fifty. My husband, Chester, died when our daughter, Wendy, was seven. I've always felt I did a really good job of rearing her as a single mother. After all, she is a college graduate, has not experienced any out-of-wedlock pregnancies, has never been arrested and, to my knowledge, has only experimented with drugs one time. Having a daughter who smoked one marijuana joint at a prom party certainly doesn't make me a bad mother. And anybody could get two speeding tickets in one week from the same police officer, in the same school zone, with just a stroke of bad luck. All in all, in my unbiased opinion, I have produced a very decent human being, an upstanding citizen, a proud American, and a wonderful daughter. It is probably my biggest accomplishment to date, and one I take great pride in.

I still live part-time in my own home in Shawnee, Kansas, where I had been volunteering as an assistant librarian at a small local library a couple of days each week. It was a nice way to pass my spare time, and it gave me an opportunity to read new books as soon as they arrived at the library. But because of the location of the inn, and because the Alexandria Inn wasn't needing seasonal help currently, I was putting in fewer and fewer volunteer hours at the library. I felt a little guilty about it, but right now Stone needed me more critically than the library did. I hadn't even found time to read a book in weeks. I was lucky to get the newspaper read each morning.

I now spend most of my time in Rockdale with Stone, operating the Alexandria Inn, which Stone had named after me. We aren't married, but we both assume marriage will be the next step in our relationship. Neither of us is quite ready to take that step yet. We are pretty content with the current situation, so why fix something that's not broken?

Stone is a bit older than me at fifty-seven, and we both carry around a few extra pounds on our shorter than average frames. Before moving to the Midwest, Stone had been a jeweler in Myrtle Beach, South Carolina. We'd first met when he helped me replace the charms on a beloved charm bracelet Wendy had lost. Technically we'd met over the Internet, but I hesitate to tell anybody that. It sounds so reckless and irresponsible.

When we first met in person during my trip back east the previous year, Stone told me he'd lost his wife of many years to cancer. Stone and I hit it off almost instantly. Shortly afterward, he sold his business there to be closer to me, and found a way to spend his time and make a little income in a small town within an hour of Shawnee.

The expansive historic home he refurbished into the bed and breakfast of today consists of two upper floors of suites, some with shared bathrooms. On the ground floor there's a large parlor, complete with a grand piano; a dining room with a table that seats twelve people; and an ample kitchen. It also has a huge living room with lots of seating and a television with a fifty-five inch screen. In the rear of the house are three more bedrooms, each with their own bath. A cozy, well-stocked library completes the array of rooms in the inn.

From the outside, the inn still resembles an old-fashioned Victorian mansion, erected in the late 1890s. The palatial home, which was built by a wealthy landowner, had employed a lot of local laborers to complete the structure. It covered half the block, and boasted an immaculate lawn with a fountain, centrally located in the circular driveway, and numerous flowerbeds. Filling the flowerbeds now was a variety of fall foliage, such as chrysanthemums and red salvia plants. Several sugar maples scattered across the lawn had already lost their brilliantly colored autumn leaves.

Like me, Stone was pretty well set financially and didn't have to make a lot of money to get by. His investments provided him with a sizable monthly income. He also carried the mortgage on the jewelry business he'd sold to one of his employees, so he received monthly mortgage checks and benefited from the interest on the loan.

But he needed something to do to keep him busy. He wasn't the type of person to enjoy hobbies, although he occasionally spoke of wanting to take up golf, more for the exercise than anything else. Despite his intentions, he still couldn't tell anybody what a mulligan or a double bogey was. He had yet to beat me in a game of Putt-Putt, and I had a tendency to bounce putts off the cars out in the parking lot.

We held hands now and spoke softly while we waited for the authorities to show up. We were speculating on the circumstances around Walter's demise when we heard a loud rap on the front door. It was the local police responding to our call. Looking out the window I noticed that numerous emergency vehicles now filled up our driveway, from an ambulance to a pumper truck. The entire Rockdale Police Department, and that of several small surrounding towns, must have responded too, judging by the number of cop cars lined up and down the street.

The Alexandria Inn was soon full of uniformed officers who were scouring the parlor for clues. Few were to be found. At first the authorities did not suspect murder, but it could not be ruled out. Wendy, who had suspected murder from the beginning, chatted with her boss, Nate Smith, in the corner. Nate was the county coroner and had already determined Walter had been dead for less than an hour. I'd had to turn away when Nate nonchalantly jabbed a thermometer through Walter's abdomen into his liver. Wendy informed me this was a common way to determine the time of death.

"Hmm. I smell a faint bleach scent, Nate, as if chloroform might have been used," Wendy said, sniffing the air around the plywood coffin. Her voice held an "I-told-you-so" tone I was familiar with from her growing-up years.

Chief Coroner Smith was a few years older than Stone and would be retiring soon. Wendy was being prepped to take his place, which is why she'd transferred from Kansas City, Kansas. There was a better and faster opportunity for advancement in the county coroner's office in St. Joseph. The chief coroner in Kansas City was only a few years older than Wendy and would probably hold the position for many years to come.

"Now that you mention it, I smell bleach too," Nate concurred. "It's barely discernable, but it's definitely there. Good job, Wendy. I just might have overlooked it if not for your keen observation skills."

Wendy was delighted with Nate's compliment. I could see the distinct look of superiority on her face. It was a trait she'd inherited from her father.

Nate turned to the county sheriff who'd just arrived. The sheriff had been out investigating a domestic dispute call on the far end of the county.

"I'd suggest dusting for fingerprints and all that," Nate told the sheriff. "Have your men give it the full-meal deal. I'm thinking, more and more, this could be a crime scene. My assistant detected the faint scent of bleach, and I smell it now too. We think chloroform might have been used on the victim."

Photos were now being taken from every angle, of Walter, the fake coffin, and nearly everything else in the room. An officer drew a circle around a small button he found, under the bench of the grand piano. A small white card, folded in half, was propped up there with the number one written on it. I hated to disappoint him, but I was sure the small button had come off the red cardigan I was wearing earlier. It had popped off while I was setting up props, and after several minutes of searching, I gave up looking for it. It was a non-essential button anyway, since I never buttoned up the sweater.

As soon as the investigative team was finished, the coroner's office would take possession of the body, perform an autopsy on it, and then store it at the county morgue until further notice. Nate obviously wanted to make sure all I's were dotted and all T's were crossed before this occurred. Unfortunately, not much evidence could be found, which would make the difficult task of tracking down a suspect much harder. That's assuming a suspect existed and this really wasn't just some fluke thing like an aneurysm or a heart attack. Walter was young for a heart attack, but such things did happen on occasion.

Maybe the smell of chloroform was just imagined by both Nate and Wendy, even though I never used bleach in the house. Laundry just wasn't my thing, and Stone didn't raise much of a fuss about wearing pink socks and t-shirts. I found myself praying poor young Walter had suffered a massive heart attack, even though that possibility was looking less and less probable.

The local detectives asked Stone, Wendy, and me for the names of all the people we could remember who had passed through the haunted house that morning. It was just barely noon, and among us we came up with a mere handful of names, no more than six or seven. A lot of the people were strangers to us, since we'd only recently become acquainted with the area.

And most of the guests at our haunted house had been small children. Teachers were bringing classes to the inn on field trips, so we often had a line of twenty or more kids at a time. None of them had appeared capable of cold-blooded murder. A few of them looked as though they could commit a number of unspeakable crimes, but certainly not murder. Is there such a thing as an illegal temper tantrum? Assault with a deadly mitten? I saw one boy poke another one in the eye with a green crayon, but that's the extent of any violence I'd witnessed all day.

I noticed one of the detectives standing back in the corner of the room. He'd been involved in the previous case of Mr. Prescott's murder and had been a close friend of ours since. He was a tall, strapping, good-looking young man named Wyatt Johnston. Wyatt could ingest an entire Chinese buffet and not gain an ounce. I had tried to fill him up a couple of times and never could succeed at the challenge. He waved at me from across the room, and I made my way over to speak to him. He'd just ended a conversation with my daughter when I greeted him.

"Any ideas what happened to young Walter?" I asked.

"Not yet," he said.

"Do you think there was foul play involved, Wyatt?"

"The coroner is certain there was, so it looks likely. Wendy told me she suspected foul play from the very beginning. She said she could sense a crime had taken place in this room the moment she stepped in to it."

Wendy would definitely tell Wyatt that kind of thing; it was the portion of her nature she'd inherited from her father coming out in her again. Like Chester, she could be extremely dramatic. She carried a lot of his traits and mannerisms, considering she was such a young child when he died.

Reaching into a pocket inside his jacket, Wyatt extracted a small notebook. He pulled a pen out of his front shirt pocket, and asked me, "Did you see or hear anything unusual before discovering his body? Did you hear an argument taking place or a conversation of any type? Any sounds of a scuffle, perhaps?"

Detective Johnston had asked me those exact same questions the winter before, without much success. He didn't look awfully optimistic this time around either. He merely nodded after I answered in the negative.

"He's much too young for a heart attack, but you never know," he said. "Stranger things have happened. My nephew had heart surgery while still in the womb to avert a major heart problem after his birth. It was unbelievable."

"Yes, it is incredible what they can do these days. Look at how much modern medicine has extended the average life span," I said, instantly feeling remorseful for talking about long life spans when Walter would never even reach the age to drink legally. Wyatt nodded at my remarks and continued to speak.

"Personally, I couldn't make out a bleach scent near the coffin. Nate and Wendy could possibly be mistaken about the chloroform thing, even though they are trained to pick up scents like that."

"I was just thinking along those same lines, Wyatt. Let's hope so, anyway. I'd hate to think another murder has occurred right here in the inn."

"Yeah, me too, and it's certainly plausible he was born with some kind of heart condition. But it could be nearly anything, really. And since Nate thinks chloroform might have been present, there's sufficient reason to process this room as a crime scene and to require a full investigation into the circumstances surrounding Walter's death," Wyatt said. "We should be done here soon, and I'll make sure to let you know anything I find out. The first thing, of course, will be to notify the family. And it goes without saying, but please preserve the purity of the crime scene, at least until the detectives are through scrutinizing it. They may have to come back for further review."

"Of course. I know the drill. Do you know any of Walter's family members?" I asked.

"His mother, Melba Sneed, is an odd woman," Wyatt said. "We get domestic dispute calls to her house every month or so. She gets off her medicine and goes berserk. She has a tendency to get into fistfights with door-to-door salesmen for some reason. She nearly killed a girl scout selling cookies last year. She threatened to bash the poor little girl's head in with her cane. She's one pup short of a litter, but still, she'll be horrified when she learns of her son's death. I heard one of the detectives say Walter's father lives in Albuquerque. Mr. Sneed and Melba divorced several years ago."

"Melba sounds dangerous," I said.

"She can be," he replied. "She is in and out of the mental ward at the hospital all the time. She's been mentally handicapped for years."

"Did Walter have any siblings?"

Wyatt rubbed his chiseled chin for a few moments, and replied, "I know he has a sister in town named Sheila Talley. Why do you ask?"

"Just curious," I said.

"Yeah, right." He chuckled. "I know how you are, Lexie. I promise to let you know anything interesting I discover about the case. And you promise me you'll stay out of trouble. I'm sure our team of detectives can figure out what happened to Walter and make any necessary arrests—yes, even without your assistance."

"Yeah, whatever. Say, there are some homemade pastries in the kitchen. Would you like a couple before you leave?"

"I thought you'd never ask."

THREE

An hour later Stone, Detective Johnston, and I sat around the kitchen table sipping coffee and eating pastries. The team of detectives had finished up, and Wendy had left with Nate Smith to transport Walter's body to the county coroner's office, which was located right next to the county morgue. Naturally, we were discussing the possibilities and circumstances surrounding Walter's death. None of us could believe tragedy had once again struck at the Alexandria Inn. This death was even more tragic than the last one. A young man in his prime had been struck down. Walter should have had a long life ahead of him.

"If it weren't for the Alexandria Inn, Rockdale would never need to borrow officers from St. Joseph's homicide division," Wyatt said. I chuckled, but Stone did not find any humor in the remark. Wyatt noticed Stone's silence and changed his tune. "Seriously, Stone, I really hate that this has happened here again. I couldn't believe it when I got the call from the dispatcher that a dead body had been found here at the inn. I was the first one to respond, not certain who'd been discovered dead on the premises. I shouldn't say this, but I was relieved to see Walter's body lying in the coffin. I didn't want to think something had happened to either of you, or to Wendy."

"I hate it, too, that another death has occurred here. I also hate that we had to close down the haunted house a few days before Halloween. It was going so well," I lamented. "Oh, and I also hate that poor Walter is dead. He seemed like such a nice, quiet, and polite young man. And don't forget, accidental death has not been ruled out yet."

Stone nodded in agreement, and Wyatt snatched another cream puff off the pastry tray. Stone set his cup down on the table and said thoughtfully, "I wonder how this death's going to affect business here at the inn. Our reputation is already a bit shaky after Horatio Prescott was murdered during our grand opening. People are going to start worrying this place really is a haunted house. We've put so much time and elbow grease into the inn. Not to mention money. A death in the first year of operation, much less the first day, is uncanny. But two deaths in the first year? That's just unbelievable. Customers are going to be afraid to stay here."

"I hadn't thought of it that way," I said, although I had thought of almost nothing else since the death was discovered. "Hmm, I wonder—"

"No, Lexie! I don't like the look in your eye or the sound of your voice. I know what you're thinking. I feared this was going to happen. You want to jump into this investigation feet first, don't you?" Stone asked. He had begun to pick his coffee cup up but set it back on the table forcefully. "Don't you, Lexie?"

"No, not really. I just thought we might ask around a bit. Make sure nothing or no one is overlooked. We're intimately involved you know. Walter did die in your establishment. We have the reputation of the inn to protect."

"I've got you to protect," Stone said. "You are my main concern, and my number one responsibility."

"And I appreciate it. I really do. But we've gotten involved in the past and no harm was done."

"No harm was done?" Stone looked at me incredulously. "You were nearly killed several times!"

"Yes, but I wasn't."

"Only by the grace of God you weren't. And speaking of

God, that is why he created policemen like Wyatt. Let them do their jobs, Lexie. I appreciate your concern. Believe me, I do, but I'm more concerned about you than I am about any brick and mortar building. And I don't want to get involved. I have enough to do already, taking care of the inn. The authorities will have a cause of death determined shortly, and if there was foul play involved, a suspect will be apprehended and brought to justice. Case closed. What do you think, Wyatt?"

"I think this cream puff is delicious," Wyatt said. When it came to eating Wyatt had a one-track mind. He picked up another cream puff. It disappeared in two bites. "Can you teach Veronica to make these things, and those cherry tarts you make too?"

Veronica was the only daughter of the late Mr. Prescott and was currently dating Wyatt, with whom she'd reconnected during the ensuing investigation of Horatio Prescott's death nearly a year ago. They'd been classmates in high school, but never dated back then.

After her father's death she'd moved to Rockdale from Salt Lake City, where she'd recently lost the graphic design job she'd held at a local advertising firm. The firm decided to downsize when business slowed down, and they laid off a number of employees. She had the least seniority and was the first to go. Wyatt rehashed the story now to remind Stone and me what had brought Veronica back to Rockdale.

"That was a bad break for her, but it turned out to be fortunate for you, didn't it? You were meant for each other. I'm so glad things have worked out so well for the two of you. How is Veronica, by the way?" I asked.

"She's doing fine. She just landed a new job at a casino in St. Joseph. It isn't really what she was hoping for, but it will do for now. She has her inheritance to live on for the time being, but she'd really like to find another job involving graphic design.

After all, she went to the University of Kansas to earn a degree in that field. She submits an application whenever she hears about an opening in the graphic design field. She'd love to work for a large advertising firm."

"I remember she inherited her father's old place and moved into it. Is she planning to sell it?" I asked.

The magnificent house was an Italianate mansion in the historic region of Rockdale, not far from the Alexandria Inn. Her father, Horatio Prescott, was about to be inducted as the president of the local historical society when he was murdered in our nicest suite. It was a big deal here in Rockdale, a small town that took a lot of pride in its history and quaintness. It was Rockdale's uniqueness that brought a lot of visitors in to town to leave their money in restaurants, gift shops, gas stations, and so on. Antique stores littered Main Street, and these were also popular with tourists. One small company in town offered a tour of homes in the historic region, so passenger vans often stopped in front of the inn while a tour guide narrated, explaining the design and history of the Alexandria Inn.

"I think she's planning to list the home with Sunflower Realty," Wyatt said. "It's too much for her to take care of, and she really has no interest in antiques or historic homes. She'd like something smaller, easier to maintain, like a condo or townhouse. Unfortunately, as you know, the housing market in Rockdale is not at its best right now. There are far more houses on the market than there are buyers wanting to buy them."

"Not only that," Stone interjected. "Credit is easily accessible at banks across the country, so many people are building brand new homes, when they once would have bought an older home in an established neighborhood and fixed it up. Buyers are getting mortgages with little or no down payments. Contractors are building new spec homes, and buyers are getting into bidding wars over them. Subdivisions are popping up everywhere, except in smaller towns like ours. Walnut Ridge Estates is really the only new subdivision in Rockdale. But in places like Johnson County, every plot of vacant land is being sold for a mint and developed into a new subdivision. Eventually the housing bubble will probably burst and people will find themselves upside down in their new homes, owing more for them than they appraise for."

"That's true," I said. "Eventually her historic home will sell, and maybe, in the meantime, Veronica could make a little extra money by taking in boarders, either short-term, or long-term. There's a shortage of rentals in this town, you know, and we do draw a lot of tourists. We haven't done too badly here at the inn so far."

"Good idea, Lexie. I'll suggest it to her when I stop by her place tonight. Are you sure you wouldn't mind a little competition?" Wyatt asked, winking at me over the top of his pastry. He knew the inn was more of a labor of love for us than a quest for money.

"Of course not. There's always room for one more, and her Italianate is ideal for a bed and breakfast," I said. "We'll help her in any way we can. As you know, we have a tendency to fill up in the summer months, and we'd be glad to send customers her way. We'd recommend her bed and breakfast as a substitute."

"That would be so nice of you guys. She might just jump all over an idea like this. She could certainly use the extra money. A place like hers is expensive to maintain," Wyatt said.

"You can say that again," Stone said.

The subject of us doing a little investigating of our own had been dropped, but it wouldn't stay that way for long. Of that, I was certain.

The phone was ringing in the kitchen later that afternoon as I walked in to get a refill on my coffee. I could tell by the caller

ID it was my daughter.

"Hello, Wendy."

"Hi, Mom. How are things going over there?" she asked. "Did the plastic hanging skeleton come to life, or a white-sheeted ghost make off with the silver since I left? The Alexandria Inn is a hotbed of crime, you know."

"No, nothing new has happened here," I told her. She was getting way too much enjoyment out of this terrible situation. "But Wyatt called and said they'd had to take Walter's mother, Melba Sneed, to the hospital again because she became so distraught after hearing the news. Wyatt said she was nearly out of her mind and only half lucid when they first showed up on her doorstep, as if she already knew that something bad had happened. He thinks she might have forgotten to take her meds today, or possibly all week. She forgets to take them regularly, he said."

"I've heard through the grapevine she's a bit off-kilter, even on the best of days," Wendy said.

"Yes, but I still find it disturbing she'd had some kind of premonition about the devastating news she was about to hear before she was told about her son's death. Doesn't that seem a bit odd to you, Wendy? Maybe I'll go up and visit with her tomorrow."

"Oh, boy—"

"I just—"

"Mom—"

"But I—"

"Please tell me you aren't going to get involved in this investigation," Wendy pleaded. "Do you remember what happened, or almost happened, the last time you did that? Granted, everything worked out okay in the end, but the outcome could have been much different. You are lucky to be alive."

"Oh, Wendy, I have no intention of getting involved to that

extent," I said. "I only want to ask a few questions here and there. You know, just to protect the integrity of the inn. Even Stone said he was worried about how the news of Walter's death could affect the business. I feel it's the least I can do."

"Oh, boy—" she said again. "A shiver just ran all the way up my spine. I almost hate to tell you what we found out in the autopsy."

"Oh, tell me," I said, much like a cat in heat in my intensity. "Come on, Wendy, tell me. Please."

"Well, it was chloroform, as we suspected, which was used, presumably to sedate Walter. We found it in the tox screen we ran. The unusual thing is that Walter had a blood sugar reading of nine, which is way, way below normal. The official cause of death was listed as hypoglycemic coma."

"What's the normal range for blood sugar?"

"Generally between eighty and one hundred and twenty, and Walter has no history of diabetes or hypoglycemia. There was a small red puncture mark, a sign of a recent injection, on his lower right anterior abdominal wall. I was the one who discovered it," Wendy stated proudly.

"What does that mean, in layman's terms?" I asked. Wendy could be wordy when it came to descriptions of autopsies. I wanted her to cut to the chase.

"Walter died from a hypoglycemia coma due to insulin shock. Apparently, someone injected him with insulin after they sedated him with the chloroform. He may have known the intruder, and therefore didn't make any noise when he saw him or her come into the parlor. The perpetrator no doubt knew we were in the house and wanted to commit a silent murder so as not to alert us. This would allow him time to sneak out of the house and make a clean getaway, which is exactly what happened. Granted the inn is immense, but we still would have heard Walter shout or scream. He was probably unconscious before he even realized what was happening. A low blood sugar reaction can cause great confusion along with light-headedness."

"Yeah, and he was alone in the parlor most of the day," I said. "We only popped in there occasionally with a group of kids."

"Yes, and think back, Mom. No one but Walter had been in the parlor for over an hour. We had shut the place down for lunch, and you and I had a sandwich in the kitchen and spent the rest of the time rearranging the props in the library and on the back porch."

"I guess someone could have sneaked in the front door and gone into the parlor while we were busy in the back of the house," I said. "It is a huge house. Still, we should have heard any noises coming from the parlor from where the kitchen is located at the back of the house."

Wendy nodded. "But like I said, if Walter knew the intruder and didn't view him or her as a threat, he wouldn't have any reason to shout out. And it wouldn't have taken but a matter of seconds to sedate and inject Walter with the insulin. It was probably a very large dose that took only a matter of minutes to take effect."

"Yes, I guess you're right. Was there anything else interesting you discovered in the autopsy?"

"No, that's about the size of it, although the cause of death is fairly substantial. Isn't that enough to satisfy you for now?"

"Uh-huh. Okay then. Bye, honey," I said, practically hanging up on her in my haste to go tell Stone the news. The subject of doing a little investigating of our own was about to be broached again. Walter's death was officially a homicide.

Sitting at the kitchen table with Stone at dinnertime, I found I had very little appetite for the corned beef and cabbage I'd prepared. Normally, it was one of my favorite meals. Even my much beloved asparagus just got pushed around on my plate, as I thought back to what had happened earlier in the day. While fixing supper, I'd called the hospital to check on Melba's condition and was told she was resting comfortably, under heavy sedation.

I needed to have a reason to leave the inn tomorrow. Stone had indicated he didn't want to be personally involved in the investigation, and I knew he genuinely was busy maintaining the inn and the lawn. He'd also made it clear he wasn't happy about my desire to do a little snooping and prying, so it would be best to keep my own involvement in the case to myself as much as possible, to avoid causing Stone undue stress and anxiety.

Stone had been very open to helping me investigate two murders in the past, but after my life had been threatened in a variety of ways the last time around, he was no longer as willing to get involved as he'd once been. And he didn't want me involved in any way at all, but he knew he couldn't force his will on me, so he tried pleading with me instead. That was only effective to a certain degree.

I caught my reflection in the highly polished serving bowl in the center of the table and realized it was time to have my short brown hair permed again. The span between perms seemed to be getting shorter and shorter. There were still quite a few blond highlights left in my hair, at least. Getting my hair permed would give me a viable excuse to be out and about.

As I looked back up, I caught Stone staring at me. He had noticed I was deep in thought. "Are you thinking about Walter, like I am?" he asked.

"Yes," I said, not wanting to admit I was thinking about making an appointment for a perm. I liked to let Stone believe I was very low-maintenance, even though the maintenance routine was getting more and more complex with each passing year.

Fortunately, Stone was pretty unobservant when it came to my appearance. I could have been wearing a do-rag and an eye patch for all he noticed. Thank God he loved me for all the right reasons and not just my physical appearance. At five-foot-two and 125 pounds, I wasn't exactly model material. But Stone wasn't David Beckham either, and I was glad he wasn't. Excessively handsome men could be excessively vain too, and I loved Stone exactly the way he was: warm and caring, and sensitive to my needs.

"I can't get Walter off my mind," Stone admitted. "I feel so damned bad about him getting killed right beneath our very noses."

"You were outside most of the morning. Did you see anything unusual?" I realized the detectives had already asked him these same questions, but I was hoping to jog a memory he might have forgotten.

"I don't recall anyone pulling into the driveway at around the time of the murder, but then I was in the garden shed out back, tweaking the engine on my lawn mower," Stone said between bites of the new potatoes he was eating. His appetite had not been affected by the untimely death of Walter Sneed. "I did find out, however, that as the mail carrier was dropping off our mail, he spotted someone dressed in dark clothing leaving the front yard on foot. He said the person cut through the hedges into the yard next door as if to get out of sight as quickly as possible."

"How did you find out about that?"

"The mail carrier mentioned something about it to Willard next door when he went up to the house to deliver an Express Mail package. I've already phoned Wyatt to tell him about it."

"Would he be able to give a description of the person or make an identity?" I asked.

"I doubt it," Stone said. "He was busy and didn't think much about it at the time. According to Willard, he only recalled the dark clothing, and that the person seemed to be in a hurry."

As I cleaned up the dishes after supper, Stone watched the television in the front room. He called me into the living room when a piece on Walter's murder was being shown on the evening news. The reporter didn't mention the presumed cause of death or give any other useful information. I'm sure releasing too much information to the public could impede the investigation process, so I was not surprised at the lack of details. I felt a new sense of grief when they showed Walter's senior high school photo. He seemed so young and innocent, like a young man looking forward to a whole life ahead of him. And I knew from talking to him that he'd had a full and rewarding life planned for himself.

I went to bed early that evening. The emotions of the day had left me exhausted. Tomorrow I would begin to see if I could find out something that might lead to the killer. I would be as low key as possible about it, so as not to worry Stone. He had enough on his plate as it was.

FOUR

I called the hair salon early the next morning and was delighted to discover I could get an appointment for eleven o'clock. This appointment would serve two purposes. It gave me a reason to drive downtown, and also I wanted to look good for Walter's funeral, which I knew Stone and I would be expected to attend. But then, I wouldn't miss it for the world.

In the meantime, I wanted to visit Melba in the hospital and see how she was doing and, yes, ask a few prying questions. I don't know what it says about our society, but when a murder occurs, the first suspects who come to mind are those people who were closest to the victim—the spouse, lover, children, and even parents. I can't imagine how a mother could drown her own children in a bathtub, but it happens.

"Can you tell me what room Melba Sneed is in, please?" I asked the receptionist at the information desk. She had a phone in one hand and was pulling something up on her computer screen, using a wireless mouse, with the other. She looked harried and perturbed. She didn't turn to look at me, and I wasn't even sure she'd heard me.

After gazing at her computer screen for a few more seconds, she sighed and replied, "Just a second."

She pulled up a new screen, ran her finger down a list, and said, "She's in the psychiatric ward, room four-sixty-four, ma'am."

"Thank you."

I made my way to the elevators, wondering what I was going to say to Melba, particularly knowing how distraught she was following the news of her son's untimely death. As I neared her room on the fourth floor, I could hear her shouting at a nurse. "I've got to get out of here! What's the matter with you people? Get away from me, lady, before I have to hurt you! Let me talk to the warden!"

I could hear the nurse talking slowly and soothingly to Melba as I entered the room. Melba was clearly not sedated today, at least not yet. The nurse looked at me and shrugged as if to say, "Good luck," and then walked out of the room.

"Melba," I said, "I'm Lexie Starr. I've come to see how you're doing. Is the staff here taking care of you adequately?"

"Get the hell out of my room, unless you're here to release me!" she yelled.

"I just might be able to do that if you will answer a few questions for me." I was lying, of course, but my words calmed her down instantly. This might be her ticket out of here, I'm sure is what she thought.

"I was very fond of your son. Walter was temporarily working for us at the Alexandria Inn to earn a little extra cash."

"Doing what?" Melba said, with indifference in her voice.

"We were hosting a haunted house at the bed and breakfast my partner, Stone Van Patten, owns, and Walter was portraying a vampire lying in a . . . er, in the, uh, well . . . lying in the parlor." Oh my, "lying in a coffin" did not sound like an appropriate thing to say at a time like this. Fortunately she didn't delve any deeper into what her son was doing lying in our parlor.

"Well, whoever you are, I'm glad you are here. Go tell the warden I demand to be let out of here right now! And get me my lawyer while you're at it. I think I might just have to sue somebody."

"Melba, dear, you are in the hospital, not prison. And I don't think you have any need for a lawyer, at least not at this juncture," I told her. "You were very shaken up after the news of your son Walter's death, as anyone would be."

"That unappreciative scamp is no son of mine. If he were, he'd be here right now talking to the warden for me. I never could count on that sorry excuse for a son."

"But he's gone, Melba. He suffered a tragic and untimely death yesterday. I'm sure he would be here if at all possible."

"Yeah, right."

"By the way, Melba, do you know of anyone who would want to kill your son? You surely wouldn't harm your own child in any way, would you? Do you know anyone who might have a grudge against him?" I asked.

"Oh, sure. Who doesn't? I'm a little mad at him myself. Where is that boy, anyway? He should be here helping me. What kind of no-account son is he, anyway?"

It was obvious Melba had a severe mental deficiency. Just how incapacitated was she? I wondered. Could she, in a moment of pure oblivion, perhaps, have done something dreadful to her own son? No, surely not. Once again I wondered how any mother could hurt her own child. I'd slash my own wrists before I'd harm a hair on Wendy's head. And I'm sure the same is true of most mothers. Usually there's no stronger bond than between a mother and her child. But there is always an exception to every rule.

"Say, Melba, where were you yesterday before noon? You don't happen to be diabetic, do you?" I asked. Someone once told me, you should leave no stone unturned when investigating a crime. This theory had worked for me before, so I thought I'd utilize it again. "Have you ever been to the Alexandria Inn? Did you happen to stop by there yesterday? Where were you at about eleven yesterday?"

Melba didn't respond, just looked at me with a hollowness in her eyes I couldn't describe. I felt like I was talking to a hamster. Why did I even bother to ask questions? Melba wouldn't know where she was yesterday if she didn't even know where she was at the moment. I told her to get some rest and left the hospital. My hair appointment was in fifteen minutes.

Finding a parking spot on Main Street near the Klip Joint was next to impossible, so I parked two blocks down the street in front of a nail salon. It was a beautiful autumn day, great for walking. Before I drove off, I would stop in the nail salon and make an appointment for a manicure and pedicure. I'd only recently started having my nails done. In years past, I never even polished my own nails unless it was for a very major occasion. The day I married Chester was actually the only time I could remember offhand.

I was never this high-maintenance before Stone came into my life. Now I even got my teeth cleaned twice a year, like my dentist recommended. What had happened to the lackadaisical lifestyle I'd come to know and love? Sometimes I actually missed it. Being in love could be very exhausting and time-consuming. It could also be a little expensive at times. It was fortunate for me Chester had invested wisely before his death.

I was happy to see Beth was working today; she was my favorite hair stylist at the Klip Joint. Most of the time I had my hair done in Shawnee by a stylist I had used for years. I agreed to wait for Beth to finish up the customer she was currently working on. It looked like the customer was only getting a wash and style.

I grabbed a *People* magazine and took a seat next to a heavy-set woman about my own age in the waiting area. I needed to catch up on all the celebrity gossip in Hollywood, and the scandals going on in Washington, D.C., not to mention the current fashions, as if current fashion trends would ever affect my jeans and t-shirt wardrobe. In this new high-maintenance routine of mine, I drew the line at giving up my comfortable clothing.

"How are you today?" the heavy-set woman asked.

"Fine," I answered politely. "And you?"

"Not too bad. I'm here for a cut and style. I have a wedding to go to tomorrow. It's in Leavenworth, you see. My nephew is finally getting hitched to this woman he's gotten knocked-up. I didn't think I'd live to see the day he'd bite the bullet and settle down with a wife and kid."

She laughed, so I smiled back at her in return. It was obvious I wasn't going to be able to read the magazine any time soon, so I took a deep breath and replied, "How nice. I'm here to get a perm. My name's Lexie, by the way. It's nice to meet you."

"I'm Nadine. It's nice to meet you too, Lexie. Say, did you hear about that Sneed boy? Melba's son? I heard at the pharmacy he died, or was killed or something."

"Yes, you're right. Yesterday, about this time in fact. It happened at my boyfriend's inn, actually," I told her, for no good purpose. Too late it occurred to me it would be better to leave the inn entirely out of it. Telling Nadine anything might be akin to telling the story to the town crier. She obviously enjoyed gossiping, and spreading rumors was probably one of her favorite pastimes.

"What happened to him? Was he murdered?" Nadine's voice rose an octave as her second and third chins rippled dramatically.

"It looks that way," I admitted. "The autopsy showed evidence of foul play, though no one can fathom a motive. Who would want to kill a nice young man like Walter?"

"Maybe that long-time, slutty girlfriend of his, Chelsea—no, I think it's Cindy, or something of that nature. I heard their relationship has been shaky recently."

I laid my magazine down on the table, no longer interested in who was sleeping with whom in Hollywood these days. Nadine seemed to have an inside track to the local grapevine, and I wanted to pump her for as much information as I could before Beth called me back to the shampoo basin.

"Tell me more." I turned toward her to give her my full attention.

"Well, they'd been going together for over three years, I take it, when this girlfriend found out Walter had gotten hooked up one night with one of her archenemies."

Archenemies? Who was this girl? Cat Woman? Nadine was being a little melodramatic, but I encouraged her to continue.

"A nasty breakup ensued, as you can well imagine. Both girls were on the cheerleading squad at the community college and ended up getting into a catfight right in the middle of campus. God, I would have loved to see that one," Nadine said. I could see she thoroughly enjoyed passing on the scuttlebutt she'd collected through gossip. Whether or not there was any truth to what she was telling me remained to be seen. Still, I kept pumping.

"And then what happened?"

"Then Walter cut off ties with both of them and went out with yet another coed at the college, pissing both of the girls off. I heard this other date was with a girl named Roxie Kane. I know the girl's mother. In fact, I think Roxie's mother used to cook at the Red Rooster Café downtown. But, anyway, last I heard, this Cindy gal and Walter were trying to work things out."

"Do you know how I can find out the names and addresses of either or both of those girls you mentioned?" I asked. I could hear Beth calling my name from what seemed like a million miles away. I continued to look into Nadine's eyes with intensity.

Who knew I could obtain such valuable information at the hair salon?

"Huh? Why would you want to do that?" She asked.

"Lexie, I'm ready for you now," Beth called.

I waved my hand in a "just a moment" gesture and said, "Well, uh, I'm somewhat involved with the investigation, you see. It did happen at my boyfriend's inn, you know, which makes me intimately involved. I'd like to speak with the girls, if possible. I've been known to help the police department solve crimes before."

"Lexie—" I heard in the distance. Beth could be so persistent and annoying.

"Oh, I see. No, I'm afraid I can't tell you their names or addresses. I don't really know any of them. But I do know the cheerleading squad practices on Wednesday nights and Saturday mornings in the college's gymnasium."

"Thanks, Nadine." Bingo! I got the answer I needed on how I might locate this Cindy gal, Walter's long-time girlfriend.

"Good luck, Lexie," Nadine said as I walked back to the washbasin.

I made a nail appointment for later in the week, and then drove around the college campus on my way home. I found the gymnasium without any problem. Tomorrow was Saturday, and I planned to get up bright and early so I wouldn't be late for cheerleading practice. I'd been a high school cheerleader myself, but that now seemed a hundred years ago. I hadn't gone on to college, marrying Chester right out of high school. We'd begun dating in ninth grade, so Stone was really only the second man in my life. And there had been a long, dry period in between them. I'd been reluctant to start a relationship with another man, but I couldn't help falling in love with Stone. A widower himself, he had felt the same way. We hadn't gone looking for love; love had come looking for us. Now I was extremely glad it had found us.

I stopped by the grocery store next and bought several bags worth of non-perishable items, stashing the full bags in the back seat of my Jeep. I would need to walk into the inn with them tomorrow after an imaginary visit to the market. I'd want another excuse to leave the house for a while. Sometimes it was best not to tell Stone every little detail of my day. We got along better that way, and my little omissions seemed to keep his blood pressure down to a tolerable level. Since he wasn't exactly thrilled about my decision to participate in the investigation, the less he knew of the extent of my involvement, the better. I didn't like lying, but being the impulsive creature I am, not divulging the whole truth was sometimes in my best interest.

I wasn't surprised to find Detective Johnston in the kitchen with Stone when I returned home. I was even less surprised to find him wolfing down a huge bowl of chili from the pot I'd prepared before leaving for my hair appointment.

Stone stood up and kissed me, and Wyatt, with his mouth full, nodded and winked. As it was nearly noon, I dipped out a cup of chili myself and sat down at the table. I was anxious to see what had brought the detective to the inn.

"Any new developments, Wyatt?" I asked.

"Not really," Wyatt said, after swallowing a mouthful of chili. Wyatt tended to eat like a rottweiler tearing through a raw rump roast. He had an insatiable appetite, but no sign of one molecule of fat on his large frame. He must have a membership at the local gym, I decided. "We've mostly been notifying relatives this morning. The story leaked out to the media before we could locate everyone, and that's never a good thing. Nobody wants to hear their loved one has been murdered on the evening news."

"Yeah, that would be awful," I agreed. "What other relatives could be found, other than Melba?"

"Like I said before, Walter has a sister living here in Rockdale, just west of the historical district. Her name's Sheila Talley. We also found out he has a half-brother, Chuck Sneed, who lives in Chillicothe, which is on Thirty-Six Highway, straight east of here," Wyatt said for Stone's benefit, since Stone hadn't lived here long enough to be thoroughly knowledgeable about the area. "Walter's father, Clarence Sneed, was married to Chuck's mother prior to being married to Melba. Chuck's biological mother is dead now, and Clarence lives in Albuquerque, New Mexico. Chuck's a few years older than Walter or Sheila."

"I'm sure Sheila and Chuck were shocked and dismayed by the news," I said.

"Not really," Wyatt said. "They took the news pretty matter-of-factly, the chief of police told me. He was surprised by their lack of emotion, in fact. Close family ties do not seem to be a feature of the Sneed clan. They're your typical dysfunctional family."

"Could either Chuck or Sheila have a possible motive for getting rid of their brother?" I asked.

"The local police are looking into it," Wyatt said. "Both stood to inherit quite a bit of money from Melba, which they would naturally have had to split three ways. Melba owns the small home she lives in and had received a sizable sum from her husband, Clarence, in the divorce settlement. Clarence owned the local lumber mill downtown for many years before moving to Albuquerque to start a new business. The lumberyard sold for a pretty penny to a group of investors, so Clarence is apt to leave the kids a substantial amount of money, as well. For such a screwed-up, dysfunctional family, they are not without means."

"I guess greed can be a powerful motive," Stone said. "Probably second only to jealousy and/or retribution."

"Yes, unfortunately. Money is the root of all evil, they say. It's been the driving force behind more murders than any of us can imagine, I'm sure," Wyatt said. "And it can tear a family apart too, particularly when an inheritance is involved."

"I suppose you are planning to speak to Sheila and Chuck, aren't you?" Stone directed his question at me. Knowing the answer without waiting for me to reply, he continued. "I know you better than you think I do, Lexie. And I'm not sure it's such a wise idea, particularly if one of them is capable of murdering their own brother. Wyatt has said the police are looking in to it, so I can't see any reason for you to do so also."

"We'll see—" I said, jumping up to grab the coffee carafe. "Would anyone like a refill?"

"No, but thanks for the offer. I've got a pretty full schedule today, what with the murder and all. So I guess I better get back to work." With that Wyatt stood up, tipped his hat at us, and walked out the door leading to the back porch. "Later."

I spent the next couple of hours putting away the haunted house props and setting the inn back in order. I was disappointed the haunted house idea hadn't gone as planned. Stone had convinced me it wouldn't be in good taste to reopen it, considering the circumstances. People would be thinking the place might really be haunted from the souls who passed on here.

As instructed, I left everything in place in the parlor. More investigating of the crime scene might be necessary, I'd been told. But every time I glanced at the coffin I got the willies. I found it less traumatic to walk the long way around the house to avoid the parlor entirely.

We didn't have any guests currently staying over at the inn. But we did have a couple from Oregon due in the next afternoon, and I needed to get the inn ready for them. We didn't have a housekeeper/chef on the payroll because autumn wasn't the busy season at the inn. We would be hiring one in the spring when business picked up again.

Our new guests, the Dudleys, were coming to town tomorrow for a family reunion to be held the following weekend, and they planned to make a vacation of it. I spent a few minutes setting their room up for them. I put fresh bedclothes on the bed, dusted and vacuumed the room, and placed a fresh bouquet of fall flowers in a vase on the slide-out shelf of the armoire, next to the TV. Antique furniture complemented the four-poster bed, the Belgian lace curtains, and the age-old feel of the room. Although the inn had quite a number of rooms and suites, this was my favorite in the house. I always assigned it first, before using any of the other ones.

At this point I was tired of housework and went downstairs to pour myself a cup of coffee and look through the daily *Rockdale Gazette* that Howie Clamm had delivered earlier that morning. I went out on the back porch for a much-needed break. It was a bit chilly, so I grabbed my jean jacket on the way out. The back porch was inviting with its long flower planter, filled with bright orange mums, that ran around the far edge of it, and its comfortable outdoor lounge chairs. I needed frequent caffeine fixes, and this was where I usually took my breaks.

I sat my cup down on the wrought-iron table and opened the paper. As I'd expected, Walter's face was plastered all across the front page. Under what appeared to be a picture of him taken during a basketball game, the headline read, "History repeats itself! Local man killed at Alexandria Inn—again!"

Oh, swell. Stone's nightmare had come to life. There's nothing like free advertising in the city newspaper. I'm sure this headline would encourage Rockdale's citizens to recommend our inn to their families and friends. The thought made me more determined than ever to find out what was behind the death of young Walter Sneed. How dare the reporter be so flippant when a young man's life had been taken, and a perfectly respectable lodging establishment's future was at stake?

The article following the headline told me little more than I already knew. The only tidbit of new information I garnered from it was that Walter's father, Clarence, was in town from Albuquerque, and had been for over a week. Hmmm. This seemed like an odd coincidence. I wondered what, if anything, Clarence might stand to gain from the death of his son. Nobody was beyond suspicion, the way I saw it. History would prove more fathers killed their own children than mothers did. Men were just naturally more physical and violent than women in most instances.

Apparently, Clarence now owned a company called Sneed Heating and Cooling in the Sandia foothills of Albuquerque. Isn't late October a busy time for a business that deals with furnaces? Granted, Albuquerque had a milder climate than Rockdale, but people who lived there still had occasional use for their furnaces. October seemed like the ideal time to have a furnace serviced, repaired, or replaced, right before cooler weather set in. Why would Clarence take time off from his work now to come back to Rockdale? He'd divorced Walter's mother several years earlier. Could his visit possibly have something to do with his son's death? I made a mental note to check out this possibility.

I'm sure Clarence was being questioned thoroughly by the detectives, but I wanted to talk to him too, if I could find him. I might just pick up on some clue the police overlooked. Finding Sheila Talley was probably the easiest and fastest way to find Clarence, and she was another person who might benefit from Walter's death. I'd hoped to talk with her, anyway.

Sheila lived in Rockdale, I recalled Detective Johnston saying. I also recalled him saying she wasn't particularly upset about the news of her brother's death. Maybe I could find her number and address in the phone book and pay her a visit. If she happened to be unlisted, I could contact the local funeral home. There was only one such establishment in the town of Rockdale. I was, obviously, interested in the funeral arrangements, considering that Walter's death occurred in the Alexandria Inn.

FIVE

Saturday morning brought cloudy, misty weather, and I woke up wondering if cheerleading practice would still be held over at the small college campus. I knew I'd be there, one way or the other, to make sure I didn't miss an opportunity to talk to Walter's girlfriend and maybe even his ex-girlfriend.

I needed to think of a ploy that sounded reasonable to explain my presence at the practice. Just being a former cheerleader myself a hundred years ago didn't warrant a visit to their practice. I knew I could come up with something plausible though. The ability to create schemes and execute them was one of my best, and worst, traits.

While I mulled this over, I checked the guest record to make sure the Dudleys were not due in until mid-afternoon, poured myself a cup of strong, black coffee, and headed out to the front porch to sit and relax before it was time to leave for the college. The sun had broken out for a few minutes and I wanted to take advantage of it. The front porch was in full sunlight, and the warmth from the sun felt good on my skin. The shaded back porch was still a bit too chilly this morning.

Stone had repaired his lawn mower as best he could, and was making a circular route around the front yard on his John Deere. He loved mowing, and he enjoyed tinkering with his lawn equipment. He mowed every time he could reasonably justify it. He waved and I waved back as I watched him make cornrows of mulched leaves. I could tell he was having fun.

It suddenly occurred to me that if I hurried, I could make my exit without having to discuss my plans with Stone. Then I wouldn't have to come up with any long-winded half-truths that could only come back to haunt me in the future. As I have always maintained, it is easier to ask forgiveness than permission in most instances, particularly instances that involve me.

I nearly burnt my throat as I took huge gulps of coffee. I probably should have just poured the remaining coffee down the drain and headed out, but I knew I couldn't proceed without my caffeine fix.

Just a few minutes later I ran out the back door, fired up my yellow Jeep Wrangler, and pulled down the driveway with one final wave to Stone. He looked at me quizzically as he waved back in return.

"Excuse me, ladies. Is one of you here named Chelsea or Cindy, or something like that?" I asked the group of sullen-faced girls I had found in the end zone of the school's football field. I had walked around the campus after discovering the gymnasium was locked up. For a while I'd feared the practice had been canceled. Clouds again filled the sky, and there was a slight feel of moisture in the air.

I noticed all but one of the girls had long blond hair tied back in a ponytail. All of them were thin, nearly emaciated, and wore red and white sweatpants to match their cheerleading jackets. By their perfectly straight, bright white teeth, I could tell they'd all run up high dental and orthodontic bills in their pasts. I was also aware they'd all heard of Walter's passing by the frequent tears, mixed with gossipy chatter, and the shocked expressions on all of their faces. Cheerleading seemed to be the farthest thing from their minds. No one seemed to notice my presence until I spoke out.

"My name is Sidney. Sidney Hobbs," one girl volunteered.

50

Her eyes were watery and nearly swollen shut. "And it's probably me you're looking for. Walter Sneed, the guy who was just murdered, was my boyfriend. Oh, God, I just can't believe he's gone. I loved him so much. Oh, God—"

With that, Sidney burst into a new round of tears, sobbing so hard she ended up on her hands and knees, pounding the ground as if a hill of attacking fire ants had just invaded her space. I wasn't sure if I'd find out anything from Sidney while she was so overcome with grief. The possibility appeared remote.

"What do you need?" Another girl asked me. She was the only brunette in the bunch. "I'm Sidney's best friend, Paula Browne, and maybe I can help you. I know as much as anybody, I'd reckon. At least I can try to help you as best I can."

"Well, maybe you can, Paula. I'm Rhonda Reed, a contributing writer for the *Rockdale Gazette,* and I've been assigned to do an article about the recent murder. It's kind of an investigative report. I've been told Walter is, er, I mean was, Sidney's boyfriend, and therefore I'd like to interview her for the article."

After my slip of the tongue I now had the entire gaggle of girls crying and felt like I was losing ground rapidly. Waiting patiently for Paula to compose herself, and grasping her upper arm, I led her away from the group.

"I thought you were probably with the media," Paula said. I had never really thought of the little *Rockdale Gazette,* or any of its writers, as being "part of the media," but at least she hadn't called me a member of the paparazzi.

"Let's talk over here, Paula." She nodded her head as I continued. "As Sidney's best friend, I assume you are privy to what goes on in her social life, her private life, even her love life."

"Yes, pretty much. She tells me everything, as I do her."

"Were Walter and Sidney getting along? Have they been on good terms recently?"

"Very good. They've always been extremely close, but since they got back together they've been tighter than ever. They went to a party at my dorm together just the night before he was killed. They were like soul mates," Paula said dreamily. "Everybody envied their relationship. We all knew they'd eventually get married."

"Do you know where Sidney was the day after the party, the day of Walter's demise? Can she account for her whereabouts at the time the murder occurred?" I asked. Maybe Paula was not aware of an argument the on-again, off-again, lovestruck pair had engaged in after the party. Perhaps Walter had broken it off with Sidney again. According to Nadine at the beauty shop, the couple's relationship did seem to be on a rocky footing lately, so anything was possible. If he'd been caught cheating on her, twice, I should think there had to be some lingering tension between the pair.

"Oh, my God, Rhonda!" Paula exclaimed. "Is Sidney a suspect? That's just not possible. She would never hurt Walter. She loved him with all her heart and was so excited they'd been able to patch things up after a rough spell in their relationship."

"Oh, no, I didn't mean to infer she was a suspect. I'm just trying to cover all the bases for my article. I'm sure the police do not list her as an official suspect at all. They haven't arrested anybody yet."

"Well, I sure hope they won't consider Sidney as a suspect, because I can tell you it's impossible. Sidney was with me. All day, in fact. We'd gone to the Legends area, over by the Kansas Speedway, in Kansas City, Kansas. We were shopping for new shoes and winter coats at the stores there. Sidney's dad had given her two hundred dollars to spend and even gave me a one hundred dollar bill. He suggested we make a day of it. We were thrilled, as you can imagine. So we found her a pair of black Crocs and this cool navy blue parka, and I got a pair of Crocs like hers, in brown, and a new windbreaker. Then we ate lunch at Jazz and went to see a movie afterward," Paula said. "We didn't get back home until late in the evening, so I can vouch for her whereabouts the entire day. Not to mention, she talked about how much she loved Walter all day long."

"That's good. Not that anyone suspected her of doing anything wrong. How long had the two been dating?" I asked.

"I'm not sure exactly, but over three years at least. I've known Sidney for three years, and she was going with him when we first met. They started going together in high school, the summer before their senior year, I think. They broke up for a few weeks recently, but they worked it out and made up. Like I said before, they are closer than ever now."

"What happened to cause the recent rift in their relationship?"

"Well, I don't know what made Walter do it, but he went out with Audrey McCoy one night. Sidney and Audrey have always hated each other, and I imagine Audrey coerced him just to get to Sidney. The two bicker constantly on the cheerleading squad, which makes it hard to get anything done at our practices. We all wish Audrey would just quit the squad, because nobody likes her very much. She's a hothead and a royal bitch. Now she's the one who ought to be considered a suspect! She was really ticked off when Walter got back together with Sidney."

"I'm sure she's on the list," I said sincerely. She was definitely on mine. "Do you have any idea where Audrey was at the time of the murder?"

"No, but it wouldn't surprise me if she was at that bed and breakfast place, killing Walter. I don't know how much she really cared for Walter, but I do know she would do about anything to hurt Sidney. They've been rivals since Sidney beat out Audrey in a run for class president. The campaign was brutal, but Sidney won by a landslide in a class vote. Like I told you, nobody likes Audrey very much."

"Is Audrey here today?"

"No, which also makes me wonder if she could be responsible for—"

"Do you know where she lives?" I asked, cutting off her train of thought. I had been thinking along the same lines myself.

"Well, I've never been to her house, but I do know she doesn't live anywhere close to the campus, maybe not even in Rockdale anymore. She moved out of her parents' house as soon as she graduated from high school. She and her dad didn't get along," Paula said. "I'm sure she's in the phonebook. Or you could contact her mother, Norma McCoy, and get the information from her."

"What kind of person is Audrey, other than competitive?" I asked.

"She wasn't much of a student in high school, barely passing most of her classes. Her grades were just barely high enough to graduate. I couldn't believe when she enrolled in this community college. She doesn't have many friends, kind of keeps to herself most the time. She's not really the cheerleader type at all. And Audrey has a terrible hair-trigger temper. She's into it with somebody all the time, but usually it's Sidney. They absolutely despise each other," Paula explained. "They've clashed since the day they met."

"How about the other gal? Roxie something. Do you know where she lives?" Paula didn't seem to question the fact I knew all about Walter's love life, including the name of his most recent one-time date. "What was her last name again?"

"Kane. No, I have no idea where she lives. I don't really know her, or anything about her. She's a student here at the college, though, I do know that much. I've seen her a couple times in the anatomy lab. I still can't believe Walter went out on Sidney with that girl. That nearly slammed the door shut on his relationship with Sidney. If she didn't love him so much, she would have never taken him back after he went out one night with Roxie Kane."

"Thank you very much, Paula, for all your help. I appreciate you taking the time to talk with me," I said. I felt I'd gotten all the useful information I was apt to get for the time being, and I needed to get home and put away the non-perishable items I'd bought yesterday as if I had just purchased them this morning. Mostly, I was just stocking up on paper products and cleaning supplies. The cupboards were already full of food products.

I still wanted a one-on-one with Sidney, but it would have to wait. I looked over at the rest of the cheerleaders to see if Sidney was still bawling, but I couldn't spot her. The girls were talking among themselves, but Sidney wasn't in the group.

"Glad I could help, Ms. Reed," Paula said, heading back toward her friends.

Later that afternoon, I called Sidney Hobbs' home after looking up her number in the phone book. Her father answered the phone. I explained I was Rhonda Reed, investigative reporter, and I was writing an article for the local newspaper. I needed to ask his daughter just a few simple questions and promised I would make it quick.

"Didn't I see you driving out of the parking lot at the college campus when I went to pick up Sidney from her cheerleading practice this morning? Sidney told me there was a reporter at the practice. Was that you?" he asked. He didn't sound too pleased about it.

"Yes, that was me. I spoke with her friend, Paula, because Sidney was in no shape to speak with me at the time. Is she available now?"

"No, she still isn't in any condition to speak with anyone regarding Walter's death, especially reporters. She's devastated, as you can well imagine. That's why she had called me to pick her up early," Mr. Hobbs said.

"But I was under the impression practice hadn't even begun when I left."

"She called me to pick her up early because she couldn't function enough to participate in practice. She's still enduring a lot of anguish and pain, and I absolutely refuse to let the media hound her, which could only cause her more suffering. She knows nothing about the young man's death and has nothing to say, so please leave this family alone." Mr. Hobbs hung the phone up rather noisily, which I thought was quite rude under the circumstances.

I would surely get an opportunity to speak with Sidney in the next few days, at least when her parents weren't around to protect her. I could understand why they didn't want the media involved. Their daughter had already been through enough. But a few simple questions couldn't hurt her much, could they? Did she have something to hide? Did her parents think she might have something to hide? Could they be right? Was that why they were shielding her? Did she go shopping with Paula that day to have something to use as an alibi while someone else did the dirty deed for her? I would have to steal a few minutes of her time, one way or another.

Six

"I got the lawn all mowed, Lexie. The lawnmower is still not running properly, but it's probably the last time this season it'll need to be done. I noticed the trees have already lost most of their leaves. I think I'll do some fertilizing today too, on the front lawn, at least. What have you been up to this morning?"

"Oh, you know. Groceries and such."

"Uh-huh. Have you heard from Wyatt or anyone? When are our guests due to arrive? Are you ready for them? Is there anything I can do to help?" Stone asked me when he came in from outside. He sounded like my daughter, firing one question after another at me. This reminded me I did need to call Wendy in case she'd learned anything new on the murder case.

"Just picked up some things from the store," I replied. "And no, I haven't heard from anyone yet today. I was just getting ready to bake some apple tarts for dessert tonight. The Dudleys are due here in a couple of hours. I'm baking a pork roast to serve with fried potatoes and fresh green beans for supper tonight."

"That sounds great. I'll grill us all some steaks tomorrow night," Stone said. "The rib eyes are on sale at Pete's Pantry this week. I'll pick up several extra packages to freeze for later on. Did you buy any meat this morning?"

"No, I bought mostly paper products today. We were running low on toilet paper and paper towels. I also bought several bags of candy to hand out to trick-or-treaters."

The Alexandria Inn was billed as a bread and breakfast but offered much more. Breakfast was served, as well as dinner, in the formal dining room. Tea or coffee, and an afternoon snack was also available in the parlor, at least when coffins and/or dead vampires were not on display in that room. I even served lunch when the occasion called for it.

Free museum excursions and walking tours were offered, as well as shuttle service to nearby casinos and shopping areas. I'd led groups through the local museums more times than I cared to count. Other personalized arrangements could be made, as well. We did whatever we could to ensure we had thoroughly satisfied guests in hopes they'd return often, and would also encourage others to visit our establishment. It was basically an all-inclusive inn, with Stone and me, and our seasonal help, taking care of every want or whim our customers could come up with. It wasn't even unusual for us to lend out our personal vehicles.

Stone joined me in the kitchen for a cup of coffee and a piece of a store-bought crumb cake I'd just brought in from my Jeep, before heading back outside to clean up his mower and park it back in the maintenance shed. I was relieved my whereabouts that morning never came up in conversation again. I rinsed off our dishes and placed them in the dishwasher as Stone stood up to leave.

"Why did I install a brand new dishwasher if you insist on washing the dishes before you put them in the dishwasher?" he asked me in jest.

"I'm just rinsing off the chunks of food so they don't clog up the pipes. I'm not actually washing them, and you know it," I answered playfully, as I snapped the back of his jeans with my damp dishtowel. "Now get your buns out of my kitchen!"

As soon as Stone left, I picked my cell phone up off the counter and dialed Wendy. She answered on the first ring. She was living in a small apartment in St. Joseph, but spent many evenings with Stone and me at the inn. She even occasionally spent the night with me in Shawnee. She claimed to get very lonely in her studio apartment. She'd always been a very social person, unlike me, who enjoyed time alone now and then. Having less personal time had been one of the adjustments I'd had to make when I became involved with Stone. Now I missed his company when I was by myself.

"Were you just sitting around waiting for the phone to ring?" I asked Wendy.

"Actually, I was just getting ready to call you when it rang," Wendy said. "What's up?"

"Not much," I answered. I didn't mention my morning episode with the cheerleaders, as she could be as annoyingly protective as Stone. "Have you learned anything new about Walter's murder?"

"No, I was just going to ask you the same thing. I thought maybe you'd heard from the police department. I know Wyatt stops by the inn just about every day."

"That's because I bake fresh pastries just about every day," I said, with amusement in my voice. Wendy knew I was very fond of the detective, and she liked him a lot too. If she weren't so infatuated with Stone's nephew, Andy, who lived on the east coast, she probably would have been interested in dating Wyatt. But Wyatt had not been on the market since Veronica had come back into his life.

Wendy still spoke with Andy nearly every day. She'd met him shortly after I met his uncle, Stone. He'd flown back several times in the following months, and Wendy and Andy spent much of his time here together.

"Yes, I'm sure that's part of it, but I also know Wyatt enjoys visiting with you and Stone. It gives him something to do when police business is slow in Rockdale. Fortunately, random murders, like that of Walter, are very rare in your neck of the woods. Not that they are all that frequent here in St. Joseph."

"Yes, well, at least they were rare in Rockdale until the Alexandria Inn opened for business, according to Wyatt."

"The inn did liven up the police department, didn't it? Before long the Rockdale Police Department will need its own homicide division," Wendy said.

"You sound just like Wyatt now."

Wendy chuckled over the phone. "Well, I've got to take my car for an oil change this afternoon so I'll let you go for now. Give me a ring if anything comes up."

"Okay," I said. "You do the same."

I glanced at the clock as I heard a car pulling up in the driveway. It was ten minutes after three, so I knew the Dudleys had arrived. Eleanor Dudley had informed me on the phone they expected to arrive no later than four in the afternoon. I'd just placed the pork roast in the oven, and now I quickly turned the tea kettle on so the water would be warmed up by the time Eleanor and Steve Dudley had stowed their luggage and washed up. I didn't know if they preferred tea or coffee, so I was prepared for either case.

When I stepped out on the back porch to greet them, I noticed Detective Wyatt Johnston talking to Stone over by the maintenance shed. Stone was pouring fertilizer into a walk-behind spreader. I was anxious to see if Wyatt had anything new to report. His friendship with Stone was just one more reason I appreciated him. He gave Stone someone to buddy around with.

I quickly led the Dudleys to their suite. As the only guests, they were ensconced in the nicest suite on the second floor. Tea was their preference, so I told them it would be served whenever they were ready for it. They could take their time unpacking and freshening up from their long day on the road. I was trying, unsuccessfully, to keep my eyes off an unsightly growth on the side of Mrs. Dudley's chin. It was the size of a quarter and had sprouted something that reminded me of a Chia Pet I'd once owned.

The rest of Eleanor's face bore a week's worth of boldly colored makeup, taking away from the brilliance of her strikingly beautiful blue eyes. She was shaped very much like a pear, with almost no shoulders, and a butt that spanned the entire width of the suite's door. She wore a white tennis dress, stretched taut across her backside, and spiked white heels with shiny sequins across the top. Had no one told her you shouldn't wear white after Labor Day? And you really shouldn't wear any color of spiked heels with a too-tight tennis dress. I could hardly wait to see what she chose to wear to their family reunion the following weekend.

At least Steve Dudley, in comparison to his wife, was very bland and average in appearance. He was the type of person you could talk to for an hour, and then not recognize the next day. He kind of blended in with the woodwork, but he seemed like a very nice gentleman.

I got the Dudleys settled into their suite and made a beeline for Wyatt and Stone in the backyard. As I approached, I could hear them discussing the intricacies of a 200-horsepower Mercury motor. I stood silently for a minute or so, trying to appear interested as Wyatt told Stone about his new Ranger bass boat. I failed miserably and lost my patience with the present conversation. Needing a segue, I leapt at the first opportunity I could grasp.

"Thrust?" I asked innocently. "Did you say something about thrust? Speaking of thrust, Wyatt, I'm so sorry another murder case has been thrust upon you. Oh, yeah, and about that, have you heard anything new on the case?"

"Well, we've been interviewing relatives, and the few adult visitors to the haunted house you could remember," Wyatt Johnston said. "None of them have had much input. None claim to have any involvement in the murder or have any information about it to relate. Most of the haunted house visitors had never even heard of Walter Sneed."

"I'm sure that's true," I said. "Most were young mothers, or grade school teachers."

"As you may already know, Walter's mother, Melba Sneed, is still in the hospital. She's become even nuttier than ever, impossible to question. When the name 'Walter' was mentioned by a detective, she thought he was the housekeeper. She asked if he could come sweep under her bed. She was sure she'd heard sounds of mice scurrying beneath the bed, and wanted to assure there were no food scraps scattered about that would attract more varmints.

"It appears her mental state has become completely unstable in her grief and anguish," Wyatt said, with compassion in his deep voice. "I hope she can come around enough to attend her son's funeral. I think I read in the paper it's scheduled for Wednesday morning at ten, with a wake Tuesday evening."

"Where will it be?" Stone asked.

"I have no idea, I've forgotten what the paper said," Wyatt said. "But I could—"

"I know where," I interrupted. "I called the funeral home this morning. The visitation will be held at the Catholic Church at Fourth and Cyprus, from six to eight. Walter will be laid to rest at St. Mary's Catholic Cemetery, directly behind the church."

"Okay," Stone said. "I'll have to find something to wear."

"Your brown suit has just been dry-cleaned, Stone, but I'll have to go home and bring back some decent clothes to wear to both the wake and funeral. I don't have anything here that's appropriate."

"It looks like Walter's father will be in town for the funeral. While we were notifying the next of kin, we discovered Clarence Sneed had come back for the Rockdale High School thirtieth class reunion," Wyatt said. "At least he won't have to make a special trip back here."

That answered one question I had. It had seemed like too much of a coincidence to me that Walter's father would show up in town the same week his son was killed. At least he had a logical reason to be in Rockdale right now. For some reason, I was kind of disappointed by the news.

"Do you know who made the funeral arrangements?" Wyatt asked.

"I'm not certain if Chuck or Clarence were involved, but I got the impression from the funeral director his sister, Sheila Talley, took care of the details all by herself. He said she complained bitterly about every charge incurred, like the cost of their cheapest casket, a flower spread to drape over the casket, transportation of the body, the necessity of a vault and embalming, and so on. Sheila was considering cremation, even though it goes against her personal beliefs, but she finally decided against it."

Wyatt nodded, and said, "I'm sure the financial aspects of it do concern her. Funerals cost a mint these days, and I don't think she has a lot of money to spare. Most likely she resents having to spend what little she does have on her brother. She doesn't make much money as a clerk at the local pet store. Sheila lives over on Oak, close to the hardware store her father once owned. I think it's the old family homestead Sheila and Walter grew up in."

"Does she live with Melba?" I asked.

"No," Wyatt answered. "Her mother moved to a much smaller house downtown when the old family home got to be too much for her to take care of. Not that Sheila has taken very good care of the poor old house either. It's an older, two-story home, pretty run-down, with peeling pale yellow paint and a sagging front porch. Last I knew, there was an old toilet propped up against a tree in the front yard."

I filed this information in my memory bank, intent on speaking with Sheila myself the first opportunity I got. I could surely find Sheila's home. How many old pale yellow houses with toilets in the front yard could there be on Oak Street?

SEVEN

Dinner with the Dudleys went perfectly, except for the fact that Eleanor, like Walter, was a vegetarian, and Steve was allergic to pork. Other than pork, he told me, he was very receptive to meat. The fried potatoes I prepared were burnt to a crisp and the green beans tasted like wax imitations of themselves when I sampled them. They obviously had needed to be put on the burner earlier. I'd been too preoccupied while fixing supper, I guess.

I called the local pizza shop and ordered a large meat lover's pizza for the men, a medium veggie lover's special for Eleanor and me, and an order of breadsticks. I'm not a vegetarian, but I'm not a big meat eater either.

Thank God the Dudleys were extremely fond of pizza. I scrapped the potatoes and beans, and put the roast in the fridge for Stone to munch on later. I'm sure he could coerce Wyatt to help him take care of the leftovers.

I somehow managed to polish off two pieces of the veggie pizza while I watched the growth on Eleanor's chin quiver as she chewed. I had to take deep breaths to keep from upchucking. Still, like a train wreck about to happen in front of my eyes, I couldn't force myself to look away.

Chatting with Steve and Eleanor over supper, we learned they planned to spend the following day at the riverboat casino in nearby St. Joseph. They were anxious to try the casino's big buffet so they wouldn't be around the entire day, including dinner. Tomorrow was Sunday, when the casino restaurant offered all the seafood you could eat on the buffet, which appealed to Steve. I was sure they'd be happy to try any buffet after my dinner fiasco. Eleanor told me the buffet offered a wide variety of fresh vegetables and a great salad bar, also. I was sure Stone considered inviting himself along with the Dudleys for the Sunday buffet, after my disastrous dinner.

I found out later Stone had already made plans for Sunday. As I was washing up the plates, so I could wash them again in the dishwasher, he told me he and Wyatt were going to tow Wyatt's boat down to Smithville Lake so Wyatt could try out his new purchase. While there, they were going to see if they could catch a mess of crappie. Wyatt thought, other than during the spring spawn, fall and winter were the best times to fish for crappie. Stone had taken up fishing with Wyatt on occasion, and I was glad to see he enjoyed it. Fishing was now the closest thing Stone had to a hobby.

"I'll barbeque the steaks on Monday, and we'll have crappie on Tuesday, if I can catch enough of them," Stone promised. "If not, I'll buy some tilapia fillets at Pete's Pantry. Can you fix something Eleanor will eat? Vegetarians can be such a pain in the ass, can't they?"

"Yes, I'm finding that out right now. I've never had to cook for one before."

"Well, hang in there. They'll only be here for a week or so."

"Thank God," I said, before changing the subject. "How can you spend the whole day fishing when we have this murder investigation going on? For that matter, how can Wyatt get away? Isn't he on the investigating team?" I asked. It seemed to me as if the detectives were not giving enough attention to Walter's murder case.

"Yes, but tomorrow is his scheduled day off," Stone said. "And there really isn't much I can do regarding the investigation. You'll have the entire day to yourself, Lexie. You can drive down to Shawnee and pick up some clothes for the funeral, and then spend rest of the day reading and relaxing."

"Well, I do plan on going home to pick up some clothes, but I think I'll spend the afternoon asking a few people some questions." Damn! Why'd I have to say something like that, instead of just agreeing with his ideas for my day?

"Oh, no—" Stone said with an exaggerated groan, followed immediately by an exaggerated sigh. "Why does that make the hair stand up on the back of my neck?"

"I have no idea."

"Listen, Lexie, you know how much I worry about you. And we both know how much trouble you tend to get yourself into without even trying. Let the police do their work. I'm sure they'll have a suspect in custody shortly. You could use a day of R and R, couldn't you? You've been putting in a lot of hours here at the inn."

"Not that many, really, and I've enjoyed every minute of it. Besides, the Rockdale Police Department is very rarely called on to investigate murders, other than the ones that occur at your establishment," I said, rather cruelly and sarcastically. "It wouldn't hurt to see what I can find out that might give them the tip they need to make an arrest. The police department hasn't made any progress so far. I promise I won't do anything risky or crazy."

"Oh, I can't tell you how much I'd like to believe that, Lexie. You're an adult and I can't tell you what to do, but it would mean a great deal to me if you could manage to not risk life and limb to try and identify Walter's killer," Stone said. "I suppose asking a few questions can't hurt, as long as that's all you do. Please try to keep your impulsive nature in check. Who are you planning to visit tomorrow?"

"Walter's sister, Sheila, for one, and his father, Clarence, if I can track him down," I said. "I probably need to represent the inn and extend our condolences anyway. If they seem open to it, I will do a little probing to learn more about their relation- ship with Walter. I surely can't get into any trouble asking a few simple, innocuous questions."

"Famous last words," Stone muttered, as he turned around and left the kitchen.

Wyatt picked Stone up before sunrise Sunday morning, and the Dudleys left for the casino soon after. I didn't want to show up on Sheila's doorstep too early in the day, so I lingered over multiple cups of coffee. I found myself singing Led Zeppelin songs and skipping down the driveway to pick up the daily paper. As hard as it was to do, I turned off the coffee maker and poured out the remaining coffee in the carafe, which didn't amount to much. I would make a fresh pot when I returned home.

The front page of our local paper had a small article about Walter and mentioned that an intensive investigation was taking place. How intensive could it be, when not one detective had even been back to the inn? Well, except for Wyatt, who'd only stopped by to devour most of the leftover pork roast.

I had a wooden coffin taking up space in the parlor and wanted it gone as soon as possible. I was tired of avoiding the room. The fake coffin hadn't bothered me a bit until someone actually died in it. Thinking about the coffin reminded me tomorrow was Halloween. We didn't know how many trick-or- treaters to expect, so I'd bought plenty of candy. With Wyatt around so much of the time, none of it would go to waste.

I scoured the rest of the *Rockdale Gazette*, surprised to find nothing else on the matter. The paper never really amounted to much, but I was still amazed a town this size could support a daily newspaper at all. Apparently a lot of the citizens supported the paper with subscriptions and ad placements. The front page offered news, or what they could pass off as news, and the rest of the paper was filled with want ads and store ads, and a small section that told who had dinner with whom the previous day.

The lack of progress on the case only served to make me more determined to find out whatever I could from the list of suspects I was compiling in my little notebook. I'd purchased the notebook when I traveled to New York the previous year. That notebook had come in handy on several occasions, and I was making use of it again now.

As I read the paper, I absent-mindedly ate way too many miniature chocolate doughnuts. I had vowed to lose ten pounds over the winter, and they weren't going to melt off me if I kept up this compulsive snacking. In my opinion, chocolate is one of the five basic food groups, but I still needed to limit myself to only one doughnut at any given time.

Before putting the newspaper in the trash, I did a quick scan of the classified ads. Stone and I were looking for a used treadmill, even though we'd both owned treadmills in the past and knew we wouldn't use this one any more than we'd used our previous ones. Like before, we'd use it a couple of times, dust it for two or three years, and then sell it for a few bucks at a garage sale. We were still trying to convince ourselves this time would be different and we'd wear the tread right off it in our attempts to get back into shape.

With that thought in mind, I closed the doughnut bag, placing it way back in the rear of the snack cabinet. Out of sight, out of mind. Besides, it was time to get the show on the road. I had things to do and people to see.

The first thing I did was check the county phone book for a Roxie Kane. I found several Kanes listed, but no Roxie, Roxanne, or R. Kane. I started with the first one and dialed the number. No Roxie lived there I was told by the man who answered the phone. The second call netted better results. The woman told me her brother-in-law, who lived in Weston, had a daughter name Roxanne, and she was a student at our local college.

Rockdale was a small town, very small to be a college town, but it drew students from a lot of communities in the surrounding area. The institution was a fully accredited two-year junior college, with surprisingly good athletic teams, and a small school band. It offered the prerequisite courses and a few specialized degrees such as nursing degrees. Many graduates went on to four-year universities, and some to work and train at nearby hospitals. Many eventually earned medical degrees.

Roxie was working toward a career in medicine, and was already working as an EMT part-time, her aunt told me. After we conversed for a few minutes she gave me Roxie's address and phone number in Weston. She still lived with her parents, the nice lady told me. I hung up and called the number I'd been given.

"Hello."

"Is this Mrs. Kane?" I asked.

"Yes, it is. May I ask who's calling?"

"Actually, I'm calling to speak to Roxie. Is she home?"

"No," Mrs. Kane said. "This is her weekend to serve in the army reserves. It helps with her college expenses, you know. She reports to Fort Riley one weekend a month."

"Oh, of course. I knew that. I just didn't realize this was her weekend to serve. Well, thank you, anyway. I'll try her back in a few days," I said.

"Can I tell her who—"

Click.

"No, sorry. You can't tell her who called for her," I said to myself. I'd try again on a weekday, or maybe even run out to her home in Weston. Maybe by then her mother wouldn't answer the phone, or would have forgotten I'd hung up on her.

EIGHT

I hummed along with the Westminster Chimes tune as it echoed inside the walls of Sheila's house. Her house hadn't been difficult to find. The stained, antique toilet still sat beneath the tree in her front yard. Wyatt had been right; the house was due for a makeover. It was in dire need of repair. The steps up to the front porch didn't even look safe. I'd held tightly to the railing as I'd ascended them. The house looked more grayish than yellow, because the paint was peeling so badly.

After a full minute had passed, I pushed the doorbell one more time and hummed along with the tune once again. There was still no answer. Even though it was Sunday, it was possible Sheila was at work. I climbed back into my Jeep and headed for the nearest "stop and rob," which happened to be a gas station and convenience store at the corner of Third and Sycamore. There I borrowed the phone book and discovered the only pet store in town was right on Main Street, next to a popular antique store.

A minute or two later, I was parking in front of The Purrfect Pet Shop. It was indeed open on Sundays, and I felt optimistic I'd find Sheila working inside, despite the fact she'd just recently lost her brother. From what Wyatt had said, I knew she needed all the money she could get and wouldn't waste the chance to earn a few dollars. She probably earned overtime on Sundays, maybe even double-time. For her sake, I hoped so.

There were two young ladies and an older man working in

the store. They all wore matching green polo shirts with a Siamese cat embroidered on the back. "Purrfect Pet Shop" was stitched beneath the cat. Other than the help, I only saw one customer in the store, a middle-aged man who was currently watching a young woman net a colorful Oscar and place it in a plastic bag full of water.

The other young lady had opened the door on a large cage, and was filling a bowl with dog food as three young beagles jumped up and down around her, begging for attention. She petted them each in turn, and then reached for their water bowl. I approached her as she filled the bowl with fresh water.

"Excuse me, miss," I said. "Could you tell me if there's a Sheila Talley here today? I was told she worked here."

"Good morning, ma'am," the young gal replied. "Yeah, Sheila works here. She's over helping a customer in the aquarium section. Is there something I could help you with?"

"No, but thank you, anyway. I need to speak with Sheila when she gets through with her customer. It's more of a personal matter. I will check out the saltwater fish in the large aquarium while I wait."

"Fine," she said, turning back to close the cage housing the beagles.

I waited quite a while as the customer picked out fish after fish. Finally he walked toward the counter with numerous water-filled bags with colorful fish in each bag. I walked over to Sheila and stuck out my hand.

"Sheila?" I asked. As she nodded, and shook my hand, I continued, "I'm Lexie Starr. My partner owns the Alexandria Inn, where your brother was killed. I wanted to extend our condolences for your loss, and let you know we're willing and able to do anything we can to help you in this time of grieving."

I noticed Sheila glance at the older gentleman who was at the cash register in the front of the store, tending to the customer with all the fish. When she saw he was busy with the customer, she responded to me.

"Thank you, Ms. Starr."

"Stone and I will be at the funeral services on Wednesday. Running the inn keeps us tied up in the evenings but we'll try to attend the wake as well," I said. "We are very deeply saddened by the loss of your brother. It was such a shock to all of us."

"Me, too. Thank you again," Sheila said. She turned back toward the aquariums.

"We're doing all we can to assist the detectives in making an arrest. And I'm sure an arrest is imminent. We want Walter's killer apprehended as soon as possible. We are also, naturally, concerned about the image of our bed and breakfast. Once news gets out that a crime has taken place there, it could have a devastating effect on our business."

Why was I telling her all this when she probably couldn't care less? I needed to stop running off at the mouth and get down to the real reason I was here. She nodded politely, and looked back up at the man at the checkout stand. I realized he must be her boss, and she was worried about being reprimanded for goofing off during working hours. I needed to do something to make it look as if this was not a personal conversation. She couldn't afford to lose her job, and I certainly didn't want to be the cause of such a disaster.

"Could you show me the angelfish, Sheila?" I asked.

She replied affirmatively, looking relieved to have something productive to do. I followed her to the angelfish tank. "The beautifully colored angelfish is a freshwater fish from South America," she told me. "They get along well with other aquarium fish, except the more aggressive species, such as the crystal eyed catfish."

"That's nice to know," I said. "The crystal eyed catfish had been my second choice. So, were you and Walter close?"

I seemed to catch her off-guard with my question, and she stammered a nervous response. "I guess so," she said. "Well, not really. We really didn't see each other all that often. We never had much in common. I was five years older than Walter."

"Do you know of any enemies he had? Maybe someone with a grudge against him for some reason? Do you have any idea of anyone who'd want to kill your brother?" I asked.

"No, nothing like that. I don't know of anyone who didn't like him. He was polite, courteous, and never in any trouble. I just can't imagine who would want to kill Walter. He had an awful lot of friends at the college. He was always popular at school."

"Who, beside you, could stand to benefit from his death?"

Sheila seemed to get the idea I had a personal agenda and was not here looking for a new pet. She made a move as if to walk away, so I pointed at the tank, and said, "I'll take one of the angelfish."

"Just one?"

"Yes, please. Small tank, you know."

"Okay," was her short, clipped response. "I may stand to benefit from his death, and I may be hurting for a little cash right now, but not enough to kill someone. And I would never, ever hurt my own brother—not for any amount of money."

"No, I'm sure you wouldn't. Are you going to be responsible for all of the interment costs?" I asked.

"No. Our mother will see I'm repaid, I hope. Or, at least, she will once she gets back on an even keel. I really can't afford to pay for the funeral. I live paycheck to paycheck as it is. I had to put the entire mortuary bill on my MasterCard, and can't afford even the minimum payment on it."

"I'm sure your mother will repay you," I said, not totally convinced, since Melba still believed Walter was the housekeeper at the hospital. Why would she want to pay for the housekeeper's funeral? "Did you see Walter often, living in the same town as you do?"

"No, not really," she said. "The last time I saw him was at my mother's house several weeks ago. There was an attorney from St. Joseph there at the time, and he had Walter signing a form to become mom's power-of-attorney when I showed up to check on her. She has medical and psychological issues, you see."

"Didn't that upset you? It doesn't seem right to not choose the eldest child for a responsibility of that nature. It would upset me. I just don't understand her choosing Walter to give power-of-attorney status to. After all, Chuck is just her stepson, and you're several years older than Walter."

"Yeah, five years older, and, well, frankly I didn't understand it either," Sheila said as she deftly netted the largest angelfish in the tank. "Will this one do?"

I nodded. What the hell was I going to do with an angelfish? Flushing it down the toilet didn't seem right. I was too much of an animal lover to do that to an innocent fish, which just had the bad fortune to be in the wrong place at the wrong time.

"I think Mom always preferred Walter over me, though," Sheila said, suddenly interested in talking. "He was her baby, and he was a real momma's boy. I always felt Walter had his own bottom line in mind, angling to get the bulk of her estate when she passed. He knew he wouldn't make much of a salary as a teacher and coach. Mom still has a lot of investments she bought with her share of the proceeds from the sale of the lumberyard. Dad used his half to start up a refrigeration business in New Mexico, but she has an investment broker who put hers in stocks and bonds. She even paid cash for her new home."

"She sounds pretty intelligent and responsible," I said. "Good for her to handle her money so wisely."

"Well, it's not really her doing. She's in no shape, mentally, to handle her own affairs these days. She hired an overseer to handle most of her affairs, and she keeps that lawyer I mentioned on retainer, too, to take care of any legal matters for her," Sheila explained. "He's always got her filing lawsuits against one company or another. She sued one pharmaceutical company for not calling her daily to remind her to take her medication, naturally a medication they manufactured. Obviously, the case got dismissed, as have the majority of them."

"I can see why. Her lawyer doesn't sound very competent or he wouldn't pursue a case like that one in the first place."

"Exactly!"

"Are your dad and brother close?" I asked. I wanted to keep her talking. The more she talked, the better chance of my picking up on any significant details.

"I'd say they're pretty tight. Closer than Dad and I ever were, at least. Dad tried to get Walter to move to Albuquerque with him, but Walter is too tied to his mother's apron strings to move away. Walter could have probably ended up inheriting the bulk of Dad's estate too, by taking over Dad's company, if he'd only moved to New Mexico. But Walter was too attached to his girlfriend, Sidney Hobbs, to move away. I imagine they would have married eventually. Then maybe he would have moved, with Sidney, to Albuquerque."

Now I was worried also about what her boss would think with all her chatting and lollygagging around. From where I now stood, I couldn't see him to tell if he was watching us, so I leaned over toward an aquarium full of swordfish to get a better angle. Just as I caught a glimpse of him, glaring at Sheila, I lost my balance and stumbled, falling squarely into the fish tank.

Suddenly the sound of glass shattering and water gushing filled the little shop. I heard Sheila gasp in horror and the sound of the manager's feet running down the aisle between the cat toys and the snake cages. I had knocked the tank off its black metal stand. Swordfish were flopping on the floor all around me, amid thousands of pieces of broken glass. One hundred flopping, gasping swordfish is a ghastly sight.

I stood as still as a statue, silently holding my new pet angelfish, unsure what to do next. Sheila stood still too. She was obviously in shock, with a hand pressed up against each cheek. She looked like the kid in the *Home Alone* movies.

"Oh, my God!" She said breathlessly.

"I'm so sorry," I said. "What should I do? Where should we put these poor swordfish?"

"Put them in the tank with the angelfish," the store manager said. His ID badge read Marc Meyer. Mr. Meyer looked very agitated. "Help her, Sheila, while I run and get the mop and a pail to clean up all this water. What have I told you, Sheila, about paying attention to what you're doing? This is exactly what happens when you don't pay attention."

Sheila looked down at her feet as I jumped to her defense. "It was entirely my fault, sir. Sheila had nothing to do with it whatsoever. She was helping me pick out fish when I lost my footing and knocked over the tank. I fully intend to pay for the tank, and whatever damage I have caused."

Mr. Meyer was not at all pleased with me, and I knew instantly he would take me up on my offer. I stayed long enough to save as many of the swordfish as I could, and to help mop up the mess. I apologized once again to both Sheila and the store manager before I left. My opportunity to question Sheila had passed.

I climbed back into my Jeep, the proud new owner of a pile of glass shards, seven dead swordfish, and an angelfish that was very much alive and in need of a new home.

Who would have thought I could cause such a stir at the local pet shop? Like Stone always said, I could get into trouble without even trying. Now I had to foist my new pet off on someone else. The only person I knew with a freshwater aquarium was a neighbor who lived up the street from my home in Shawnee. I was pretty certain the tank in the waiting room at the dentist office was a saltwater tank. It had a couple of clownfish in it that looked like they'd have this angelfish as a snack.

I was going to Shawnee anyway, so I hoped my neighbor was home and willing to adopt an orphaned angelfish. How long could a fish survive in a small plastic bag of water? I wondered. Long enough, I hoped. I'd already killed seven of its distant relatives.

In the meantime I wanted to locate Walter's father if I could. Now if I only had enough guts to walk back into the pet store and ask Sheila if she knew where her father was staying. I tried, but couldn't muster up the courage. Mr. Meyer would probably have run me out of there on a rail, or locked the doors when he saw me coming.

There were only two old antiquated hotels and a handful of franchised motels in the small town of Rockdale I would need to call. I ruled out our competition. I couldn't picture Clarence staying in a bed and breakfast. B and Bs were more conducive to attracting romantic couples and families on vacation than single men coming back to their hometown for a class reunion. And with any luck at all, he hadn't opted to stay at a friend or relative's house while he was in town.

For once I got lucky and located Mr. Sneed on my first call. He was in room sixteen at the Motel 6. I'd been quite sure they'd left the light on, just for him. I headed straight for the motel but no one responded when I knocked on the door of room sixteen, and no cars were parked anywhere near the door.

I might have to try another tactic, I thought. Most people didn't sit around in their motel room during the day. Most were overnighters and got up early to check out and leave. The guests staying for an extended amount of time usually found somewhere to go or something to do. By the time Clarence Sneed was apt to return to his motel room, Stone and Wyatt would be home from their fishing trip, and I'd be preparing supper for us at the inn.

I headed back to the convenience store I had stopped at earlier and made a call to Rockdale High School. After listening to fifteen rings, the phone was picked up by a janitor. I had forgotten it was Sunday. He left to make a call on another line. I could hear his voice faintly in the background, talking to someone over another phone. Finally he came back with the information I needed. The thirtieth class reunion was being held later that evening at the Rockdale Community Center. I had missed my own thirtieth reunion the previous year, but I wouldn't be missing this one. I hoped Clarence wouldn't be missing it either, despite the fact his son has just been murdered.

Now I needed to procure a reunion outfit, as well as a couple of outfits for Walter's Tuesday night wake, and his funeral on Wednesday. It goes without saying that I couldn't be seen in the same outfit at both events.

While I was at the convenience store, I filled up with gas and bought a cup of coffee to go. At one time I couldn't drive without smoking, and now I couldn't drive without drinking coffee. In fact, I couldn't do much of anything without drinking coffee. I'd traded one bad habit for a slightly healthier one. But then, I didn't know if this was one of the days when coffee was considered beneficial to your health, or one of those days when it would surely kill you before the year was out. The prognosis about coffee consumption seemed to change daily.

Back in the Jeep, I buckled up and headed for Shawnee with my black and white striped traveling companion riding shotgun beside me.

NINE

It didn't take me long to pick out the clothes I needed. I owned one black dress, one tan pantsuit, and one light blue skirt that went well with my white and blue cardigan. They would all work perfectly for what I needed.

I was lucky the Watsons were home and more than happy to adopt my angelfish. I was quite vague about how I'd become its owner. Before I headed back to Rockdale, I watered my drooping houseplants, and decided to load one of my Boston ferns into the Jeep to take back to the inn. I had the perfect spot for it in the library.

Then I sorted through the mail, paid a couple of bills, and checked and deleted most of my e-mails. I got the exact same George Bush joke from three of my friends. It wasn't even funny the first time I'd seen it two weeks ago. I had checked my e-mail yesterday from Stone's computer at the inn, so I only had a half dozen other messages. I didn't want to apply for a credit card, take advantage of free shipping at an online toy store, or order any pills from Canada, including one that would enlarge and enhance something I didn't have to begin with.

I poured out a carton of spoiled milk, tossing the carton into the trash. I removed some unidentified green and furry object from the vegetable bin and placed it in the trash can also. Then I tied up the trash bag and took it to the curb for a Tuesday morning pickup. With any luck at all, the neighborhood dogs wouldn't rip it to shreds before then.

Before locking up the house, and arming the security system, I checked my landline phone for messages. Good. No messages, I thought. I then headed straight back to the Alexandria Inn. I'd most likely have an hour or two to relax, and get a few chores done around the inn, before Stone and Wyatt got back from their fishing trip.

It was getting dark earlier these days, and Stone and Wyatt would probably return before five. The class reunion didn't start until six, according to the school janitor. I wanted to be out of the house by the time Stone and Wyatt came home, so I wouldn't have to explain where I was going to either of the men. But I also wanted to arrive at the class reunion fashionably late.

Since I didn't know anyone at the reunion and nobody there would know me, I hoped to arrive after the reunion was in full swing. I could sneak in, find Clarence Sneed, offer my condolences, ask him a few personal questions, and sneak out again without being noticed by any of his former classmates. I would try not to make eye contact with anyone so I wouldn't be drawn into a conversation. I could find no apparent flaw with this plan.

I figured I'd have about an hour and a half to fill, so I wanted to make good use of the time and not just drive around town aimlessly. I'd found a Chuck Sneed in the phone book, living east of Rockdale, in Chillicothe, on an old gravel farm road off Thirty-Six Highway. I decided to drive past the house a couple of times while I came up with a viable reason to speak with Walter's half-brother. I put on my blue skirt and matching cardigan, an easy outfit in which to maintain a low profile at a class reunion, and left the inn at four-thirty.

Using a city map I carried in my glove box, I found Chuck's house with little problem. It was a double-wide mobile home surrounded by overgrown weeds, cigarette butts, and smashed beer cans. There was an old red Ford pickup in the driveway, with a shotgun hanging on a gun rack behind the bench seat. There was a bashed-in trash can on the porch, and several rusty bikes propped up against the trailer.

I could hear kids playing inside as I walked up the crumbling concrete steps. The screen door was ripped and hanging from one hinge, so I reached through the mesh and knocked on the door. I didn't think my knocking could be heard over the boisterous clatter inside the house, so I rapped louder the second time.

A prematurely balding man, about thirty years old, answered the door. The snap on his blue jeans was undone, and he wore a threadbare white undershirt. He had a cigarette in one hand and a can of beer in the other. He didn't look too welcoming as he opened the front door.

"Yeah?" he said.

"Excuse me, sir," I said, looking down at my trusty white notebook, which I held open in my hand. The page I had opened it up to was actually an old grocery list. I doubted Chuck was too literate, and he didn't seem particularly interested in what was written in my notebook anyway. I put a check beside "horseradish" because I wanted to look as if I were there on official business and was checking off scheduled appointments. "Are you Chuck Sneed?"

"Yeah," he said again. He took a long drag on his cigarette and blew it out over the top of my head. I noticed his cigarette was unfiltered. I notice things like that more now that I no longer smoke. I'm also annoyed by smokers a lot more now since I quit smoking myself. And I find hypocritical people like myself annoying sometimes, too.

"I'm from the floral shop in Rockdale," I said to Chuck. "We've been hired to create a flower arrangement, and a casket spread for the Walter Sneed funeral service this week. There's a question about the order and I found your name in the phone book, hoping you were related to the deceased."

"Yeah, he's my half-brother. Got hisself kilt a couple days ago, I heared."

"I'm so sorry," I said. "At least he's in a better place now."

"Yeah, whatever. Don't know nothing about no flowers, though. Try my sister, Sheila Talley. She lives there in Rockdale with her boyfriend," Chuck said, closing the door as he spoke.

I managed to squeeze my foot in the door before it shut completely. "Listen, Chuck, while I'm here, I was wondering if you could tell me a little about your brother. It helps us arrange the flowers better if we're more familiar with the person whose funeral we are preparing the flowers for. We can match the arrangements to their personality, you see. It makes for a much more personalized and aesthetic-looking arrangement."

What a bunch of hogwash I was spouting. I was pushing my luck with such a flimsy story, but I didn't think Chuck was the type of person to have ever bought a flower in his entire life. He appeared to buy in to my excuse to ask him questions, or, more likely, he just really didn't give a rat's ass why I was standing on his doorstep.

"Yeah? Whatcha want to know?" Chuck took a drink of his beer and belched loudly.

"Was Walter well-liked around town?"

"I dunno. Guess so," he said. He took another long swallow.

"Were you and your brother close?" I asked, as if this would determine whether we used roses or orchids in the casket spread.

"Nah. I was a lot older than Walter, so we barely knew each other. I had moved out 'fore he moved in with my pa and my step-ma." Chuck finished off his beer and placed it between the palms of his hands, smashed it, and flung the empty can out into the yard. He reached over to his right inside the trailer and came back with a fresh beer. He pulled back the flip-top on top of the can with one of the three teeth I could count in his mouth.

"How did you find out Walter had been kilt, er, killed?" I asked. He was hard to hear above the yelling and shouting going on inside the trailer. It sounded like a good old-fashioned free-for-all was taking place behind Chuck. He must have a whole pack of wild kids, I decided.

"Bubba told me."

"Bubba?"

"Neighbor down the road a spell," he said. "He told me 'bout the funeral and all. Then some damn cop showed up to ask me questions, but I didn't know nothing to tell him."

"Are you and your family planning to attend the funeral services?" Gee, if you are, maybe we can include your favorite ferns in the arrangement, I wanted to add. How do you feel about baby's breath?

"Nah, can't go to the wake 'cause I got a hog-tying contest I wanna go to. Don't got no suit neither," he explained. "Besides, I never really liked the whiny brat anyways, so don't give no never mind that he's done gone and got hisself kilt."

With that final gem, Chuck must have felt I had enough insight now to prepare the perfect arrangement for the funeral, because he shut the door in my face before screaming at his children to shut the hell up and go to their rooms.

I backed away from the door with my mouth hanging open. I don't know exactly what I had expected of Chuck, but I hadn't expected a redneck with such a callous attitude about Walter's death. I wondered if he cared more for Sheila than he did Walter. I actually wondered if he cared much for anything other than smoking and drinking.

I looked at my watch. If I stopped at McDonalds for a cup of coffee and drank it slowly, I could arrive at the Rockdale Community Center around six-thirty. By then, most of the reunion attendees should already be there. I felt confident everything would go smoothly. I expected to have all the information I needed from Clarence and be back home by seven-thirty. The best laid plans of mice and men . . .

"Marian! Come on in!" I heard as I walked quietly in the opened front door of the community center. I noticed the woman who'd spoken was looking directly at me. I tried to walk the other way, to no avail, as she rushed up to greet me.

"I'd know you anywhere," she said. "You haven't changed a bit in the last thirty years, since you got married and moved out to Montana."

"Uh, you haven't changed either," I said, quickly walking away from the woman as I spoke. "It's wonderful to see you again. I'll catch up with you a little later so we can visit."

I walked over toward a table of refreshments while I tried to determine the best way to figure out which man in the room was Clarence Sneed, if he had indeed attended the reunion. A gentleman walking on the other side of the table looked up with a questioning expression on his face. He stared at me from behind the punch bowl before speaking.

"Why Marian, I thought your RSVP stated you'd be unable to attend due to the failing health of your mother, who was suffering from Alzheimer's. I didn't expect to see you here. Is your mother still hanging in there?" he asked.

Whoever this Marian was, I must really resemble her. According to her RSVP, she wasn't going to be there, and most likely none of the classmates had seen her recently, so I decided maybe I could use this resemblance to my advantage. Fortunately, I'd only met a handful of people in Rockdale and I wasn't likely to run into any of them at this reunion.

"No, she finally passed," I said. Sorry about that, "Mom," but I needed to be able to explain my ability to attend the reunion after sending back an RSVP stating I couldn't. Besides, both of my parents were deceased, so I didn't feel like my answer was a complete lie.

"Oh, please accept my condolences. I'm so sorry to hear about your loss."

"Thank you, Mister, uh—" I said, followed by the standard line, "but at least she's in a better place now."

"Yes, that's for sure. Say, a lot of people here will be happy to see you again after all these years," he said. "I don't recall seeing you at any of our previous reunions."

"No, it seemed like something always interfered with my plans to attend, Mister, um, uh, I'm so sorry, but I don't recognize you," I said.

"Oh, I'm sorry. I'm Pete Franken. I guess I did have a lot more hair and a lot less gut back then," Mr. Franken said. "Since we dated for over a year, I thought you'd recognize me, even without the hair. I flew in from south Texas for the reunion."

"Oh, but of course. I should have recognized you, Pete, but we've all changed so much over the years," I said, moving on down the table toward some deviled eggs and petit fours. Then, after a thought occurred to me, I moved back down to where Pete Franken was now filling his cup with punch.

"Excuse me, Pete. Have you seen Clarence Sneed? Speaking of losing a loved one, he just lost his son recently, and I wanted to offer my condolences."

"Well, yes, Marian. He's standing right behind you. I'm surprised you didn't see him. I guess maybe he's changed a lot too," Pete concluded. "It has been thirty years since you've seen any of us, I reckon. I'm sorry to hear about his son. No wonder he's got such a crowd around him."

"Oh, yes, there he is. Silly me. I never was any good with faces. Thanks Pete."

With the news of Walter Sneed's death all over the news,

Clarence was understandably surrounded by a bevy of class-mates, no doubt offering up words of compassion and comfort. Many of the classmates probably still lived in the area and had seen the news about Walter's death on television and in the papers. I moved over to the corner of the room where I could keep an eye on Clarence, while hiding behind my plate of refreshments. I would wait to move in until after the crowd had thinned out.

After about five minutes of nibbling on the same sugar cookie, I noticed several ladies walking my way. I glanced around quickly, but I could see no way to escape, especially after one of them called out my new name.

"Marian, how are you? We're all so thrilled to see you. You missed our last three reunions, and we didn't expect to see you at this one either. How have you been getting along? I don't imagine Rayburn is still alive?" One of the ladies asked me. I assumed Rayburn was Marian's husband, and he must have been afflicted with some serious health problem. I didn't have the heart to kill him off too, after just killing off Marian's mother.

"Yes, actually he's doing fine. He's recovered remarkably well," I said. "I was going to bring him along, but he was scheduled to have some medical tests performed this week. Just a routine checkup, you see."

Suddenly, all three women looked at me as if I'd said my husband was busy shooting a porn film, or if I had grown my very own Chia Pet on the side of my chin.

"You were going to bring a champion quarter horse to the reunion?" One lady asked, astounded. "Why in the world would you bring a horse to a class reunion?"

"A very, very old one, I might add," another lady said. "After all, you won the county championship with Rayburn over thirty years ago. Isn't that at the high end of a quarter horse's average life span?"

The third lady just stood there with her mouth gaping open. Crap. I knew I should have just killed him off too. Now I had to wiggle my way out of my ridiculous remark.

"Oh. Rayburn, you said. I'm sorry. I must have misunderstood you. No, I had to have Rayburn put down several years ago," I said, putting my hand over my ear to hide it from their view. "You'll have to excuse me. I experienced some hearing damage a few years ago, in an explosion. And I'm sorry, but it appears the battery in my new hearing aid needs to be changed. Please pardon me while I go see to that in the ladies' room. It was nice to see you all again."

I walked away with my face as red as my cup of fruit punch. Maybe I shouldn't approach Clarence Sneed until my nerves had calmed down and my face had returned to its normal color. The crowd around him had thinned somewhat, and I could just move in a little closer and eavesdrop on the conversation, until I felt comfortable stepping in and visiting with Mr. Sneed myself.

But first I had to make a quick trip to the restroom, as I was sure the three women were still staring at me, talking amongst themselves about their old friend who had gone completely batty in her old age. They must be thinking I'd experienced some brain damage, along with the hearing damage, as a result of the explosion. For Marian's sake, I hoped she didn't make the trip back to Rockdale for any future reunions.

After spending an adequate amount of time in the restroom to replace a hearing aid battery, I sauntered back out to inch my way closer to Clarence. I wanted to talk with him as quickly as possible and get out of this place before I made another major screwup.

Clarence was a rather slovenly looking man; his suit was wrinkled, his greasy hair was sticking out in numerous direc-tions, and he wore old battered sneakers instead of the dress shoes a suit demanded. Chuck may have come by his "redneckness" naturally.

When I finally got within hearing distance of Clarence, there were five or six men conversing with him. I didn't want to step right into the middle of the men, but thankfully, with the benefit of the imaginary new hearing aid battery, I was able to make out the gist of the conversation.

"I can't imagine who would want to kill your son," one man said.

"Me neither," Clarence said. "He was really too much of a sissy to get into it with anyone capable of cold-blooded murder. I never knew him to run with a rough crowd, just athletes most the time. When he wasn't with his girlfriend, that is."

"Did you get to spend much time with him in recent years?" Another man asked him.

"No. Unfortunately, I haven't seen him in over two years. I tried to get him to move out to New Mexico with me, so I could train him as an apprentice. He could have taken over my company some day. I wanted to get him away from his mother and try to make a man out of him. I tried several times, but he refused every time. Now I guess it's too late to change his mind. This wouldn't have happened if he'd been with me," Clarence said, with a catch in his voice.

"Yeah, that's too bad. Have you seen Melba since you've been back?" The same gentleman asked. "I've heard she's in the mental ward at the hospital."

"No, but I'll probably run into her at the funeral. She's such an off-the-wall nutcase now that she drives me crazy if I have to be around her very long. She completely lost her mind a few years ago. We got divorced, but she wouldn't leave me alone. That's the main reason I relocated to Albuquerque, to put as many miles between us as I could."

"I heard she was in the hospital, too," a woman broke in. "She might or might not be able to attend the funeral, depending on her mental condition at the time."

"I hope she's unable to attend," Clarence said. "I don't wish any ill health on her, but I could do without the unpleasantness."

It seemed to me, although Clarence had little use for his ex-wife, he didn't appear to have any qualms with his son. He may have considered Walter a sissy and a momma's boy like his sister did, but he'd still tried a number of times to get Walter to join him in New Mexico. He had expressed wishes of turning his company over to Walter in the future, so he must not have felt any animosity toward him. I felt confident Walter hadn't harmed his son in any way.

I continued to eavesdrop. I was learning more this way than if I'd been asking Clarence questions myself. This way there'd be no awkwardness when I ran into him at Walter's funeral, which I was sure to do. He would surely question why Marian, an old high school classmate, had attended his son's funeral. Clarence was now relating a story about taking Walter on a hunting trip when his son was still a young boy.

"He squalled every time I shot a quail. He refused to touch the gun or the dead birds. He was much too sensitive to make a hunter of, so I never took him hunting again. At least he was a pretty good athlete, which is why he wanted to be a coach and a gym teacher. He made the varsity basketball team his sophomore year in high school and was currently on the college team. He was too scrawny for football though. He would have gotten his neck snapped in half. I still can't quite believe someone would want to kill him."

Another man who'd just joined the group told Clarence he'd heard Walter had been dating the same girl for several years. He said he'd read in the paper the young girl, Sidney Hobbs, had been unable to be questioned by the police, but they had spoken briefly with her father. According to her father, she had a solid alibi: shopping all day with a friend. She was temporarily cleared of any wrongdoing, he told Clarence.

Not that anyone suspected Sidney Hobbs in the first place, the man said. After talking to Paula, I'd already figured this was probably the case. I'd observed her falling to pieces in agony and grief, and knew no actress could perform that brilliantly. Still, I wanted to talk to her if the situation arose. She would know as much about Walter as anybody.

"Yes," Clarence said. "Walter had told me about Sidney. He wanted to marry her. The last time I talked to him, he'd already proposed to her."

"What did she say?" Several men asked in unison.

"She was kind of waffling back and forth, I take it. She wanted to marry him, but I think her folks might have thought they were still too young. I think they wanted her to finish college before settling down," Clarence explained. "Walter was anxiously awaiting her decision, he told me that day on the phone. He felt Sidney wanted to marry him right away but didn't want to disappoint her parents."

"Marian," I heard over the squealing loud speaker, "Marian Welch. Where are you, Marian? I know you're here."

I froze in place, hoping I wasn't the only Marian in the room, and the Marian in question would quickly step up to the stage while I snuck out the back door.

"Come on, Marian. I know you're here somewhere," I heard a man's voice say again, as heads were starting to turn my way. "We've nominated you to sing the National Anthem to get the festivities rolling. You were always the best singer in our class. As you all may remember, Marian sang the National Anthem before every home football and basketball game. We'd like to hear it one more time, just for old time's sake. I'll accompany you on the organ, Marian, just like in the good old days."

Everybody began to cheer, urging me up to the microphone.

Someone was pulling on my arm, trying to drag me to the stage. Another person was giving me a gentle push from behind.

Now I was in a full-blown panic. I couldn't carry two notes in a row that were in tune, and couldn't have remembered the words to the National Anthem right now if my life depended on it. In fact, I always lip-synched whenever it was sung at ball games just to spare those standing around me.

"Wait a minute." Thinking quickly, I said to the crowd. "My throat is very dry from talking so much. I haven't seen any of you in so long and I'm already getting hoarse from visiting with everyone. Let me step out in the hallway and get a drink from the water fountain. Then I'll be delighted to go up on stage and sing the National Anthem for you."

Everybody in the room seemed okay with this plan. Little did they know that a bulldozer could not have shoved me up on that stage to sing even a tune as simple as "Happy Birthday to You." I'd fake a heart attack before I'd sing the National Anthem.

Why did this Marian have to be so damned talented? I'd been learning a lot by listening to Clarence talk amongst his old schoolmates. As I turned to head toward the hallway, I heard Clarence say to his friends, "I once cut a fart that lasted longer than the entire first verse of the 'Star Spangled Banner.' "

Okay, so Clarence was definitely just as much a redneck as his son. That would be the last thing I learned from Clarence, because the class reunion was over for Marian. I walked out to the hallway and then scurried as fast as I could out the side door to the parking lot, where I drove off in my Jeep and never looked back. I found myself humming the "Star Spangled Banner" on the way back to the inn.

Thanks to the National Anthem, I made it home close to seven-thirty. Stone was sitting with the Dudleys in the family room.

They were all watching the Sunday night football game on television, and sharing a large bowl of buttered popcorn. The game had barely begun, but the Chiefs were already behind by seven points.

"Hey Lexie, where have you been?" Stone asked. He walked over and hugged me as I entered the room, placing a tender kiss on my forehead. "I was just getting ready to call your cell phone."

"Just listening to Walter's dad, Clarence, talk about his son," I said. "I ran into him at the convenience store when I stopped to pick up a cup of coffee for my drive to Shawnee. He had a shirt on with 'Sneed's Heating & Cooling' stitched across the pocket and was waiting behind me to pour a cup of coffee."

Good Lord, what a liar I'd become. I can remember back to when I couldn't tell a lie without stuttering all the way through it. Out of pure nervousness, I'd crack my knuckles until my fingers swelled up. But now I lied at the drop of a hat. I vowed to stop all this impromptu lying just as soon as Walter's killer was apprehended. I didn't like the person I was becoming, and I knew it wasn't fair to Stone to keep the truth from him. But for now, I continued with another falsehood.

"We had a nice conversation," I said. "I'm convinced he had nothing to do with his son's death."

"That's good," Stone said. I was glad to see that Stone wasn't interested in the details of our meeting, even though I was ready to gloss over them. My prefabricated story didn't even sound believable to me. But the truth sounded even more phony than my made-up story.

"Find out anything?" he asked.

"Just a few things, such as Walter had recently asked his long-time girlfriend, Sidney Hobbs, to marry him and she was having trouble making up her mind. She was wild about Walter but wasn't sure she wanted to marry him right away. Her parents weren't anxious for them to marry until she finished school," I said. Stone nodded, so I continued.

"Walter was a momma's boy, but still a decent athlete, at basketball at least. I guess I learned nothing of any importance really, but I just got the distinct impression Clarence couldn't, and wouldn't, have harmed his son. He was too determined to get Walter to move out to Albuquerque and learn the heating and cooling business so he could take over the reins of Clarence's company some day," I explained.

The Dudleys had no idea what I was talking about but showed polite interest. "I wouldn't say the same about his half-brother, Chuck, though. I think there's enough dislike there to warrant a closer look. One of the detectives talked to him, and I don't know what conclusion he came to, but I think he should be on the suspect list, if he isn't already."

Just then there was a great deal of commotion on the television screen. The Chiefs had returned a punt for a touchdown, and were now tied with their opponents. Stone's attention was riveted back to the ballgame, so I went up to undress and take a long, hot bath.

I was no closer to identifying a killer than I'd been at the beginning of the case, but there were a couple of suspects I felt comfortable in taking off my list. I hoped the investigation team was having better luck than I was. It just didn't seem to me they were making much of an effort. I needed to soak in the tub and think of a way to rectify the situation.

TEN

It was raining when I woke up on Monday morning. There was even a touch of sleet hitting the windowpane. The sound made me want to stay in bed, but we had guests at the inn and I had things to do. I jumped out of bed before I could talk myself out of it. I could hear Stone's electric razor humming in the bathroom.

"Hi, babe," he said as I joined him in the bathroom. "I'm about done here and then the bathroom is all yours."

"Okay, thanks. I need to get around and fix breakfast for the Dudleys and for you, too, if you want some."

"What are you fixing?"

"I thought I'd make some biscuits and gravy, and make some patties with the rest of the sausage for you and me," I said. "How does that sound?"

"That sounds good to me. Count me in!"

After I got dressed and made the bed, I went down and found the Dudleys in the library of the large house. They looked bright and cheery for such a gray, dismal day.

"Happy Halloween. What are your plans for today?" I asked. "Are you guys going out?"

"No, we really don't have any plans. Since it's a rainy day, we thought we'd just sit around and read. That's why we're hanging out in the library," Eleanor said. "You have a very nice selection of books in here."

"I work as an assistant librarian on a volunteer basis. The

library occasionally has a book sale to make room for new books on the shelves. I get a crack at them before they're put out to sell. It's just a small library and doesn't have much spare space," I said. "I'll have Stone light a fire in the fireplace in the living room today. A fire will make it nice and comfy."

"Well, I'm looking forward to reading this latest Jill Churchill cozy. She's my favorite author," Eleanor said. "I've read all her books except this latest one."

Steve put down a book he was glancing through, and said, "I'm still trying to decide which book I want to read first. There's a Sidney Sheldon book that's caught my eye, as well as an old Zane Grey western. By the way, I noticed there's a large wooden box in the parlor. It looks just like an old-time coffin. What do you use it for, may I ask?"

"Well, it actually is a make-believe coffin—"

"That you keep handy just in case any of your guests get out of hand?" Steve asked, chuckling at his own comment.

"Yes, and keep that in mind if you don't like the breakfast I'm getting ready to cook. You better compliment the food no matter how bad it is," I said. I noticed that Steve laughed but was still looking at me inquisitively, waiting for the real reason the Alexandria Inn kept a coffin in its parlor.

I couldn't tell them the truth and make them uncomfortable. Many people wouldn't stay at a place where someone had just been murdered. And there was a chance they'd be outraged they weren't informed of the crime earlier. Fortunately, the crime scene tape around the parlor had been removed before their arrival. The tape had been placed around the parlor to keep potential guests from disturbing any possible evidence still remaining at the scene. But, at my request, Wyatt took it down on Saturday morning, convinced no more evidence could be found.

"Actually," I continued. "We were going to have a haunted

house here for the area kids, but something came up and we were unable to do so."

"Oh?"

"Yes," I said.

Before he could ask me what came up to thwart the haunted house plans, I excused myself to go begin preparing breakfast. I really did need to get started. I would have to make two bowls of gravy, one with sausage, and one without for Eleanor and Steve, who I'd almost forgot was allergic to pork. Like Stone had said, vegetarians could be a real challenge to try to plan meals around. Allergies could make for a hassle too, I was discovering. I'd have to fix a lot of vegetables and meatless casseroles while the Dudleys were here, to serve along with the meat, which Steve and Stone would want. As long as the meat didn't come from a pig, I'd be fine.

With breakfast over, and dishes "pre-washed" and in the dishwasher, it was time to relax over a cup of coffee. As I was pouring myself a cup, there was a sharp rap at the back door off the kitchen. I could see Wyatt through the glass and waved him in.

"Good morning, Lexie. What smells so good?"

"Good morning. I fixed some biscuits and gravy for breakfast. If you'd gotten here a little earlier I could have made a plate for you too. But there's a plate here with some extra sausage patties you're welcome to. I really don't have room in the refrigerator for leftovers. You'd do me a favor if you could eat them."

"Anything for you, Miss Lexie," Wyatt said. "You don't have to ask me twice when it comes to eating. Where's Stone this morning? Did he tell you about that sixteen-inch crappie he caught? Man, it was a slabber!"

"No. Actually I forgot to ask him about your fishing trip yesterday. I was too busy—"

"She just doesn't care about me anymore, Wyatt," Stone said, as he entered the kitchen. "It's all me, me, me with her these days."

"Oh, you poor son of a bitch. Pardon my French, Lexie," Wyatt said with a wink.

"I know. It's an awful state of affairs. So, how are you this morning, Wyatt?" Stone asked with laughter in his voice. I poured a cup of coffee and handed it to him.

"Fine. Just taking care of these leftover sausage patties for Lexie. I felt it was my duty as an officer and a gentleman."

"I'm sure you did," Stone said.

"So, how many did you two catch yesterday?" I asked. "I'm sorry I didn't think to ask about your day out fishing last night, Stone. I got home late, and by then I was hungry, tired, and wanting to go soak in the tub."

"Oh, that's okay, honey. Wyatt caught about eight or so. I only caught three, so he felt sorry for me and gave me his so we'd have enough to fix for the Dudleys tomorrow night. Remember, Lexie, I'm grilling steaks tonight. We'll have plenty of fish tomorrow, knowing Eleanor won't eat fish if she's a true vegetarian. Several of the crappie we caught were real slabbers."

I didn't know what a slabber was, but Wyatt had used the same term, and it sounded big. I'd have to make some kind of casserole without meat to serve with the slabbers. An eggplant casserole sounded good to me.

"It was generous of you to give Stone all your fish, Wyatt," I said.

Wyatt snorted, and said, "Not really. I had a date with Veronica last night, and I didn't have time to clean them. But there's always more where those came from. There are several area lakes Stone and I need to try out. But as much as I like Stone, frankly, I just didn't want to be late for my date with Veronica."

"I thought it was too good to be true," Stone said, laughing as Wyatt shoved the final sausage patty into his mouth. "So, what brings you around this morning, Wyatt, or was it just for the sausage?"

"I just wanted to tell you what we know so far concerning the murder, although I have to admit it ain't much."

"Go ahead," Stone said.

"Well, do you remember it rained early in the morning before Walter was killed?" Wyatt asked.

"Yes," Stone and I answered in unison.

"Well, we found a couple of muddy footprints on the sidewalk, made by someone who appeared to come out of the door by the parlor. I wanted to ask you if either of you or Wendy might have made them. It looked like a pair of military-type boots left the prints. They were about a size nine or so. The footprints didn't match any of the detectives' shoes."

"I'm sure it wasn't me," Stone said. "I wear a size eleven, don't own any boots, and came in and out the back door all day. But isn't that about the size you wear, Lexie?"

"No, it wasn't me either," I answered, rather insulted. "I wear a six and a half, and Wendy was barefoot all day. She wears a size seven. However, I do have an idea of who might have made those prints."

"Who?" Both men wanted to know.

"Has anyone spoken with a gal named Roxie Kane?"

"Who's that?" Wyatt and Stone asked simultaneously.

"She's a girl Walter went out with. It was just one date, but it's still possible she was somehow involved. She might have felt used or taken advantage of by Walter. And I do know she owns military boots, because she's in the army reserves, and this was her one weekend this month to serve."

"Ah, we may be on to something," Wyatt said. "I'll see if someone can't look in to Roxie Kane. What else do you know about her, Lexie?"

I went on to tell Wyatt everything I could remember her aunt telling me. Stone came up with a valid point that hadn't occurred to me yet.

"If she happens to work as an EMT, she might have been one of the responders to our nine-one-one call. If I remember right, there were a couple of young women on the scene, a brunette and a blonde," Stone said. "That would explain how she could have made a footprint on the sidewalk. What color is Roxie's hair?"

"I don't know. I haven't actually met her. But you are right. How many female EMTs could Rockdale have? But Roxie lives in Weston, so she's probably on the EMT team there."

"True," Wyatt said. "The blonde is a gal named Bobbie. I didn't recognize the brunette. Either woman, or even a man with fairly small feet, could have left the footprints. Still, I'll see what more I can find out about this Roxie Kane. Thanks for the tip, Lexie."

"You know I'm always ready, able, and willing to help. How about if I go and talk to her and relate back whatever I can find out about Roxie to you? It would free you up to pursue other angles."

"Well, I guess that would be okay, if you're sure you want to do it. I'd keep it between you and me, though. The department might not be too thrilled to have civilians out interrogating suspects," Wyatt said. "And I know how determined you can be."

"Oh, I promise not to say anything to anybody but you about what I learn from 'interrogating' her. And seriously, Wyatt, I only engage suspects in friendly conversation, to see if I might glean some useful information."

"Of course you do," Wyatt said. "Well, engage Roxie in a 'friendly conversation,' and see if you can 'glean' anything from it."

"Do you have to encourage her, Wyatt? Do you remember what happened the last time someone died in the inn?" Stone asked. "Do you recall her nearly being killed twice, and possibly even three times?"

"Yes, I do, and you are probably right that she shouldn't—"

"I promise to be careful and do nothing but speak with her," I said. And before either man could reply, I asked, "Have you learned anything else, Wyatt?"

"Just that Melba Sneed had very recently changed her will, making Walter the sole inheritor. According to both Sheila and Chuck, they knew nothing about it. Neither one of them was too happy about the change. All three were in the original will. Even though Chuck is only Melba's stepson, she had raised him since he was very young. Seems like quite a coincidence, and certainly moves those two higher up on the suspect list," he said. "Some lawyer out of St. Joseph arranged for the new will to be executed."

"Yes, I would think losing an inheritance would move them up on the suspect list," I agreed. It moved Walter's two siblings up a notch or two on my list also. "I know Sheila didn't indicate to me she knew about her mother changing the will, but then, I don't imagine she would have admitted it to me if she did know."

Stone glanced at me sharply. I hadn't mentioned speaking to Sheila until that moment. I guess I never was exceptionally good at subterfuge. I often spoke before I thought.

"When was that?" Stone asked, as I was sure he would.

"Yesterday, while you two were at Smithville Lake, catching slabbers. I guess I just forgot to tell you about it."

"Yes, I'm sure you just 'forgot' to tell me about it," Stone said, with a wink at Detective Johnston. "Forgetting to tell me things is becoming a habit with you."

"Would anyone like a refill on their coffee?" I asked. I wanted to steer the topic of conversation away from my forgetfulness.

ELEVEN

Before Wyatt or Stone could attempt to talk me out of it, I wanted to go speak with Roxie, if I could be lucky enough to find her. It was Monday morning, and I had nothing else to do until it was time to serve afternoon tea to the Dudleys. I quickly fixed a cheesecake to serve with tea later on. I made it right out of a box because I didn't have time to make one from scratch. I had more important matters to attend to.

Once the cheesecake was chilling in the refrigerator, I called the Kane home again, hoping Roxie would pick up this time. Unfortunately, I found myself speaking to her mother again. Her mother didn't seem overanxious to talk with me. Her responses were short and snappy. She must have recognized my voice.

"Is Roxie home this morning?" I asked.

"No."

"Will she be home soon?" I asked Mrs. Kane.

"No."

"Do you know where she is?"

"She's got classes today," she replied.

"Oh, yeah, that's right. It is Monday, isn't it?"

"Yeah, she's in physiology right now, and then she goes to her anatomy class." At least she supplied me with a little more information than I was beginning to think I could dredge out of her. I thanked her and wished her a nice day before hanging up. I wanted to be pleasant to her in case I had to speak with her again in an attempt to track down Roxie. Not that I'm not usually pleasant to people, but I did make a special effort this time.

If I hurried right over to the college I might be able to speak to her between classes. I could ask around, try to locate the anatomy classroom, and catch her before she went in to class. Stone was still chatting with Wyatt in the kitchen, so I blew through the room with a quick, "See you later. I'm going out for a bit this morning."

I got to the college a little later than planned, and I had to ask a half dozen or more people before I found the anatomy classroom. It wasn't anywhere near the lab as I'd expected. By the time I arrived at the room, class was already in session. Looking in the window, I saw the teacher down below, standing at a podium. The seating was stair-stepped up from the podium, in an auditorium-styled setting. It was fairly dark at the top of the auditorium where the door was located, so I stepped in quietly and sat down in the closest seat. Looking around, I was happy to see several older students in the crowd. None were as old as I am, I'm sure. I was closer to retirement age than college age.

I asked the young man next to me if he knew where Roxie Kane was sitting. He didn't know who she was but, after speaking to several people down the aisle, he was able to point her out to me. She was located about halfway down toward the stage. I thanked him and slowly crept down to where Roxie sat. I bypassed a number of vacant seats. She looked up at me as I plopped down in the empty seat next to her.

She was a brunette like Paula Browne. She had her long hair tied back in a ponytail this morning. She was a good-sized girl, not fat by any means; she just had a large bone structure and broad shoulders. She looked every bit the part of a National Guard recruit.

"Good morning," I whispered. "Are you Roxie Kane?"

"Yes, I am. Who are you?"

"My name is Lexie Starr," I said. I had thought about trying to pass myself off as a student who had come back to school later in life to try to further my education. Then I decided it would serve no purpose to lie to her about who I was. She was apt to find out the truth eventually.

"Do I know you?"

"No, but I think you know the young man who died at my boyfriend's bed and breakfast a few days ago. My partner's B and B, that is." Boyfriend sounded so adolescent, but partner could be construed as about any kind of relationship.

"Walter? Walter Sneed?" She asked, incredulously. I could tell she was flabbergasted that I could know who she was, and also know she'd gone out with the man who had died in the inn.

"Yes, Walter. There was a muddy set of footprints outside the door the detectives think were left by you," I told her. Of course I was stretching the truth a little, as you know I'm prone to do in circumstances such as this one. "Apparently, you were the last to see him alive, which indicates you could have something to do with his death, or at least know something about what happened to the young man. I thought I'd approach you before the authorities did, just to kind of give you the heads-up."

"Ladies. You over there," I heard spoken over the microphone. I looked up to see the professor pointing straight at Roxie and me with a laser pointer she'd been using to highlight various bones on a hanging skeleton. The skeleton looked realistic, as if it were actually made of bone and marrow. It would have been a nice addition to the haunted house. I thought it was so much better than the skeleton we'd been able to find at the department store.

"Yes?" I answered meekly. My response was barely audible in the massive auditorium.

"Could you hold it down a little? This is a classroom, and the other students in the class are here to learn, not to listen to you two visiting," the professor said. "You on the right. Would you like to tell the class where the patella bone is located?"

I looked at Roxie. She pointed at me. Damn it! I was on the right. But thank goodness for childhood sports, making knee surgery necessary a few years ago. I actually knew the answer to her question.

"It's the kneecap, ma'am."

"That's correct. I'm surprised you heard me point it out with all the visiting you're doing. Now quiet down and pay attention, or leave the auditorium."

Several minutes went by until I had enough courage to speak to Roxie again. I couldn't waste this opportunity learning about carpal and tarsal bones.

"What do you know about Walter's murder?" I whispered. "What were you doing at the inn that morning?"

"Shush!" She whispered back. "I'm trying to listen to the instructor."

Roxie and I both looked up to see the professor glaring at us. She shook her index finger at us and continued her lecture. Roxie began to scribble furiously on a sheet of paper she'd been taking notes on. She wrote for what seemed like a very long time. When she finally finished, she handed the note to me. According to the note, she knew absolutely nothing about his death. "Yes, I was there for a few minutes," she had written. "But only to let him know how disgusted I was with him. He used me, and he hurt and humiliated me, so I wanted to give him a piece of my mind. And I did. Then I went back out the front door, and down the sidewalk, the way I'd entered. There was a sign on the door that said 'Welcome. Come on in,' so I did. I didn't see anyone else but Walter in the house, but then, I had walked straight into the room where he was lying in a fake coffin. Coffin or not, he was very much alive when I left."

This sounded reasonable to me, but it could also be a convenient story she'd made up. I wrote back, "Can anyone confirm your story? What size shoe do you wear?"

Her next message stated no one else knew she'd gone to Alexandria Inn to confront Walter. She was too embarrassed by the whole thing to tell anyone. But she swore she had nothing to do with Walter's death, and didn't know anything about it either. And it was none of my business what size shoe she wore. If the detectives wanted to know, she'd tell them, she said, but she was under no obligation to tell me.

"Did you see or hear anything while you were there?" I wrote.

"No," she answered. "But I noticed Walter was sweating, shaking, and seemed extremely confused at the time. I wasn't sure he even realized I was there or what I was saying to him. I felt like I was wasting my time trying to tell him off. But I have no idea what was wrong with him, and I swear I had nothing to do with his death."

"What?" I said out loud, after reading her response. "But that means—"

That was the first time I'd ever been kicked out of a class. The professor had stopped her lecture, pointed her laser light at me, and motioned for me to exit the auditorium. As I stood up to leave, all eyes were on me. It was a long walk of shame up the stairs to the door. I heard the teacher say, "You too, miss" as I climbed the steps. Darn it, I hadn't meant to get Roxie kicked out of her anatomy class. I'm sure she needed those credits to get her degree.

"Thanks a lot!" She said to me outside the classroom door. "Now I'll have to talk with Mrs. Herron to see if I can get back into the class. And tomorrow there's a major test I need to do well on to pass the course."

I apologized. I was sincerely sorry. I really was. I had certainly not planned to get her in trouble. But she didn't accept my apology very well, stomping her foot and turning to leave. I looked at her feet as she stomped. Yes, I'd estimate them to be somewhere between size eight and nine. I'd say the footprints were definitely hers, even though she was wearing tennis shoes today, not boots.

"Good luck with your test," I said inanely as she walked away. She said nothing in response. With her back still to me, she lifted her left hand in a one-fingered salute. Wow! Kids these days were sure a lot ruder than they were in my day.

At least I'd found out it was Roxie who'd most likely left the footprints and why she claimed to have been at the inn in the first place. If Walter was in the shape he was in at the time Roxie arrived at the inn, he must have begun to come out from under the effect of the chloroform, and had already been injected with the insulin, which was taking effect. I'd have to ask Wendy if sweating, shaking, and confusion were symptoms of low blood sugar. Once his blood sugar dropped to a certain level, he would have collapsed into a coma and eventually died, which is exactly what had occurred. He might have been too confused and out of it to call out for help, not cognizant of what was happening to him.

Could this be a ploy on Roxie's part? I suddenly wondered. If she were a diabetic herself, she would know the symptoms of low blood sugar and might be using this story to steer suspicion away from herself. If the authorities already knew it was she who'd left the footprints, as I had indicated to her, then she'd want to concoct a story to make them suspect the killer had already come and gone by the time she arrived at the scene. It was definitely something to think about. Being a diabetic, as more and more Americans were each year, would give her access to the insulin too.

"Hey, are you a diabetic?" I hollered down the hallway. There was no response. Even if Roxie hadn't already left the building, I doubt she would have given me a response. I was not her favorite person right then.

I called Wendy on my cell phone, and she confirmed the symptoms Roxie claimed Walter exhibited were indeed those of a low blood sugar reaction. She was somewhat surprised to hear Walter had already begun to regain consciousness from the affect of chloroform, but deduced he might not have been given a full dose, or a strong enough dose, of it.

Then, as Wendy is prone to do, she began telling me everything she knew about chloroform. I listened politely for a minute or two, although I didn't really care that chloroform was forty times sweeter than sugar, or that it could also be made by the chlorination of methane by using free radicals to create a reaction in the presence of ultraviolet light. When she lapsed into a story about the American chemist Dr. Samuel Guthrie, who first prepared chloroform, I broke in to tell her I was in heavy traffic (in Rockdale, no less) and needed to pay full attention to the road.

After putting my cell phone back into my purse, I thought about what I'd learned by speaking with Roxie. I now felt as if I'd created more questions than I'd found answers to. I walked out to the parking lot and headed back to the Alexandria Inn in my Jeep, not sure if I'd ever get the chance to speak with Roxie Kane again. I hoped so. I still wanted to get an answer to my last question. If she were a diabetic, she would most likely jump to the top of my suspect list. Being the last known person to see him alive put her in a questionable position. How coincidental was it that she was with him just minutes before he died?

TWELVE

I stopped by Pete's Pantry on the way home from the college to pick up a few groceries. Stone was grilling some rib eye steaks for supper, and I wanted to get the ingredients to make an eggplant casserole so Eleanor would have something substantial to eat in lieu of the meat.

The selection of eggplant was pretty lame, even though it was still eggplant season in the Midwest. I also picked up some carrots so I could serve them in Stone's favorite way—boiled, dipped in milk and cracker crumbs, and then fried in butter. Hopefully, the Dudleys would like them fixed that way, as well.

While I was at the grocery store, I picked up the ingredients I would need to make a broccoli/rice/cheese casserole on Tuesday, and some rather sorry-looking green beans to snap and cook. I would add a bit of bacon grease to add flavor, and serve them along with the casserole. Maybe Eleanor wouldn't notice the hint of bacon flavor in the beans, and not realize she was eating the by-product of a pig. If I didn't help raise her cholesterol level, who would?

Then it occurred to me that if her husband's tongue swelled up like a blowfish and he developed unsightly blotches all over his face due to his pork allergy, Eleanor might catch on that a meat by-product was somehow involved with the supper I was feeding her. I quickly replaced the limp green beans with a large head of cauliflower.

Standing in line at the checkout counter, I heard the clerk

talking to the customer in front of me, asking her if she planned to attend the football scrimmage scheduled for that afternoon. The college team would be competing against another nearby community college team, a game that wouldn't affect their league records. The game would be in lieu of a regular practice for each of the two teams.

"Do you know if the cheerleaders will be cheering at the game?" I asked the clerk, who gave me an odd look. "My niece is a cheerleader and I enjoy watching her cheer."

"Oh, of course," she replied with a smile. "I should think the cheerleaders will be cheering tonight. They're competing against another college team, so it'd stand to reason both sides might have cheerleaders present. I'm sure they could only benefit from the practice. You might call the college and ask though, before you go to the trouble to attend the game."

Stone loved to watch college football on television every Saturday and pro football on Sundays. I wondered if he'd be interested in going to watch the scrimmage game after supper. The Dudleys would be left alone at the inn tonight, but entertaining the guests 24/7 was not one of the services the inn offered. I still wanted to speak with Sidney, Walter's long-time girlfriend, or possibly even to her best friend, Paula, again, if Sidney was still too overwhelmed with grief to talk. Either girl might be aware of someone Walter had issues with before his death.

I called the college as the lady had suggested, and was told the cheerleaders would be attending the game and practicing some of their new cheers. Stone agreed to go, because he enjoyed football on any level.

The stands were fairly empty when we arrived at the college stadium around three in the afternoon. It was cool and windy, so we'd worn windbreakers over thick sweaters to ward off the cold. We stopped at the concession stand on the way in. Stone wanted a cup of hot chocolate and I, of course, wanted a cup of coffee.

We took a couple of seats together about halfway up the bleachers on the fifty yard line, which Stone assured me was a great vantage point to watch the game. He didn't expect a large crowd, since the game was being played in the afternoon while many people were still at work. And after all, it was just a scrimmage game, not anything that would affect the teams' rankings, or their official records.

The cheerleaders were mingling with the crowd. They looked cold to me. They'd have to cheer their little hearts out to keep warm this afternoon in the skimpy outfits they were wearing. I could still remember those days when I was a cheerleader. I hadn't had a clue to what was taking place on the field. I didn't know the difference between a kickoff and a punt, and really hadn't cared to know. Now that it no longer mattered, I found myself shouting "clipping" at the TV, and could explain what a nickel or dime package was in detail.

I thought it best to enjoy my cup of coffee and wait for the game to start before I went down to the sidelines and tried to steal a few minutes of Sidney's time, assuming she even showed up for the game. Stone held my free hand while he pointed out the few players and people in the stands he was acquainted with. I was surprised by how many businessmen he knew from around town. He had dealt with a lot of them while restoring the Alexandria Inn.

Listening to people chattering around us, we found out the band would not be present at the game and, as I already knew, the cheerleaders had only chosen to attend to try out some of their new routines. Like the football players, the game would count in lieu of cheerleading practice this week. The opponent's team had not brought along their cheerleaders for this Monday afternoon scrimmage. They had but a handful of fans in the bleachers on their side of the field. The officials for the game were merely volunteers from around town. They weren't completely schooled on all of the rules of the game.

"Don't forget there's a wake tomorrow night we need to attend," Stone reminded me. "We'll need to serve an early dinner, so we can get dressed and get to the church by six-thirty."

"You're right. I don't want to be late," I said. "There will be a lot of key players at the wake, and it might prove useful to mingle around and chat with them."

"You aren't going to turn this young man's wake into an interrogation, are you?" Stone asked. Why does everyone use that word when they're describing my technique of investigating? I was slightly insulted by his question, even though there was a lot of truth to it.

I could tell he was a bit appalled at the idea of my questioning Walter's family and friends at the funeral services, and I agreed I would only talk to them about the murder if the subject came up in conversation. I probably would do very little talking at all, I told him. Still, it wouldn't hurt to visit a bit, offer my condolences, and maybe ask a question here or there as long as I wasn't too intrusive. I would try to refrain myself from "interrogating" anyone at the memorial services.

"Okay, then. But let's let the mourners have their time to grieve and reflect on Walter's life. Most likely the killer will not even be at the services. If he disliked him enough to kill him, why would he come to the memorial services to mourn for him?"

"Of course, you're right," I said. He was right unless a close family member or a so-called friend thought it would raise suspicion if he didn't attend.

Rockdale was ahead ten to three at the end of the first quarter.

It took some doing, but I finally convinced Stone of my need to speak with Sidney for just a minute or two. I hadn't been able to ascertain if she were among the group of cheerleaders or not. They all tended to look alike from a distance. I could only pick out Paula due to her brunette hair. I excused myself and went down to the sidelines, after first stopping off at the Johnny-on-the-spot to get rid of some of the coffee I'd been drinking all day long.

I noticed Paula right off the bat and waved at her when she caught my eye. She waved back, then she turned back to the other cheerleader she was conversing with. I made my way through the throng of cheerleaders to where she and the other girl were standing.

"Hi, Ms. Reed," Paula greeted me. She seemed surprised to see me. I was equally surprised she'd remembered my fictitious name.

"Hello, ladies," I said to both girls. "I love your uniforms."

"Thanks," said the other girl. "I'm Jennifer, by the way."

"Hi, Paula. Hello, Jennifer. I'm Wanda Reed, an investigative writer for the *Rockdale Gazette*," I said, for Jennifer's benefit, in case she didn't recognize me from their practice on Saturday.

"I thought you told me your name was Rhonda," Paula said quizzically.

"Oh, I'm sorry. I meant to say Rhonda. It's just that some of my closest friends call me Wanda, so I misspoke. It's kind of an inside joke, you see," I explained, fumbling for a reason to have forgotten my own name. Paula was still young; her memory was better than mine. "Rhonda or Wanda. I answer to either."

"What are you doing here, Ms. Reed?" Paula asked. She didn't want to use either name, apparently.

"I had hoped to speak with Sidney. I'm still working on my article for the paper. Is she here today? I've yet to see her," I said, glancing from one cheerleader to the next.

"No, she's still too upset. She doesn't feel like she has anything to cheer about. Her parents are keeping her home from school and all the other school activities this week. It's to give her a chance to recover from the shock and grief of losing Walter. We might see her tomorrow at the wake. Most of the cheerleading squad is going to go to the wake together," she said. "Sidney told me on the phone this morning her parents didn't want her to attend the wake or the funeral. They think it'll be too much for her to handle. Still, I imagine she'll try to talk them in to letting her attend. I know her well enough to know she will want to see him one last time, even if it's in a casket. It will be difficult for her to let go and get on with her life."

"I understand, and I can see why she'd want an opportunity to say goodbye. But I also understand her parents' concern. Have the detectives spoken with her yet?" I asked.

"I'm not sure. I haven't been able to see her since Saturday, and she didn't mention talking to the police on the phone. I doubt they've spoken to her, though. She's been holed up in her house," Paula said. "Her mom and dad have been fending off authorities and media, not even allowing her friends to see her. She's just too distraught to see anyone right now, I'm sure."

Maybe I'd get a chance to speak with Sidney for a moment at the wake, if she was able to attend, but the likelihood didn't sound too promising. I'd probably have to go through the parents to get to her. They sounded very protective of her, and there was nothing wrong with that. I'd always been over-protective of Wendy too. When you're a single parent, it's hard not to spend most of your time worrying about your children. And parental concern wasn't something you got over, no matter how old your child was. It was just part of the job description of being a parent.

"Well, maybe I'll see you at the wake tomorrow," I said to

her. I really had no intention of getting too close to Paula at the wake, however. I didn't want her to figure out I wasn't really Rhonda "Wanda" Reed, a newspaper journalist. Lying could be such a nuisance sometimes. It was so easy to get caught up in a web of lies. Like I said before, I never used to be such a liar, but murder seemed to bring out the worst in me when it came to telling the truth.

Just as I turned from Paula to leave, I was struck by what felt like a Mack truck. I felt a painful impact to my midsection, and my neck snapped forward, as I was pushed backward with a lot of force. My breath was knocked out of me. I remember falling to the ground with a heavy weight on top of me, and the next thing I knew I was looking up into Stone's eyes as a paramedic was strapping an oxygen mask on me. I noticed I was no longer on the sideline, but off to the side of the bleachers, lying on a canvas stretcher. I must have blacked out for a short time. Stone patted my arm and spoke reassuringly.

"You'll be okay. They're just going to take you to the hospital for further observation. They want to X-ray you to make sure you have no broken bones. And they want to watch you for signs of a concussion," he said. "They examined you for fractures and didn't find any sign of one. Your eyes are not dilated, and your pupils responded normally to light, so they don't suspect a concussion either, but they do have to make certain."

"What happened?" I asked, from beneath the oxygen mask.

"You got tackled by a wide receiver. He was running along the sidelines toward the end zone when a Rockdale player knocked him out of bounds. You had your back to the field and got taken down with him," he explained. "So we're off to the emergency room, a place you're very familiar with."

Yes, I had been to the emergency room a few times in the past, but this was my first ride in an ambulance. I had a severe headache by that time and was relieved they didn't have to turn the siren on just to transport me to the hospital for further observation. I just hoped the hospital didn't find a reason to admit me. I had a wake to go to the following evening, and not even a concussion and a few broken bones would prevent me from being there.

THIRTEEN

Several hours later, after a battery of tests, I was released from the Wheatfield Memorial Hospital in St. Joseph with a few bruised ribs and a headache. It was almost midnight when we returned to the inn in Rockdale. I'd been given pain medication at the hospital, which had alleviated the pain in my ribs and eliminated my headache completely. I didn't feel half bad for someone in my condition. I knew there was a reason I stockpiled pain pills.

The house was eerily quiet as we entered the kitchen. The message light on the phone was blinking. I pressed the button and listened.

"Mom, Stone, this is Wendy. I have some great news for you. I want to tell you about it in person, though, not on an answering machine. So, I'll be over tomorrow morning," she said in her recorded message. "You'll both be excited about it too."

"Wonder what that's all about?" Stone asked.

"Hard to say, but she sure is happy about something, isn't she?"

"Guess we'll find out in the morning. Let's get your poor, battered body to bed. I'm sure you'll be even sorer in the morning. Do you still have some pain pills on hand for tomorrow?" Stone asked.

"Of course."

Normally, after hearing a message like Wendy's, and getting knocked out cold at a football game, I would find it hard to get to sleep. But after a long evening and a shot of Demerol, I found falling asleep came very easily to me. I didn't awaken again until I felt Stone rubbing my shoulder at eight-thirty the next morning. As predicted, it hurt to even breathe, much less move my body. I groaned dramatically as I sat up in bed.

"I brought you some coffee and your favorite granola cereal for breakfast," Stone said.

"Thanks, honey. What about the Dudleys? I need to get downstairs and fix them something for breakfast too."

"Don't worry about Steve and Eleanor. I fed them some cold cereal and toast, and they've headed out to meet with a cousin in Kansas City."

"I hope they weren't disappointed about having toast and granola cereal for breakfast," I said.

"Actually, they had Honey Nut Cheerios. I explained to them about your accident last night, and they were fine with their breakfast. They're both watching their cholesterol levels. They both seemed quite concerned about you too, and wanted me to wish you a quick recovery."

"No headache this morning, but my ribs are sore, and I feel stiff all over."

"I figured you would be, but at least your head feels all right today. Stay in bed as long as you want. There's nothing pressing this morning," Stone assured me.

"I think I'll come down to the kitchen for a coffee refill in a little bit and wait for Wendy to arrive with her big news."

Before Wendy's foot even touched down inside the front door, she blurted out breathlessly, "Andy is flying in here tomorrow afternoon to spend a few days. He told me to tell you guys, and to tell you he'll be staying here at the inn with you, as usual. It was a last minute decision on his part."

"Fantastic!" Stone and I spoke in unison.

After giving both of us a hug, Wendy sat down at the kitchen table. "He'll arrive here at four-fifteen tomorrow at Kansas City International Airport. I'll go and pick him up."

As I poured her a cup of coffee, I said, "I can't wait to see him. It's been such a long time. He hasn't been here since Fourth of July weekend."

"That's wonderful news, Wendy," Stone said. Andy had always been Stone's favorite nephew, possibly his favorite relative. Andy was the son of Stone's older brother, Sterling, and he lived not too far from Stone's former residence in Myrtle Beach, South Carolina. Andy was a pilot and owned a small charter flight business there. "Is there any particular reason he's coming to Kansas City, or is it just for a visit?"

"You know how Andy always wanted to own some land? He noticed an ad for a place on the Internet quite a while ago, and he just found out it's still on the market. It's like a farm, I guess. He'd like to move back to this area, and thought maybe this was his opportunity to do so. He's got an appointment with a realtor to look at the place Thursday morning," Wendy explained.

"I remember you talking about that before, when he first saw the ad," I said. "Then when nothing came of it, I figured he'd changed his mind about moving back to the Midwest."

"Me too," Stone said. "And as much as I'd love to have Andy close by, I'm a little skeptical about his giving up his business and becoming a farmer. He has no experience in farming, and even experienced farmers are having a tough time of it these days."

"He's still planning to pilot charter flights on the side," Wendy said. "He has a friend who owns a charter company in Kansas City, and he offered Andy a part-time job if he moves back. That's the only reason he would even consider a move like this. He knows he has no experience living on a farm and making it work. He wants something to fall back on with some guaranteed income. He's saved enough for a nice down payment, he told me."

"He always was good with his money. Where is this farm? I don't recall. Wasn't it west of here?" Stone asked.

"Yeah, just west of here. It's a couple miles north of Atchison, Kansas."

"How much are they asking for the place?" Stone asked Wendy.

"Andy never said, but he thought it was a very reasonable price. He said they've dropped the price considerably since he first saw the ad months ago. They're desperate to sell. The price includes an old farmhouse, which needs a little repairing and remodeling."

"How much repair and remodeling?" Stone asked. It didn't surprise me that Stone was being practical and pragmatic. As much as he loved Andy, he wanted what was best for him, not what was best for himself. Above all else, Stone wanted Andy to be successful and happy. Stone's first wife had been unable to have children, and I knew he thought of Andy as if he were his own son.

"Well, I don't know what shape the place is in. I don't think he does either, because he's never seen it except for some digital photos I sent him when he first mentioned the place. I drove out there to take the photos from the road, and as I recall it didn't look like it was on the verge of falling down, or anything. But he's very handy, you know. And he definitely wants you to go with him to look at the farm on Thursday, Stone."

"Good. I'll be anxious to see it. Yes, he is handy. But he doesn't want to jump into something like this without careful deliberation, and consideration for everything that's involved in a decision such as this," Stone said. "Personally, I hope it works out because I've missed him greatly."

"So have I," Wendy said a little shyly.

"Tell me more about what he's told you about the farm," Stone said. "What kinds of crops are grown on it?"

"Well, it's six hundred and forty acres. I don't know anything about crops, but there's a chicken coop on the property and some chickens, and a pigsty with some pigs. Also, there's a barn full of hay, and a goat or two, a nearly new John Deere tractor, and most importantly, ninety-three head of Black Angus, twenty of which are this year's calves."

"It sounds like he wants to be a cattle rancher rather than a farmer. That's a relief. That would make him a little less vulnerable than a farmer raising wheat and soybeans, where he'd be totally dependent on the weather," Stone said. "As you know, it's feast or famine around here. We can have severe droughts, or we can have deluges of rain, flooding the fields. Cattle are pretty resilient if you have barns and water tanks and all. I feel better about the move already. Did Andy mention why the current owners are selling out?"

"Andy said the couple who own the farm are getting up in years, and the husband has several medical conditions, making it more convenient for him to be closer to the VA Hospital in Leavenworth, so they're going to look for an assisted-living place there. He even mentioned something about the new owner adopting his beloved dog, which he doubts will be allowed at their new home," Wendy said.

"Well, I'm kind of excited about the idea," I said, breaking into the conversation. "It might turn out to be the best thing that ever happened to Andy. I believe all things happen for a reason, and I have faith whatever happens in this instance is what's meant to happen."

"I'm excited too, now that I've heard more about it," Stone said. "Ninety-three head of cattle is a nice-sized herd."

"I'd just be thrilled to have Andy living back here," Wendy

admitted. "We've established a great friendship, just talking on the phone, ever since I got back from the east coast. He's going to take me out to eat Thursday night. I recommended the new little steakhouse in town. It's called Smoking Joe's, and all of their steaks are grilled over an open fire."

Wendy was beaming at the thought of spending time with Stone's nephew, and I hoped Stone didn't bring up my visit to Wheatfield Hospital last night. I didn't want to do anything to put a damper on her ecstatic mood. And I wasn't in the frame of mind for a scolding from my daughter either. She could be very intolerant of my impulsive nature.

Wendy finished her cup of coffee while we discussed the arrival of Andy and other current issues. No new developments had come out of the coroner's lab, so I told her what I'd learned, being as vague as possible. Nothing good could come of relating everything that had happened to me in the last couple of days.

Naturally, she was concerned when Stone got around to telling her about my accident at the football game. I should have known he couldn't keep a story like that to himself. She didn't say much, just shook her head in disgust. I quickly changed the subject to talk about our guests at the inn, the Dudleys, before Wendy got up on her soapbox, which she was prone to do.

A few minutes later Wendy stood up to leave. She wanted to get her hair cut, her nails done, and possibly even do a little clothes shopping before she picked Andy up at the airport tomorrow. I could tell she was nervous about his arrival and was hoping something of a romantic nature would come of his visit. I walked her to the door, moving a little tenderly with my bruised ribs and stiff, aching muscles. She told me to take it easy for a few days, kissed me, and headed off to a nearby mall.

"Do you think this budding romance between Wendy and Andy will amount to anything, or is it just wishful thinking on Wendy's part?" I asked Stone after Wendy had left.

"Last time I talked to Andy, he couldn't say enough good things about her, so I'd say there's a fighting chance something will develop."

"Do you know if he's dating anyone right now?"

"I don't think so. At least he hasn't mentioned anyone. He's never dated anyone seriously in the past, so he brings no excess baggage with him, anyway. I certainly hope something develops between Andy and Wendy. They deserve each other, and I think they'd make a good pair," Stone said. "Andy's spent most of his time building up his charter flight business in the last few years. He doesn't give himself a chance to sit back, relax, and enjoy life very often. I admire his ambition and dedication, but I wish he'd loosen up a bit and give himself an opportunity to have some fun and find someone special to share his life with. I hope it's someone like Wendy."

"I hope so too, Stone," I said. "I'd love to have Andy as my son-in-law. As you know, the first son-in-law didn't work out so well."

Stone agreed and left to go check the mailbox. He was waiting on a part for his lawnmower, which he'd ordered over the Internet. I poured myself another cup of coffee and got the Bunn coffeemaker ready for a fresh pot.

I was glad the Dudleys had gone to visit relatives in Kansas City, because I didn't feel up to dealing with guests for a couple of hours. I'd wanted to check in on Melba to see if I could catch her in a more lucid state, but even that didn't appeal to me this morning. I felt more like relaxing in the chaise lounge on the back deck with a good book.

After reading for several hours and nodding off a few times, I heard Stone come out the back door. He was carrying a paper plate with a turkey sandwich, and a few potato chips, on it.

"Thought you might be getting hungry. How are you feeling by now?" he asked. "Are you still pretty sore?"

"Yes, but I feel much better," I said. "I'm kind of getting accustomed to you waiting on me hand and foot, Stone, and I like it. I should get hurt more often."

"No. I don't want you getting hurt and getting used to this kind of treatment," he said, with a chuckle. "Seriously, I'm glad to see you're resting."

"I've been resting and reading for hours. Now I'm thinking I might run over to visit Melba for a few minutes. I'd like to take her a colorful potted plant to brighten up her room, because it's so stark and depressing."

"Yes, I'm sure that's the only reason you want to go visit her," Stone said rather sarcastically. "I'm sure grilling her with questions about her deceased son never crossed your mind."

"Well, sure, the subject might come up in passing—"

"I'm just kidding you, Lexie," Stone assured me. "I can't imagine you could get into any trouble just speaking with Melba for a few minutes. But, then, I couldn't have imagined that speaking with a cheerleader could land you in the hospital either."

Fourteen

I could hear loud snoring as I walked up the hallway to room 464 at the Wheatfield Memorial Hospital, where I had just spent the previous evening. Melba was sound asleep, and a man I didn't recognize sat quietly in a chair next to her bed. He looked to be in his early-to-mid-forties with slicked-back jet-black hair, a thin mustache, and dark bushy sideburns. He had on a pair of aviator-style sunglasses that were out of place in the artificially lit hospital room.

I noticed the man was writing something in a black, legal-looking, notebook. I figured him for a detective with the St. Joseph Homicide Division. If so, I was going to leave the flowers and go, after first asking him if there were any new developments in the case, which he was unlikely to answer. But it would be worth a shot.

"Hello, there. I see Melba is resting. I'm Lexie Starr. And you are?" I spoke loudly to be heard over Melba's snoring, which had intensified. I'm sure she was medically sedated.

"Sheldon Wright, ma'am."

"Are you a detective, sir?"

"No."

"Are you a relative?" I asked.

"No."

"Part of the medical staff here?"

"No."

"A reporter, perhaps?"

126

"No."

"Let me make this easier for both you and me. How do you know Melba, Mr. Wright?" I asked him. I could tell he was being intentionally evasive just to annoy me.

"I represent Ms. Sneed," he replied without looking at me. "I'm a partner with the law firm of Hocraffer, Zumbrunn, Kobialka, and Wright, out of St. Joseph, and she is one of our clients."

"Hocraffer, Zumbrunn, Kobialka, and Wright? That's quite a mouthful, isn't it? Is Melba filing another lawsuit?" I asked. This was obviously the lawyer I'd heard about before, the one who assisted Melba in filing foolish and ill-advised lawsuits. I didn't trust him at all.

"No, no lawsuit. Not yet at least," he said, as if she were considering one. "We heard about the death of her son and knew she'd need to make some changes in her last will and testament, and also her power-of-attorney. I felt I should come without delay to update her documents."

"Are you saying she didn't contact you herself to request your services?" I asked with an air of disbelief, as if I found his actions totally unacceptable.

"No, she didn't have to. At Hocraffer, Zumbrunn, Kobialka, and Wright, we pride ourselves on being able to anticipate our client's every need. We are at their side before they, themselves, even realize they need our services." He beamed as if he'd just been awarded the Nobel Peace Prize. What a lot of hot air this man was, I thought.

"What took you so long to get to her side?" I asked, sarcastically. I felt his presence was an intrusion at this point, as if mine wasn't, and I wanted him to leave so I could get down to the business of waking Melba up and plying her with questions. Why couldn't the law firm have waited until after the funeral to make alterations in her legal documents? I mean, really, what were the chances of her dying, or needing someone to decide whether to pull the plug or not, in the next few days? Her ailments were primarily mental, not physical.

He was finally looking directly at me, so I glared at him without even trying to disguise the contempt written on my face. "Is Hocraffer, Zumbrunn, Kobialka, and Wright always this thorough and efficient, Mr. Wright? Is your law firm in the habit of encroaching on the survivors of murder victims before their loved ones are even in the ground? What exactly do you personally have to gain by getting Ms. Sneed's legal documents into order with no regard for her mental and emotional state? In simpler terms that I'm sure you'll understand, what is the frigging hurry?"

"There's no time like the present, Ms. Starr," he said with a great deal of annoyance in his voice. "And I resent your implication. One never knows what's going to happen. Who could have predicted the death of such a healthy young man as Walter Sneed? What's to say something equally dreadful couldn't strike Ms. Sneed and require someone with power-of-attorney status to make a life-or-death decision on her behalf? What if something unforeseen happened, and the person with power-of-attorney had predeceased her? What then? Who would make decisions for her? She could find her life and well being in peril, don't you agree?"

"Uh-huh," I said. I was tired of being lectured to by a man who looked like a member of the Italian mafia. He was talking to me as though I was a misbehaving child, and I thought he was being condescending. "I understand all that, but still, the woman's son is barely cold, and she's obviously in no condition to deal with important, possibly life-altering, decisions like that right now. Can you not see that for yourself?"

"And just how are you connected with Ms. Sneed?" he asked, clearly disgusted with me now.

"Her son, unfortunately, was killed in my partner's establishment."

"And?"

"I came to check on her and see if she was doing better, and to bring her this African violet," I said. I held it up for him to admire.

"Yeah, like a stupid flower is going to solve any of her problems right now. They'll take the flower pot away, anyway," he told me smugly. "Anything she can throw or hurt herself with is prohibited and removed from her room. They wouldn't want her pitching that pot through the windowpane, or at their heads."

As if on cue, a nurse walked into the room, checked to see if Melba was still resting comfortably, picked up the potted African violet, said, "this will have to go," and left. Mr. Wright just looked at me and smiled arrogantly.

"I told you so. Like she needed a stupid flower—"

"Oh, shut up—"

"Do you know Melba personally?" he asked.

"Well, no, but—"

"So, you believe she's up to dealing with a complete stranger, but not her lawyer, who's here on official business, acting in her capacity and looking out for her best interests?" he asked.

I was feeling very defensive at this point, and our voices were rising to such a level that Melba had ceased snoring and was now stirring in her bed. "I have every bit as much right to be here as you do, Mr. Wright! I was very, very close to Walter, and I know he would have wanted me to look out for his mother's welfare."

That was a stretch, I'll admit. I'd barely known the kid's name until he was killed within earshot of me, but I felt I knew him as well as the attorney probably did.

"I'm also looking in to his mother's welfare, and am here in my desire to protect her," he said, a little calmer now so as not to alarm his client. He turned to the woman in question, who was sitting up in bed now, with a bewildered expression on her face.

"Good afternoon, Ms. Sneed. I'm so sorry to learn of the death of your son. How are you feeling?" Mr. Wright asked with obvious insincerity. The sickeningly sweet voice he used to speak to her was almost nauseating to me. "We'll need to make some alterations in your legal documents."

"Who are you?" She asked. She pointed a long, gnarly index finger at him, and then at me, and asked, "And who's your wife here?"

"I'm your attorney, Ms. Sneed. I'm Sheldon Wright, of Hocraffer, Zumbrunn, Kobialka, and Wright," he said. Then he pointed my way with his thumb, and spoke in a disparaging manner. "And, trust me, this woman is not my wife."

"You're an attorney? Am I being sued?" Melba asked. "Have I done something wrong?"

"No, of course not. As you know, your son has recently passed. I'm here to update your power-of-attorney, and of course, your will. It's routine for my law firm to keep these documents current, just in case the unexpected happens," he explained. "We always put our clients first, because we need to protect your interests, of course."

"The only thing I'm interested in is finding out why I'm here and when I'm getting out." She spat out, literally. Bits and pieces of God knows what flew out all over the bed. Melba ran the back of her hand across her frothy mouth. I now was in danger of puking up my lunch.

I'd sat silently up to this point during Mr. Wright's conversation with Melba. I reached out now and patted the hand she hadn't swiped across her mouth as briefly as I could. "I imagine they'll be releasing you soon, my dear. I'm sure they'll let you out to attend Walter's wake this evening. You know, you really don't have to deal with all this legal stuff today if you don't want to. Next week is soon enough, after things have settled down, and by then you'll be in a better condition to deal with them."

"Okay," she responded. It was clear she was confused, and I was sure she didn't have a clue what she was agreeing to. Still, I couldn't resist tossing Mr. Wright an "I told you so" look. Two could play at his game, I thought.

"And who are you again?" Melba asked me. I realized then that nothing beneficial or informative was going to come out of this visit with Melba. I doubt she could have come up with her own name, much less mine, or Mr. Wright's.

"I'm Lexie Starr, Melba. Your son was working for my partner and me when he mysteriously died. The police have determined that an unknown assailant killed Walter, so I'm trying to help the detectives discover who that person is. I also feel I should make sure you're being treating adequately. I feel a bit responsible—"

"Aha!" Melba exclaimed. "So you're the one who's responsible for all this?"

"Oh, no, Melba—"

With Melba's last remark, spittle had sprayed all over my shirt. I couldn't wait to get home, remove my clothes, and boil them.

"So, Ms. Starr, *are* you responsible for all this?" Mr. Wright asked. Now he had the same "I told you so" look on his face I'd worn moments earlier. "Why exactly do you feel so responsible? Is it guilt? Negligence? Or what? Are you here to try to talk Ms. Sneed out of her money? What exactly do you have to gain personally from being here, trying to pretend you honestly give a damn about what happens to Melba?"

"Don't be ridiculous!" I nearly shouted. "I honestly do give a damn, you jerk! Walter was working for me when he was killed. I was at the house when it happened, but I had no idea what was going on in the parlor while I was in another part of the house. That's what I meant by feeling responsible. I had nothing to do with his death, I have nothing to gain from it, and I certainly don't want a dime from Ms. Sneed. Like I said before, I was very close to Walter. I would give anything, and do anything, to bring his killer to justice."

"Of course you would," he said snidely.

"At the very least I feel I owe it to Walter to look after his mother," I told the attorney. "Which is more than I can say for the folks at Hocraffer, Zumbrunn, Kobialka, and Wright. I think I should have the authorities check you for an alibi and a monetary motive. You seem terribly concerned about Melba's will, and what will happen to her money if something happens to her. I might also see what I can do to have you disbarred."

"Humph! Fat chance, lady!" he said as he laughed in disdain. He knew he hadn't technically done anything unjust, remotely illegal, completely immoral, or anything else he could be disbarred for doing. He had pissed me off, and that's about the size of it. Pissing people off was merely part of the job description of a lawyer. There weren't a zillion lawyer jokes for no reason.

"Watch me, you pompous ass," I hissed.

With that final declaration I stormed out of the room. I knew I didn't have a chance in hell of getting the man disbarred. Cats would eat with chopsticks before I could pull off a trick like that. But at least my threat gave the creep something to chew on for a while.

FIFTEEN

I was still fuming when I stepped out of the elevator on the ground floor. Instead of going straight out the door to the parking lot, I turned and followed the signs down a long hallway to the ladies' room. I wanted to splash some cool water on my face to help me calm down, and I had to use the restroom. All the coffee I had consumed in the morning was catching up with me, which was not to say I didn't already want another cup.

So after using the restroom, I detoured to the front lobby and picked up a cup of coffee at the little snack station located near the reception desk. There you could buy lattes, frappachinos, cappuccinos, macchiatos, caffé mochas, caffé breves, and a dozen other things I'd never heard of before. I told the gal at the counter I just wanted something hot and strong. She gave me a hammerhead, which she said had a shot of espresso in a regular cup of a Columbian blend. Whatever. It tasted like strong coffee to me, so I was satisfied.

I got the hammerhead with a lid, because there's nothing I hate worse than spilling coffee down my shirt. I've had to change clothes three times in one hour before because of coffee spillage. I use more Spray 'n Wash than anybody else I know.

As it turns out, the lid didn't stop me from wearing the entire cup of coffee on my shirt and jeans. Once I'd exited the building, I was paying more attention to drinking my coffee than I was to the cars pulling in and out of the parking lot. I looked up just in time to see a dark-colored sports utility vehicle heading straight for me. Instead of applying the brakes, it seemed to speed up as it got closer to me. The SUV was bearing down on me, and I stood frozen in time for what seemed like a full minute.

At the last second I leapt to my right as the car swerved slightly to the left, catching me on the outside of my left thigh. The cup flew out of my hand as I was knocked to the ground. Hot coffee rained down on me from above. I remember feeling a sharp pain run up my leg, and the burning sensation of steaming hot liquid soaking through my clothing, just before I heard the engine racing and tires squealing on the SUV as it sped out of the parking lot.

A woman just leaving the hospital screamed and yelled, "Stop that car! Somebody get a license number!"

Unfortunately, there was no one else in the parking lot but the two of us, and the car was too far away to see the license number, anyway. She hurried over to check my condition, and helped me get up off the pavement enough to limp over to a grass median strip so I could get out of the line of traffic. She told me she'd be right back with some help and headed back into the building. What seemed like mere seconds later, the lot was filled with police cars and emergency medical personnel. I found it very embarrassing to be the center of attention once again.

The nice lady who'd come to my rescue was giving a statement to an officer from the St. Joseph Police Department, while two young men in scrubs were checking me for broken bones and lacerations. I had a large, bleeding scrape on my right elbow from striking the pavement, a severe pain in my left thigh, a throbbing right wrist, and a hammerhead dripping off every part of my body.

I knew I was quite a sight, and it didn't help my embarrassment any to recognize a couple of nurses I'd seen last night in the emergency room. One of them even called me by name as she approached me.

"Lexie? My, you are having a bad week, aren't you? Would you like me to call that nice gentleman who was with you last night? I'm sure they'll be taking you inside to the emergency room to get some X-rays, and you may be here a while," she said. "You know how that goes."

"No thanks," I said. "I'll just give Stone a call so he won't worry about me."

I knew I would have to call him or he would definitely worry about me. He was very protective of me. But I wasn't sure how to tell him I'd just been run down by an SUV and was being taken inside the hospital for X-rays without worrying him.

The phone rang numerous times before Stone answered. He was breathing hard, as if he'd had to race for the phone. I spoke quickly into the phone, and then there were a few seconds of silence.

"You've been what?" he asked incredulously. "You're in the hospital again?"

"Someone ran into me with a dark SUV in the hospital parking lot, and it seems to me like it was deliberate. I'm in the emergency room right now. They just want to make sure my wrist isn't broken, or any other bones, I guess."

"Tell me what happened, slower this time," Stone said.

I explained what happened in detail. "Like I told the police officer who questioned me, I couldn't see who was driving the vehicle. I was more concerned with my safety at the time to care who was driving. It all happened so quickly, and I just got the faintest glimpse of the guy behind the wheel."

"So it was a man driving the SUV?"

"Well, I'm really not sure," I said. "Something gave me the impression it was a male figure, maybe the size of the body in the driver's seat. But I could be wrong. I think I know who it was though. I don't see how it could possibly have been anybody else."

"Who?" Stone asked.

"An attorney from St. Joseph named Sheldon Wright."

"Who's that?"

I told Stone about my confrontation with the lawyer in Melba's room. I left out nothing, except maybe the "pompous ass" part. "He was the only person who knew where I was except you, and he had time to beat me to the parking lot, since I stopped to use the restroom and buy some coffee in the lobby."

"You surely didn't make him mad enough to attempt to harm you, or worse yet, commit vehicular homicide. That sounds to me like it's taking anger above and beyond any reason. If you hadn't jumped to the side when you did, he could have killed you, you know," Stone reminded me.

"I don't think he meant to kill me, or he wouldn't have swerved to his right at the last moment. I think he just wanted to scare me, or maybe injure me, to put me out of commission for a while. Do you think he could have anything to do with Walter's death, Stone? Could he somehow know I've been asking questions of various people involved in Walter's life?" I asked. "He is bound and determined to get Melba's will changed immediately. I'm even worried she might be targeted once her will is updated. I'm wondering if the hospital shouldn't be alerted and a security guard placed outside her door. He should be officially banned from entering Melba's room, at least until a murder suspect is apprehended."

"I don't think it'll come to that, Lexie. But I do imagine this Mr. Wright could have caught wind of your involvement somehow. None of this makes any sense to me. Who all have you been questioning? Maybe it was one of them. What kind of motive could the attorney have had to kill Walter?" he asked.

"Maybe he's trying to swindle Walter's mother out of her

136

money. Melba's fairly well off and, in her current condition, it would be easy to pull the wool over her eyes. He seemed like a real opportunist to me, Stone. She's so befuddled right now, it wouldn't take much for him to convince her she needs to make him her beneficiary so he can protect her money for her, or distribute it for her after her death in the manner she tells him to."

"That seems a little far-fetched, but it's probably as good a motive as anyone else seems to have. And, as you mentioned, he was the only one who knew you were heading for the hospital parking lot, and you gave him ample time to get to his car and wait for you to leave the building. Did you tell the police officers all this?" he asked.

"Yes, I did."

"What did they say?"

"Just that there would be further investigation into the hit and run case. I don't think they really took me seriously about the rest of it. But they are familiar with the Walter Sneed murder case in Rockdale, at least. They told me they first wanted to try to track down the person in the SUV, to charge him with assault with a deadly weapon, leaving the scene of an accident, hit and run, and I don't know what else."

I explained to Stone how it had been more of a glancing blow than a direct hit, but fortunately, the cops had told me, the front headlight casing had been busted out, according to the evidence left at the scene. This, they thought, could help identify the dark SUV. They'd sent out an APB, or all points bulletin, for officers to be alert for a vehicle matching the description.

"Good. Hopefully they'll be able to track it down. We'll talk to Detective Johnston about the accident and your suspicions regarding Sheldon Wright. In the meantime, do you want me to come get you? I really think it'd be best if you didn't try to drive after an accident like the one you just had. We can go back and get your Jeep at a later date," Stone said.

"No, I can drive. It's my left leg that's banged up. I might be here a while though. You know how long it takes to get seen in an emergency room sometimes."

"I know, believe me, I know. What do I need to do to get supper ready for the Dudleys? The wake is in a couple of hours."

"I made the casserole earlier. Just warm it up in the microwave and heat up a couple cans of corn. You have your fish to fry also. I'll be home as soon as I can," I promised. I had a wake to attend.

The emergency room was crowded with people harboring a variety of illnesses and injuries. My injuries felt minor in comparison to the ones afflicting many of the patients I saw seated around the waiting room. One young boy had nearly severed a finger, and blood was seeping through the towel wrapped around his hand. Another patient couldn't stop retching into a bathroom-sized trash can she was clutching tightly to her chest. I had to step outside every now and then to keep from retching myself, just from listening to her.

My left hip and thigh were still throbbing, and I found it difficult to find a comfortable position in the chair. There were small pebbles embedded in the deep scrapes on my arm, and I kept busy trying to work them out. I needed a cup of coffee in the worst way. I hadn't gotten the chance to drink the last cup I'd purchased.

The main reason I was waiting in the ER was to have my wrist X-rayed. It was red and swollen, but I really didn't think it was broken because I could bend it easily, even if it hurt like crazy when I did. It wasn't bothering me nearly as much as my hip and thigh. I had half a notion to sneak out of the hospital and drive home. If the pain got worse, I could go to my primary physician tomorrow to have it examined. Time was running out to be examined, released, drive home to Rockdale, and get to the church on time.

After another forty-five minutes of squirming around in the chair, I'd had enough. If I didn't get out of there soon, I knew I'd never make it home in time to go to Walter's wake. I decided to approach the lady who had checked me in. "How much longer do you think I'll have to wait to be seen by a doctor?"

"Can't tell you," she replied, blowing a large pink bubble with her gum. "It's first come, first serve, ma'am, unless it's a life-threatening injury. I don't think your swollen wrist is going to kill you anytime soon, so go back to the waiting room and we'll call you when it's your turn."

"Actually, I just wanted to tell you I'm going to go home. My wrist barely hurts now, and I'm sure it's fine. I'm certain it's not broken, just sprained, if anything. I have important things to do at home. I have to attend the wake of a very close friend this evening, and if I don't leave right now I won't make it there on time. Besides, I don't want to waste the doctors' valuable time when they have so many more critically injured patients to attend to."

I didn't like the woman's attitude, and it was hard to remain civil and polite. I wanted to tell her so too, but I restrained myself. I also wanted to slap the gum right out of her mouth as she blew a bubble so large it nearly obscured her face. The hospital needed someone with a little more compassion and professionalism in her patient-admitting position. I hoped they'd send me a survey to fill out so I could voice my opinion.

"I'm pretty sure that's against hospital policy," the woman said.

"And I'm pretty sure I don't care."

On the way home I stopped at a pharmacy and purchased a wrist brace, some peroxide and Neosporin for the scrapes on my arm, and a dark chocolate Milky Way bar, just because I felt I deserved one. The wrist brace would make it look like I'd actually been treated in the emergency room, because I felt sure Stone wouldn't take my word for it that my wrist was only sprained. The peroxide and Neosporin would keep my scrapes from getting infected. And the candy bar would help calm my rattled nerves. After all, it wasn't every day someone in an SUV tried to run me over and possibly kill me. An added bonus was that the Milky Way took my mind off my throbbing leg and wrist for at least as long as it took to devour it.

"Are you okay, my love? I've been so worried," Stone said, as he met me at the front door of the Alexandria Inn. "Get in here and let me have a look at you. What did they say about your wrist? I see they put a brace on it. You look terrible, honey."

"I'm fine, Stone," I assured him. "My wrist is just sprained. And there are no broken bones or internal injuries, just some scrapes and bruising. I'll be back to normal in a few days."

"Well, that's a big relief," Stone said. "I'll talk to Wyatt at the wake. I have to leave in a couple of minutes because I'm already late."

"You mean 'we're' already late," I corrected him. "I wouldn't miss this wake for anything."

"You can't go in your condition, Lexie."

"Why not? I told you I'm fine."

"You're limping, for one thing. Your arm is still oozing, and I'm sure you're in a lot of pain. You look really banged up, and more than a bit rough around the edges," he said.

I looked down and saw not only coffee stains all over my clothing, but also numerous rips in my blouse, and a huge tear down the right leg of my jeans. If a person looked close enough, he could probably also detect remnants of Melba's lunch on my shirt. "Don't worry. I was planning to change clothes."

"I realize that. Don't be sarcastic. I'm just concerned about you."

I felt bad, knowing he was only anxious and thinking about me. "I'm sorry, Stone. I didn't mean it to come out that way. I've had a long day. I just meant I won't look nearly as bad once I get into my nice pantsuit, which will cover up my scrapes, and all. I don't really care what others think about the way I look. You know how much it will mean to me to be there at Walter's wake. We don't have to stay long, but I think we should at least make an appearance."

Stone let out a long exaggerated sigh and said, "Well, you better change quickly if you really want to come. I can't prevent you from attending the wake if you're determined to go."

"Okay, just give me a couple of minutes and I'll be ready."

Sixteen

The parking lot at St. Mary's Catholic Church was full, and vehicles lined both sides of Cyprus Street. But that's what you should expect when you are twenty minutes late to a wake, Stone told me. No parking was allowed on Fourth Street, so Stone dropped me off at the front door and took his Corvette to park on Elm, the next street over. I wasn't surprised the wake of a young man like Walter would draw a large crowd. Most of the people inside the church looked to be in their upper teens and twenties. Several were dabbing their eyes with tissues. Some were openly crying, and I could hear someone sobbing uncontrollably.

I'd yet to see anyone I recognized when Stone walked through the door several minutes later. We signed the guest book and went together up to the open casket in front of the main chamber of the sanctuary.

"He looks good," I whispered, looking down at Walter's body.

I hate to say a person "looks good" when he's lying dead in a coffin, but the mortician really had done a fine job with Walter. Walter looked much as he had when we'd first hired him to portray a corpse in our own make-believe coffin. He now looked quite a bit older than his twenty years, but, like I said before, death can do that to a person.

"How are you, Ms. Reed?" I heard someone say. I didn't think anything of it until someone tugged on my sleeve and repeated the greeting. I looked around and saw Paula standing next to Stone in front of the casket. "It's nice to see you again. Have you been here long?"

"Huh?" Stone asked. "Who?"

"Never mind, Stone," I said, as I elbowed him lightly in the ribs. I had to give him some clue or he might say the wrong thing to the young gal, which could give away my true identity. "Paula, this is my partner, Stone. Paula and I met the other day when I was working on my investigative report for the newspaper. You know, the article I've been commissioned to write. She's the best friend of Walter's girlfriend, Sidney Hobbs."

"Oh, I see. It's nice to meet you, Paula. I had forgotten about the article," Stone said. He caught on quickly these days, probably from having had so much practice. "Ms. Reed and I just arrived a few minutes ago."

Then I turned to Paula and said, "It's so nice to see you again too, Paula. I just hate seeing you under these circumstances, of course. Speaking of Sidney, was she able to attend the visitation tonight?"

"Yes, she's here with her parents. I was able to speak with her briefly, and she told me she wasn't allowed to stay long. Her father hadn't wanted her to attend the wake at all, but she'd been able to convince him she needed the closure," Paula said.

"I can understand her need for closure," I said. "Do you know where she is right now? I'd like to offer my condolences."

"No. I saw her come up here to the casket, and she was in bad shape when she walked away. So, her parents might have already taken her home. She was about to lose it completely."

Damn, damn, damn. I knew I should have left the hospital when I first contemplated it. Sidney must have been the gal I'd heard weeping when I first came in to the church. Maybe I could still catch her if I hurried.

"Excuse me, Paula and Stone. I need to use the restroom." I limped away toward the restroom, and made a quick change of directions once I was out of sight of the crowd gathering around the casket, where Stone still stood. Paula had gone on to greet more mourners.

I spotted Sidney with an older man and woman, presumably her parents, heading toward the door. I rushed up to them, and said, "Sidney? I just wanted to catch you and offer my sincere condolences."

"Thank you," Sidney said between sobs. I could tell she recognized me from cheerleading practice on Saturday.

"As you may remember, I'm an investigative reporter, and I'm helping the detectives track down Walter's killer. The more I know about Walter, the more effective I can be in assisting the officers in charge of the investigation. I can only imagine how much you want to see that person brought to justice, as do I."

"Uh-huh," she said.

"Would you mind if I ask you a few—"

Just then Sidney's father stepped in front of her to shield her, and said, "She's not available for questioning, ma'am. Can't you see how upset she is? Do you really think this is the time or place for her to answer questions? This is Walter's wake, for goodness sakes. Like I told you before, Ms. Reed, Sidney knows nothing about the murder, and she has nothing to say to the detectives, or to you. I'm not sure you have the authority to ask her anything, anyway."

"Well, I, er, you see—" I'd been put firmly in my place, and I felt a little ashamed of myself. I vowed I wouldn't question anyone else at the wake. Mr. Hobbs was correct; this was neither the time nor the place to intrude on people while they were grieving the loss of a friend or loved one. I would have to find other opportunities to speak with the people on my suspect list. And now I wasn't sure Sidney even belonged on that list. No one could fake anguish that well. I'd never seen her when she wasn't sobbing over the loss of her boyfriend. "I'm just, well, you know, I—"

I was still blabbing long after the Hobbs family had turned to leave. Sidney turned at the door to look back at me.

"Sorry," I mouthed. And I truly was.

I really did need to use the restroom now, so I headed toward the ladies' room. Standing at the sink in the restroom was Walter's sister, Sheila Talley. She had tears in her eyes as she blew her nose. Sheila visibly blanched when she looked up and saw me. I knew she was recalling the incident that had taken place in the pet store.

"I'm so sorry, Sheila, for your loss," I said, sincerely. "And I apologize again for accidentally knocking over the fish tank at the pet store. I hope I didn't get you into any trouble with your boss."

"No, you didn't. The next customer to come in the store bought an eight hundred dollar ori-pei, and two hundred dollars worth of accessories for it, so Mr. Meyer got over the fish tank accident pretty quickly," she said with a barely detectable smile.

"What's an ori-pei, may I ask?"

"It's a shar-pei and pug mix. They're really cute and kind of expensive," Sheila said. "Mr. Meyer was anxious to sell this particular ori-pei, because it had a tendency to chew up and eat things it shouldn't. It had just cost him over five hundred dollars to have a dime removed from the dog's digestive tract."

"That's not a very good exchange rate is it, to spend five hundred dollars to get your dime back?" I asked with a grin. She flashed a more visible smile this time. I put my hand on her shoulder, and said, "I really am sorry, Sheila—for everything."

"Thank you. What happened to your wrist?" she asked, looking at the brace resting on her shoulder blade. "Did you hurt it when you tumbled into the fish tank?"

"No, nothing like that. I just caught myself with it when I fell on the pavement yesterday. It's only sprained, nothing serious. I'll probably only have to wear this brace a few more days, and then it'll be good as new."

I didn't want to tell her, or anybody else, that a car had struck me. I'd rather let her think I'd just tripped and fallen to the ground. It was something she'd find easy to believe. I could tell by the way she looked at me she thought I was the biggest klutz in the world. I felt for a second as though I had "Impending Disaster" written across my forehead. It did seem that way, even to me sometimes, and especially when I found myself in the middle of a murder investigation like this one.

"Well, take care," I said, and made my way to the farthest stall. I was about to wet my pants, but I was relieved to see Sheila visibly upset at her brother's funeral. I could tell she'd been crying, as her eyes were red and puffy. I really didn't want to think Sheila could have had anything to do with Walter's death, despite the money she stood to gain from it.

When I caught up with Stone again, he was speaking with Detective Johnston. Wyatt looked even sharper in a suit than he did in his police uniform. He really was a handsome fellow, I thought. Veronica, who was standing next to him, was lucky to have a man like Wyatt interested in her. She wasn't even remotely attuned to the conversation the two men were having. She was busy blotting her lipstick and looking into the mirror of an old-fashioned compact. Veronica and I were at opposite ends of the diva scale.

Stone and Wyatt were discussing the benefits of using an artificial bait called a "gulp" to fish for walleye. It wasn't exactly what I was expecting to hear when I joined them. How do you segue from gulps to murder? I wondered. Finally, when there was a pause in their conversation, I asked Wyatt if there was any news on the murder investigation.

"No, not much," he said. "They're kind of at a standstill right now."

"Why does that not surprise me?" I asked.

"These things take time, Lexie," Wyatt said. He sounded defensive. I hadn't meant to imply Wyatt and his co-workers were not competent at their jobs.

"Oh, I know." For the second time in an hour I had to explain that I hadn't meant what I'd said to come out the way it did. "I'm just being impatient. Do you know who all have been questioned by the police, so far? Has anyone been named a suspect yet?"

"Well, we haven't had sufficient reason to name any suspects yet. But we've spoken to several members of Walter's family and a number of his friends," Wyatt said. He went on to mention most of the same people I had also spoken with. I noticed Walter's girlfriend, Sidney Hobbs, was not one of the people he listed.

"How about his girlfriend?"

"The current one?"

"Yes. Sidney Hobbs," I said.

"No, her parents won't let us speak to her yet, and we have no reason to think she's responsible, so we haven't pressed the issue. Her father just gave a brief statement on Sidney's behalf, and her alibi checked out to be relatively airtight."

"I've tried several times to speak with her too," I admitted. "I haven't been able to break through the wall her parents put up either."

"Lexie, I know you mean well, and I know you have helped bring a couple investigations to an end in the past—"

I could feel a "but" coming, so I broke in. "Listen, Wyatt, I'm just trying to help out. It's important to me that this murderer be apprehended and brought to justice, since it happened almost beneath my nose and in Stone's establishment. I'm only trying to assist the authorities. I'm really not attempting to interfere with the official investigation."

"You're not interfering, Lexie, and that's not what I'm concerned about. Stone told me about the accident you were involved in today in the hospital parking lot. Accident may be the wrong word, though, because it doesn't sound like it was an accident at all. It sounds like it was intentional and a direct threat to you and your safety. I just noticed you were limping and have a brace on your wrist. Is all that pain worth it? Is investigating Walter's murder really worth you getting injured, or worse? I don't think so."

"I don't either," Stone agreed. He looked pleased that Wyatt was taking a stand and trying to convince me to back off and leave it in the detectives' hands to find the killer. "I've told her I didn't want to be involved, and I don't want her to be involved either. Situations like this are why we have men like you, Wyatt."

"But—" I said.

Wyatt nodded in agreement. "He's right, Lexie."

"But—"

"I do want to ask you some questions about what happened today, but not right now. I will stop by your house in the morning," Wyatt continued. "Lexie, it would mean a lot to me, and to Stone as well, if we could get you to stop your personal investigation into this murder. It's causing us both a lot of stress we don't need right now. We couldn't stand to see anything else happen to you. You need to trust the authorities to handle the case. We are bringing in a few detectives from St. Joseph who are in the homicide division, and it shouldn't take long to identify a suspect. Please let us take care of the case by ourselves. You've already been hurt badly enough. I'm sure we are closing in on the perpetrator."

I didn't think they were closing in on a perpetrator at all, or were any closer to apprehending a suspect than the moment they first laid eyes on the victim. But jeez, talk about putting me on a guilt trip. I didn't know what to say, so I said nothing. I would bring it up in the morning when Wyatt came over to question me, and of course, ingest several cups of coffee and more than a few pastries.

I turned to say hello to Veronica, and the men went back to discussing fishing for walleye. Before I left to mingle in the crowd, I heard Wyatt say, "And yums are as good as gulps at attracting fish."

As I walked through the crowd, I noticed Walter's half-brother, Chuck Sneed, was not present. He must have decided it was more important to go to the hog-tying contest. I guess we all have our priorities. But what could be a higher priority than attending the funeral of a brother, even a half-brother? This seemed to beg for further investigation.

Sheldon Wright, Melba's egotistical attorney, wasn't in attendance either, but this didn't surprise me at all. For all he knew, I might have recognized him inside the SUV, and he could be lying low lest the police were waiting to arrest him at the wake. He might be locked away in his garage at this very moment, replacing his headlight casing.

I saw Walter's dad, Clarence, speaking with an elderly couple. Then I noticed a number of the cheerleaders I'd seen at their practice and at the football scrimmage Monday afternoon. Paula was standing with some of her fellow cheerleaders when I went up to her.

"I'm sorry I didn't get to talk to you much a little while ago," I told Paula. "How is everyone holding up?"

"Okay, Ms. Reed," she said. "We just saw Audrey McCoy waltz in, and none of us can believe she had the nerve to come here. That is, like, so inappropriate."

"Oh, I agree, Paula," I replied. "Why do you think she decided to come?"

"To irritate Sidney, probably. She knows Sidney can't really confront her at Walter's wake. Fortunately, I think Sidney has already left, or there could've been an ugly scene between the two of them."

"Sidney has left," I assured her. "I saw her leave with her parents a little while ago."

"Good. She's torn up enough as it is, without having Audrey instigate more heartache for her. You should speak to her, Rhonda, for your newspaper article," Paula said. "Audrey's the gal in the purple sweater up by the casket. I still think she's capable of murdering Walter."

"Really?"

"Yes. She'd do just about anything to hurt Sidney. They absolutely hate each other's guts. And she can't have been too thrilled when Walter dumped her after just one date to go back to Sidney, her archenemy. It had to have been humiliating for her."

There was that "archenemy" thing again. Guess what, people? DC Comics called, and they want their characters back. Good grief! I wonder what special superhuman powers this young lady possessed. What was up with that, anyway?

"Hmm, I see your point, Paula. Maybe I'll go see if she knows anything," I said. I didn't know how or when I would get another opportunity to speak with Audrey. I might just have to allow this one little exception to my vow not to question anyone else on my suspect list tonight at the wake. Like Paula said, she shouldn't be at the wake to begin with.

I meandered over to where Audrey was standing next to the casket. She was looking intently down at Walter's face. She wore a very odd expression, almost a smirk. I walked up and stood beside her for a few moments. I waited quietly and watched her do something I thought was rather strange. She reached into the casket and placed her open palm on the left side of Walter's chest for about ten or fifteen seconds, as if feeling for a heartbeat. Then, as if satisfied she couldn't find one, she nodded and withdrew her hand.

"Doesn't he look good?" I asked politely. "Was Walter a friend of yours?"

"Not really," she said.

"Did you use to date the young man?"

"We went out just once, and then the bastard e-mailed me to tell me it wouldn't work out between us. He said he just didn't feel like we'd made any kind of connection, or had anything in common. He also said he missed Sidney and wanted to try to make up with her in the e-mail message he sent me."

"Oh, well, I'm sorry to hear that," I said. I hoped I sounded more sincere than I felt.

"He could have at least told me all this in person, the gutless piece of crap," Audrey said.

Audrey was being very open and talkative, considering the fact she had no clue who I was. She didn't seem to care if anyone and everyone knew she had issues with both Walter and his long-time girlfriend, Sidney. Would someone with something to hide be this informative, or this obviously hateful of the deceased?

"I think he just asked me out to make his girlfriend jealous enough to take him back. He knew Sidney and I didn't get along, and going out with me would make her more jealous than going out with anyone else could. They'd been going together for a long time and were kind of going through a rough spell. I only wanted to help him get over it," Audrey said. "But Walter really was a jerk. I don't know what she saw in him. And I don't know what he saw in her, either."

"It doesn't sound like you cared much for him or Sidney, so why did you come tonight?" I asked. "I should have thought you'd avoid this visitation like the plague."

"I don't know. Maybe just to make sure he was really dead. I couldn't believe it when I heard the news of his death. Personally, I think he had it coming. It's kind of rewarding to see Sidney get her due too. I don't see her here though."

"She was here earlier. She's very, very distraught," I assured her. "I didn't get a chance to speak with her, though."

"Good. I'm glad his death is so painful for her. That's what she gets!"

Wow, this girl was vicious. A young man was dead, and she was thrilled about it. I could understand why Sidney and the rest of the cheerleading squad didn't care for her. She was almost sociopathic. I noticed she'd never turned to look directly at me, but was staring at Walter throughout our entire conversation, as if she couldn't take her eyes off him.

"Do you know anyone who would have wanted Walter dead?" I asked.

"You mean besides me?"

"Uh, yeah, I guess."

"Not really. He was an athlete and pretty popular with the other guys," Audrey said. "His best friend, Joey Cox, was the homecoming king, quarterback, and all that in high school. Joey was easily the most popular guy in high school. Just being Joey's best friend made Walter pretty popular. He was popular by association, I think. It couldn't be his own personality, that's for sure."

"Is Joey a college student here in town too?" I asked. His best friend should know if Walter had any enemies, anyone who might want to harm him. Had the police questioned him? I wondered. He might not be responsible for his best friend's death, but he might have some insight about who could be.

"No, he went to a trade school out in Wyoming for a couple years, and he just started as a mechanic at a garage in town." She sounded more sociable now, less menacing. Perhaps she

152

suffered from a bipolar disorder.

"Is Joey here tonight?"

"He was, but he was leaving just as I arrived," Audrey replied. "He looked pretty torn up, as if he just couldn't bear to stay any longer."

"Do you know where the garage is located?" I asked. You'd think Audrey would question why I cared where Walter's best friend worked, but she didn't seem to. She still had no clue who I was, and hadn't bothered to inquire either. She didn't seem to mind me asking her questions, nor did she seem to care what kind of impression she left on me. This wasn't typical behavior for a murderer, I shouldn't imagine. Still, she was adamant in her dislike of the guy.

"The garage is next to the hardware store on Sixth Street. It's called Boney's. An old guy, who's known as one of the founding fathers of Rockdale, started the garage years ago, and Boney was his nickname. As a matter of fact, Joey changed my oil just the other day." As she finished speaking, she stepped back from the casket and faltered a bit. She looked as if she was on the verge of fainting, so I grabbed her arm to steady her.

"Are you okay?" I asked. I wondered if she might be having a low blood sugar reaction. Something told me if she had insulin, she wouldn't mind injecting Walter with some of it. Or even Sidney, if she got half a chance. "Are you diabetic, by any chance? Do you need something sweet to eat?"

Audrey pulled away from my grasp, and declared, "No, of course not. What are you implying? I haven't gotten much sleep the last couple of days, and I didn't eat much today, so I feel a little weak. That's all there is to it."

Suddenly she was distrustful of my interest in her. I doubted I would get much more information out of her at this time. Perhaps she was realizing my interest wasn't that of a casual observer.

"I wasn't implying anything, Audrey," I assured her. She didn't seem surprised that I knew her name, even though the two of us had never met. I think she was too self-absorbed to even notice. "I was only concerned when you seemed as if you might pass out. I've seen diabetics do that before, so assumed it might also be the case with you."

"Well, it isn't. Like I said, it's just due to a lack of sleep and food."

Why couldn't this young woman, who was admittedly glad Walter was dead, sleep or eat the last couple of days? Was it possible something was bothering her? Was something eating at her conscience? She sure seemed to get defensive in a hurry. What I'd been implying was simple; she seemed like she was not above doing whatever it took to get back at both Walter and Sidney. Getting rid of Walter was like killing two birds with one stone, so to speak.

"I've got to go," Audrey said. She turned around and walked straight out of the church without glancing around at anybody in the room. She steered clear of the rest of the cheerleading squad. She was obviously in a hurry to leave. Had I touched a raw nerve? Had I made her a little nervous and anxious? I wondered. Would I ever get a chance to speak with her again, maybe weasel some more pertinent information out of her? I had tried, but couldn't find her in the phonebook. She might be commuting to college from another town or merely have an unlisted number.

I rejoined Stone and Wyatt, who were now discussing the best rub to put on barbeque ribs when you smoked them. They soon switched the topic to the kind of wood chips to use. Stone preferred hickory, but Wyatt liked to use apple wood. I waited patiently, quietly observing the body language of the mourners. No one seemed to be acting odd, nervous, or in any way suspicious. Everyone seemed appropriately mournful and upset at

Walter's death.

Eventually, Stone looked down at me, and asked, "How are you feeling? Are you about ready to go home?"

"Just about," I said. "I haven't seen Walter's mother here, have you guys?"

Wyatt shook his head, and said, "I heard they wouldn't release her from the hospital today to attend. She's too unstable. She still needs constant monitoring. I heard she kept spitting out her medication, so they tried to give it to her through an IV instead. Then, when they weren't in the room, she ripped the IV out of her arm. Now they've removed the IV and are giving her individual injections. She keeps accusing the nurses of trying to poison her."

"Poor Melba. She's really a mess right now, isn't she?" I asked Wyatt.

"Yeah, but, I guess a couple of orderlies are going to accompany her to Walter's funeral service tomorrow morning. I'm sure they'll give her a shot of something to sedate her before they get her to the church. She probably won't remember much about the service, but maybe she'll at least remember she attended it," Wyatt said.

"Oh, that's good. I'd hate for her to not be able to come to the service tomorrow too," I said. "Maybe being at the funeral will help her understand what's happened. I don't think she has quite realized yet that her son is gone."

My leg was really beginning to ache, so I was ready to go home when Stone put his arm around my shoulders and led me outside. I was also starving. The only thing that had crossed my lips in a long time was a Milky Way bar.

"Wait here. I'll be around directly with the car," he said. "You don't need to be walking any more than necessary on that bad leg for a few days at least. Did the doctor tell you to put ice on it?"

"I don't recall being told to put ice on it," I said, noncommittally. "It'll help just to get off of it and get a good night's sleep. A little warmed-up eggplant casserole and a long soak in the tub sounds appealing too."

"How are your bruised ribs feeling from the hit you took yesterday at the football game?" Stone asked.

"Bruised ribs are yesterday's news," I said. "I forgot all about my aching ribs once the SUV plowed into me."

"Well, let's see if you can't make it all the way through the day tomorrow without an accident," Stone said. "Is that too much to hope for?"

"I was kind of hoping to deduct Wheatfield Memorial from my income taxes as a second home," I replied.

"You already have a second home, Lexie. The Alexandria Inn. And I hope you realize you always have the option of making this your first and only home. You can sell your home in Shawnee and move in with me full-time any time you want. You're here with me most of the time these days anyway, so why not make it permanent? I'd feel more comfortable if you were where I could always take care of you and protect you. You could benefit from constant protection, my dear. Give it some thought, okay?"

"I will, Stone. Thank you. I will give it some serious consideration," I said. And I meant it. I felt being here at the Alexandria Inn with Stone was where I belonged.

Seventeen

"Great breakfast, Lexie," Steve Dudley said. "I haven't had pancakes this good in a long time. The blueberries really added a special flavor to them. Where do you find fresh fruit this time of year? And my eggs were perfect, too."

"Thanks," I said. I caught the look Eleanor shot her husband. Either she wasn't much of a cook, or her husband was just being polite. Either way, she didn't appear to appreciate his remark very much.

"And I really appreciated the little breakfast steak you added to my plate," he said.

"Out of pure habit, I started to fry some bacon," I admitted. "Then I remembered your pork allergy. So instead I substituted the little breakfast steak for the bacon."

"Well it was delicious. The only time I get any meat is when I go out for lunch at work. I become a 'quarter-pounder-aholic' at lunchtime. Eleanor has being trying—unsuccessfully, I might add—to turn me into a vegetarian for years. She thinks red meat is bad for my health, and she has issues with the slaughter of farm animals as well. I appreciate her concern for my health, but I really do crave meat sometimes. I think I'm protein-deficient."

"Well, I'm sure Eleanor is right about the red meat. We probably all get enough protein in things like eggs, cheese, and beans. But I'm glad you enjoyed your meal," I told him. Then I turned to Eleanor, who, I was glad to see, was only a vegetarian, and not a vegan. "Was yours okay? I hope your eggs were the way you like them."

"Yes, it was all fine," she said, as she stood up and pushed her chair toward the table. "Let's get going, Steve. We have things to get done today, as I'm sure these good people do also."

"My breakfast was great too," Stone said. "As usual, everything was perfect. Like Steve, I liked the addition of blueberries to the pancakes. Now we better get the kitchen cleaned up and get ready for the funeral this morning."

The funeral went smoothly. I didn't really talk to anyone, other than a casual greeting here and there. I was hurting all over and was having trouble concentrating on anything else. Whenever I have an excuse to ask for a prescription for pain pills, I do it. Even if I don't need them for the current ailment, I fill the prescription. I never know when I'll need one and will be glad to have a stash on hand. I had utilized one of them before leaving for the church, and it was just beginning to kick in.

I noticed Melba was sitting a few pews in front of us, with a couple of young men sitting on either side of her. Those were obviously the orderlies Wyatt had said were assigned to accompany her. They looked about fourteen years old. One spent the entire service picking at his acne, when he wasn't picking his nose instead. I guess I expected them to look more like secret service men than ninth-graders.

Clarence sat on the front row, next to his daughter Sheila Talley and a man who was probably Sheila's boyfriend. Sheila was blowing her nose frequently, and her boyfriend looked fidgety and very uncomfortable. He appeared as if he'd rather be having a colonoscopy than sitting in church at Walter's funeral. I watched him brush his bangs back for about the tenth time.

It looked like most of the cheerleading squad had skipped their college classes and were lined up on the second pew in the sanctuary. Neither Sidney and her parents, nor Audrey McCoy, were in attendance, which didn't really surprise me in either case.

Walter's half-brother, Chuck, was also not in attendance, but there might have been a turkey shoot he couldn't afford to miss. It reminded me that I wanted to ask Detective Johnston how much scrutiny had been given to Chuck and his relationship with Walter.

Wyatt was sitting on the other side of Stone, listening intently, as Father Erickson gave a very moving eulogy about the deceased. There were tears in nearly everyone's eyes by the time he had concluded the service. I was dabbing at my own eyes throughout the service and heard Stone sniffle beside me. I loved the fact Stone was softhearted and sensitive in situations like this.

Afterward, the congregation filed out of the church to walk slowly to the cemetery, located directly behind the church. There was absolute silence as the crowd formed a circle around the opened pit next to the gravesite of Henry and Marian Jobe who, Wyatt later told me, were Walter's grandparents on his mother's side.

A short, somber sermon was given at the gravesite. Following the sermon, many of Walter's family and friends placed red roses on the top of his pine casket, many still with tears in their eyes and tissues in their hands. The crowd disbursed before the casket was lowered into the ground. I was relieved, because the lowering of the casket is always the toughest part of any funeral, unless, of course, taps are played, echoing off in the distance, like at military funerals. That reduces me to tears every time.

The whole thing still didn't seem real to me. Just days ago I had spoken with Walter about his ambitions, goals, and plans once he'd received his college degree. He'd wanted to be a teacher and high school basketball coach. Before settling down into a teaching job, he wanted to be a missionary and travel to places like Africa, to help underprivileged children there.

After his missionary work was completed, Walter wanted to write a book about his experiences, to help bring awareness to the need for food and clean water in many regions of the world. He was a thoughtful, compassionate young man, I thought. It was uplifting to see young people pursuing objectives such as missionary work. The next generation was the future of our nation.

Now Walter's dreams were being buried with him. I pulled my own tissue out of my pocket and dabbed my eyes once again. As we walked back to Stone's Corvette, I talked about the things Walter had told me he planned to do in his life. Just discussing Walter upset me to some degree, so Stone put his arm around my back to comfort me.

"Stone! Lexie!" We heard a deep voice holler across the parking lot. "Wait up!"

It was Wyatt, and we waited for him to catch up with us. When he got closer to us, he asked. "It was a nice service, wasn't it? Father Erickson gave a great sermon."

We both agreed. We spoke briefly about the eulogies and sermon, and then Wyatt told us he wanted to speak to us about Sheldon Wright. "One of the detectives from the St. Joseph Homicide Division spoke with Mr. Wright last night on the phone. Wright told the detective that he did indeed own a navy blue SUV, but so did millions of other people. He's right that just about every other car on the road these days is an SUV, so owning a dark SUV means literally nothing. He promised to bring it in to the police this Saturday if we wanted to look at it, and of course we do."

"But won't that give him several days to get the headlight

fixed?" I asked. "And there is still a law of averages factor to take into consideration. What are the chances of Mr. Wright, and my assailant, both owning dark SUVs?"

"Pretty good, actually," Wyatt said. "But you are right about giving the suspect too much time to fix the busted light. It doesn't take a nuclear scientist to replace a headlamp. I think they should have gone to his house and checked out the SUV last night or, at the very least, this morning. I would do it myself but the detectives from St. Joseph would not take lightly to my interference."

"Did Mr. Wright have an alibi?" Stone asked Wyatt.

"Apparently he was home alone the day of Walter's murder, and he claims he was in Melba's hospital room for several hours after Lexie left yesterday. He claimed to know nothing about the accident in the parking lot, and said it was all cleared up by the time he exited the building," Wyatt said.

"Why did he spend several hours with Melba?" I asked.

"He said they were working on updating her vital documents. There were a number of changes that needed to be discussed and made in her will and power-of-attorney. Melba was only coherent part of the time, so the process took longer than expected, Wright said."

"I would love to see the changes he made in those documents. Can't those documents be checked and scrutinized by the police department?" I asked.

"Well, I don't really know. It would probably take a warrant," Wyatt said. "And there's always attorney/client confidentiality laws."

"How can it be legal for an attorney to make important changes like this while his client is only partially coherent?" I asked. "Isn't the client supposed to be of sound mind and body when such documents are altered and signed? That's a law too, isn't it?"

"I should think so," Wyatt said. "I don't trust this attorney at all, and like you, I have reason to believe he is the one responsible for running into you with his vehicle yesterday."

After a few more remarks about the funeral, we said our goodbyes and headed toward our separate vehicles. Wyatt had to report back to work at the police station.

We'd arrived early enough to get a good parking spot, which was nice, because I was still experiencing quite a bit of discomfort in my leg. Stone helped me into the car and said, "We need to get you home and have you put your leg up for a few hours, before Wendy arrives with Andy this afternoon. You've had a long week."

"Wendy told me spaghetti and meatballs is Andy's favorite meal, so I thought we'd have that, along with a salad and garlic toast for supper," I said. "That will be an easy meal to fix, and I can make an extra little pan of sauce without meat for Eleanor."

Stone rolled his eyes, and said, "Pain in the ass."

"We're here!" Wendy called from the front door. Stone and I put down our coffee cups and hurried to the foyer. Hugs were exchanged all around as Stone asked Andy how his flight was.

"Fine, even though I could have made a lot smoother landing than the pilot did," Andy said. "It felt like we touched down without the landing gear engaged."

"Has any commercial airline pilot ever passed muster with you?" Stone asked, joking with his nephew. He had flown with Andy numerous times and knew he was an exceptional pilot. I had even flown with him and felt very safe in his capable hands.

"Rarely has a commercial pilot passed muster with me," Andy replied good-naturedly. "And this one really could have used some remedial training. But then I would need some training myself to feel comfortable behind the controls of a Boeing Seven Thirty-Seven. That's a lot of responsibility."

"I'll say! What time is your appointment with the realtor tomorrow morning?" Stone asked.

"We're supposed to meet the agent at her office at ten o'clock and then follow her to the property. Are you going to be able to go with me, Uncle Stone?"

"Sure. I wouldn't miss it."

Andy looked at me, and said, "I'd like you to come too, if you're available. Wendy is going with us, as well. I'd like as many opinions as I can get before I make a major decision like becoming a cattle baron."

I laughed, along with everyone else, and agreed to go. I'd been anxiously hoping he'd extend an invitation to me. I was aching to see the property so I could gauge both Stone's and Andy's reactions to it. There was nothing I'd like more than to have Andy living nearby. Still, if I thought buying the farm property was a bad move on his part, I wouldn't hesitate to tell him so. As Stone had said, Andy's success and happiness were the most important things to take into consideration.

After a few more minutes of pleasantries, Wendy went upstairs with Andy to help him get ensconced in one of the second floor suites. I was certain Wendy would be staying in one of the inn's suites also, for at least as long as Andy was in town. She wouldn't be content in her lonely apartment while Andy was staying at the inn.

Stone and I went back to the kitchen for another cup of coffee and discussed how good Andy looked and how happy he seemed to be. He'd recently taken a trip to the Bahamas with some friends and was sporting a nice tan. And, as always, he looked lean and fit. Like his Uncle Stone, Andy had pretty blue eyes and long eyelashes. His light brown hair had natural blond highlights in it. He would one day look distinguished, with silver hair like his uncle's.

I knew Wendy and Andy would be back down momentarily,

so I put a fresh pot of coffee on to brew. The spaghetti sauce was already simmering on the stove. Thanksgiving was just a few weeks away, so I thought a pumpkin pie was a good idea for dessert, and I had one baking in the oven.

"Man, it's almost torture sitting in this kitchen tonight," Stone said.

"What do you mean?" I asked.

"The wonderful aromas are making my mouth water and my stomach growl," he said. "How long until dinner?"

"The Dudleys will be down for supper in about thirty minutes. The salad is ready and in the fridge, but I need to get some water boiling for the spaghetti," I told him. "Why don't you make yourself useful and set the dining room table for six?"

"Glad to be of service," he said with a salute. "I'm nothing if not useful, except maybe extremely hungry."

Thursday morning dawned sunny and mild. It was a beautiful day, perfect for looking at farm property. Some of the soreness had left both my legs and hip, and my ribs. Even my wrist moved more easily, and with less pain. I had patches of deep purple bruising in several places on my body and was praying I'd made my last emergency room visit in a long time. Fifty is too old to be getting tackled by college football players and run down by large vehicles. It's a wonder I didn't break my left hip. When one turns half-a-century old, she should be living a more cautious, docile lifestyle, and sitting in a rocking chair on the front porch, knitting and sipping a lot of coffee. I had the coffee part down pat, but the knitting part didn't mesh well with my personality. That's why God created Walmart.

The cautious, docile lifestyle just wasn't me, but a cup of coffee always sounded good. No one else was awake yet, and the house sounded eerily quiet. I could hear the clock ticking on the fireplace mantel in the living room and it was grating on my nerves. So I poured myself a cup of java and went out on the porch to drink it while I read through the morning paper. An article on the front page caught my eye.

"Slain College Student Put to Rest," was the headline. A large picture beside the article showed a crowd of mourners gathered around the gravesite in the cemetery. I could see Wyatt, Stone, and me, standing together in the center of the photo. Stone had his left arm draped across my shoulders.

Everybody's head was bowed in prayer in the photo, except for one young man who was looking straight ahead, staring right at me. Why? I wondered. Who was that young man? I didn't recall seeing him at the funeral, but he obviously had been there. Maybe Stone would remember him. Did he just happen to look up and glance my way the second the photographer snapped the photo, or was he studying me for some reason? He wore an intent expression and a stiff posture.

The article rehashed the details of Walter's death, stating no one was being detained at this time on suspicion of murder, but that the investigation was ongoing. It went on to say a hair had been found on the shirt of the victim, which was nearly black, not red like Walter's. DNA tests indicated the hair didn't belong to Walter or anyone related to him. They couldn't be sure the hair wasn't deposited on Walter before he even arrived for work at the Alexandria Inn, but it was the only piece of potential evidence found at the scene that could be DNA-tested. It didn't match any records on any criminal databases either. No one had been actually ruled out, but the hair did swing the pendulum somewhat toward an unrelated perpetrator, the article said.

I found this new discovery interesting. I wondered why Wyatt hadn't told me about it. I also wondered if they shouldn't do DNA testing on Wendy and me. We'd helped Walter into his costume before he climbed into the coffin. We could have dropped a hair on him as easily as anyone. I would mention it to Detective Johnston the next time I saw him. Roxie Kane could have left the hair also. She admitted to being in the parlor with him just a short time after he'd been chloroformed and injected with the insulin. Like Paula Browne, her hair was much darker than the rest of the cheerleaders'.

Before long, Stone joined me out on the porch with his own cup of coffee. I left him with the article to read while I went inside for a refill. He agreed the hair could very likely be from Wendy's head, Roxie's, or even mine. Wendy's hair was fairly dark naturally. Mine had been about every color the beauty salon offered from being dyed and highlighted every three months. I could no longer even recall what my natural color was, because it had been so long since I'd seen it.

Stone didn't recognize the young man in the photo who was peering at me while the rest of us had our heads bowed. If he remembered to do so, he'd ask Wyatt if he recognized him. I thought I could ask Joey if I got an opportunity to speak with him. Joey would be in the same age bracket as the guy in the photo.

By eight o'clock, everyone was down in the kitchen eating breakfast. I served corned beef hash, eggs scrambled with onions, green peppers, and jalapenos, fried potatoes, and sourdough toast. Wendy, who's thin as a rail anyway, ate practically nothing. I think she was too nervous to eat. Andy, on the other hand, ate like it was the last meal before his execution.

I gave Steve and Eleanor Dudley a key to the front door so they could come and go as they pleased while the four of us were gone. At a quarter to ten, we piled into Wendy's car and headed to the realtor's office.

A short time later we followed the realtor through the front gates of the property. Over the entrance hung a wooden sign with "T-n-T Ranch" burnt into it. We drove down the long driveway and parked behind a shiny John Deere tractor next to a pole barn. The realtor introduced us to the Olsens, Tom and Tessa. They were a friendly couple, probably in their early eighties.

It was clear the elderly couple desperately needed to sell this place and get settled into an assisted-living facility as soon as possible. They were willing to let the place go for well under its appraised value to make it happen while they were still healthy enough to make the move. As it was, they were both terribly frail. I don't know how the two of them kept up with all the responsibilities of taking care of the livestock and the property. Perhaps they had sons who assisted them, or even hired hands. I didn't want to ask and infer they were too old to handle the chores that maintaining the ranch entailed.

After a few minutes of visiting, the realtor took us on a tour of the place. The house was in better shape than any of us had anticipated. We followed her from room to room.

"This old house wouldn't take all that much to remodel and bring up to snuff," Stone whispered. "I would love to help you, Andy, if you decide to purchase it."

"Thanks, Uncle Stone," Andy whispered back. "It's not nearly as run-down as I expected either. It's cosmetic work it needs, more than structural. New appliances, new flooring, a good paint job, and some furniture and light fixtures that weren't purchased at Sears in the 1940s, and this place would shine like a new penny."

"I think it's very homey and comfortable," Wendy said. "I love the rock fireplace in the family room and the walk-in pantry off the kitchen. How many bedrooms does it have again?"

"Four," the realtor said. "It also has the sewing room that could be turned into a nice office or another bedroom, if a fifth one is needed."

"It only has the one bathroom though, doesn't it?" Andy asked. The realtor reluctantly nodded, and Andy continued. "The bathroom only has the old antique, claw-footed tub. I'd like to keep it for nostalgic reasons, but adding another, more modern, bathroom off the master bedroom with a large tiled shower would be my first priority."

I knew Wendy was wondering if the house had enough bedrooms to accommodate a family. She wanted two or three children, at the very least. I didn't know how Andy felt about having children, or even getting married. He was thirty-three years old and hadn't had a serious relationship with a woman yet, according to Stone. He didn't seem to be in any hurry to be burdened with a wife and children. Settling down with a family might be his last concern. I was certain he'd want to get the ranch going strong before making another life-altering change in his lifestyle.

Stone nodded at Andy's remark about adding a bathroom. "That wouldn't be hard to do. I think the house is definitely acceptable. Let's go have a look at the outbuildings, the livestock, and the land."

Andy agreed, and the four of us followed the agent and the sellers outside. After a brief inspection of the exterior of the house, the roof, and foundation, all of which appeared to be in reasonable condition, we continued on.

Some of the outbuildings were in need of immediate repair. The roof on the chicken coop was about to fall in on the chickens. The toolshed needed to be burnt down and rebuilt. Fortunately, the barn was in pretty good shape. It looked like it had been an addition in recent years.

The Black Angus cattle we saw looked healthy and robust, as did the poultry and the swine. There was a new litter of piglets we all thought were adorable. Even the golden retriever, Sallie, had a shiny coat and a friendly demeanor. She bonded with

Andy almost instantly, as if she knew it was in her best interest to befriend him. Sallie walked around with us as we toured the property. The realtor told us Sallie was three years old, and had been spayed. She was certainly friendly and would make a great guard dog and companion for Andy.

The 640 acres were divided and fenced off into four separate areas, so the herd could be moved from section to section. The pasture the cattle were currently in was pretty barren. These cattle needed to be moved to one of the other sections, all of which had more vegetation to graze on.

There was a good-sized pond, or farm tank, in each pasture for watering the cattle. A larger pond, which was located directly behind the house, was stocked with crappie, bass, and catfish, and was fed by a natural spring, Tessa, the rancher's wife, told us.

"What do you think, Stone?" Andy asked.

"I don't see any drawbacks at all, to tell you the truth," Stone said. "The land and livestock have been well taken care of, as has the old farmhouse. But this would be a far different kind of life than the one you lead back east. Are you sure it's what you want to do?"

"It's what I've always wanted to do, Uncle Stone," Andy said. "I know it will be a big change for me, but I also know it will be a welcome one. I'm not content with the lifestyle I currently have. I'm bored and restless and anxious to make a drastic change at this stage of my life. What do you think of this place, Lexie?"

"I think it's wonderful, Andy," I said sincerely. "The property is beautiful."

"How about you, Wendy? What do you think of the ranch?"

"I think it's only lacking two things, Andy," she said.

"What's that?" Andy asked, with a puzzled expression.

"You and a couple of horses."

Andy laughed. "Yes, I'd most definitely need a couple of horses. I'm surprised there aren't any here already. I've only ridden a horse three or four times in my life, but I'm sure I could learn to ride sufficiently."

Back at the house, we found out there had previously been four horses on the property, but they'd been sold when the old couple got too old to ride and take care of them properly. Horses tended to need a lot more attention than cattle.

Knowing he had a lot to learn about ranching, Andy agreed to come out to the farm the following day and help move the cattle to another pasture. He'd do all the work as the old rancher instructed him. He also had a lot of questions to ask Tom Olsen about raising hogs, cattle, goats, and chickens. He'd never even driven a tractor, he admitted. The John Deere looked brand new, and the two goats on the back porch looked feisty and ornery. We steered clear of them as we headed back toward the car in the driveway.

Andy wanted to spend some time on the ranch before he made a final decision. But I could tell the decision had already been made. Andy was infatuated with the place. He couldn't stop smiling as he looked out over the property, petting Sallie on the head all the while.

We thanked the Olsens and the realtor and headed back to Rockdale. Stone and Andy discussed the pros and cons of purchasing the property. Andy was concerned about Andy trying to take care of 640 acres, a full section of land.

"That's a lot of land and livestock there to maintain," he said.

"I know, Uncle Stone," Andy said. "But the Olsens have fifty years on me. If they can handle it, surely with a little training and experience, I can handle it too. If it all becomes too much, I can hire some help."

"I have no doubt you could handle anything you set your

mind to," Stone agreed. "I'm anxious to hear what you think after you spend a day out there with Tom tomorrow. And I'm not trying to talk you out of it. I just want you to take everything into consideration before you make a final decision. You know how badly I'd like to have you living near me. Still, your happiness in my prime concern."

We stopped for lunch in Atchison, and were fairly silent for the remainder of the drive back to the inn. We were all lost in our own thoughts. I was wondering how I could sneak off to run back out to Chuck's mobile home west of town. Something didn't feel right about his relationship with his younger half-brother. It was something I thought needed additional attention. The detectives apparently were satisfied with his story, but I wasn't.

EIGHTEEN

Steve and Eleanor Dudley were out when we got back, so Stone used his key to open the front door. Wendy and Andy disappeared to their rooms to freshen up, and Stone joined me in the kitchen for a cup of coffee. I had round steak simmering in a mushroom gravy, cooking slowly in the Crock-Pot, and was looking through my *Betty Crocker Cookbook* for something to fix for Eleanor.

"What are you feeding the pain-in-the-ass tonight?" Stone asked. He actually liked both of the Dudleys, but knew cooking for Eleanor was creating extra work for me.

"Here's a recipe for a cheese and spinach quiche that sounds pretty good, and also easy to prepare. How does that sound?"

"Not as good as beef, but I'm sure Eleanor will appreciate it. I'm certainly glad she'll bend enough to eat eggs," he said.

"I'll serve turnip greens and dinner rolls with it, and I'll whip up some cherry cobbler for dessert," I said. "Right after I have another cup of coffee."

"You're the best," Stone said. "Even though I have no idea how you sleep at night, considering the amount of caffeine in your system."

"I manage," I said. "I think by now I'm immune to caffeine."

"You'd have to be." He leaned over and kissed me on top of the head as he stood up to answer the knocking at the back door. "I'll let you get back to your quiche."

I don't know how, but the mere mention of food brought

Wyatt to our doorstep. Real men may not eat quiche, but I was willing to bet Wyatt was the exception to the rule. It was his day off so he wasn't in uniform. He looked nice in his creased khakis and navy blue polo shirt.

I invited Wyatt to supper, but, as it turned out, Wendy had already invited him and Veronica out to eat with her and Andy. Andy had met Wyatt on a couple of occasions while visiting us in the past year. They'd always gotten along well and had become friends in the process.

"I'm here to pick up Andy and Wendy," he said. "We decided to take in a show before supper. It's kind of a chick-flick, but Andy and I decided we could tough it out since both of the gals have been wanting to see it."

"That's mighty considerate of you boys," I said.

"Well, frankly, we'd both prefer something with a little more blood and guts in it, but maybe it'll at least have a car chase in it," Wyatt said. "Speaking of which, I was involved in one myself last night."

"What happened?" Stone asked Wyatt, as he poured the detective a cup of coffee. "Was it right here in Rockdale?"

"Yes. Downtown on Main Street, in fact. It ended when the young man crashed into a street sign in front of the hardware store. I pulled him out of the car, verified he wasn't injured, and proceeded to cuff him and stuff him. It was pretty cool."

"Anybody we know?" I asked. It was obvious this was the kind of police work Wyatt lived for. Writing out tickets for people parking in handicapped parking stalls was not Wyatt's cup of tea. "It sounds like you really enjoyed yourself."

"You guys wouldn't know him. He's not from around here. He was just a dumb punk who tried to grab the purse of a lady walking out of the post office. She made a ruckus and fought him off. A passerby called the police station, and we were on him before he could get out of town," Wyatt explained. "I've been on the force for fifteen years and have never had to draw my gun. We need a little action occasionally to keep the job interesting. That doesn't happen very often in a place like Rockdale. Pulling over speeders with marijuana in their glove compartments is about as exciting as it gets here."

Rockdale's low crime rate apparently didn't appeal a whole lot to Wyatt, who was paid to serve and protect the citizens of this sleepy little town. No wonder he hung out at the Alexandria Inn. This is where most of the major crimes in Rockdale seem to take place. It wasn't a cheery thought, especially when the low crime rate was one of the things that drew Stone to this town when he first purchased the old mansion to restore.

While Wyatt waited for Wendy and Andy to come downstairs, he, Stone, and I discussed the weather, the price of gasoline, the new mayor, and ice fishing. Finally, after listening to all the attributes of the latest ice auger on the market, I asked Wyatt if there were any new developments in the murder case.

"Not too many," he said. "Clarence and Melba have both been cleared, which is not to say something might arise that will draw attention to them again. Melba is to be released from the hospital next Monday with some home nursing care for a few weeks. They have her on a new medication. It seems to be working well, so far. She's not physically ill, at least, but they need someone to keep an eye on her. She's more of a danger to herself than anyone else."

"Does she realize yet her son is gone for good? Even at the funeral she seemed dazed and confused," I said. "I wasn't sure she even knew where she was."

"I think she does have some understanding of the circumstances by this time. She's been very upset since attending the funeral. They have her on suicide watch for a few days, anyway."

"That's too bad," Stone commented. "She's had kind of a rough life. What about Clarence? Is he still in town?"

"Clarence is driving back to Albuquerque as we speak. On the morning his son was murdered, he was at a high school friend's house, involved in a friendly game of penny-ante poker. He has five friends who can back up his story," Wyatt said. "And he really had no motive to kill Walter. He had nothing to gain from the boy's death. While he was in town, he'd planned to try once more to convince Walter to move to New Mexico and learn the heating and cooling trade. Walter was killed before Clarence got the opportunity."

"How sad, although I doubt Walter would have left Sidney behind to move to New Mexico. Any news about the DNA evidence from the loose hair found on Walter?" I asked.

"Yes, we took your advice and did a buccal, or mouth, swab on Roxie Kane, and found she was a DNA match to the hair. She's still under scrutiny, and the closest thing we have to a suspect to date. No one has stepped forward to verify her alibi yet, and her story is a little sketchy. Had she not been a match, we would have tested you and Wendy next."

"I can tell you one thing, Wyatt," I said. "I think the detectives should consider Audrey McCoy a suspect. From speaking with her, I can tell you she had absolutely no use for Walter or for his girlfriend, Sidney. She even told me she only came to his wake to make sure he was truly dead. I think she deserves a great deal of scrutiny. And, yes, I'd also do some more intense delving into Roxie Kane's involvement. I found her story a bit suspect, myself. If Walter were truly in the condition she reported to have found him in, and she had no intention of killing him, then why didn't she alert someone to the fact he needed help? She admitted she knew something was wrong with him."

"That's kind of what we thought too, Lexie. I didn't see her at the wake, or I would have spoken with her. But I thought I did see you conversing with Audrey at the wake," Wyatt said. "Did you?"

"Yes, I approached her while she was standing up at the casket, glaring down at Walter's body with pure hatred in her eyes. She left immediately afterward. We had a long and interesting conversation."

"Could you write down what all you can remember from your conversation with her before you forget any of it? You might be called to testify in court if she's eventually arrested," Wyatt told me.

"Sure, I'll do that today," I agreed. "Have they cleared Walter's half-brother, Chuck Sneed?"

"Not yet," Wyatt said. "Why do you ask?"

"I still think it's odd he didn't attend either the wake or the funeral. His excuse of having to go to a hog-tying contest doesn't sound too credible to me. What kind of people actually compete in hog tying?"

"Well, he is kind of a hick, Lexie."

"You think?"

Stone had never met Chuck, so I gave him a rundown on my meeting with him. Stone and Wyatt were both laughing by the time I was through.

"He bought your flower shop story?" Stone asked. "He must be a real dandy!"

"Well, he was at least half looped. I thought I might run back out there again this afternoon, while the kids are gone and the round steak is simmering in the Crock-Pot."

"Not without me, you're not!" Stone said. "He might be a nut job like his stepmother, but he also might be dangerous."

"If I weren't off duty today and already have plans, I'd go out there with you," Wyatt said. "He's right, Lexie. Don't go out there alone. I wouldn't trust Chuck Sneed if I were you. You don't want to show up out there alone and unannounced. If he actually had the audacity to kill his own brother, just think what he could do to you."

Wyatt was right. It would be best to take a man along with me. I could be rash at times, and I was very anxious to see the killer brought to justice, but I didn't really have a death wish. I had no desire to end up in the same boat as Walter.

"Thanks for agreeing to go out there with me," I said to Stone before he could change his mind or modify his previous statement that I wasn't going out there without him—as if he'd already agreed to make the trip.

"What will be your excuse to go out there this time, Lexie?" Stone asked. "Needing his opinion for the engraving font used on the grave marker?"

I wasn't sure I cared for the tone in his voice. I only appreciated sarcasm when it came out of my own mouth. I figured Chuck had believed I worked at the flower shop the first time so I'd stick with a story along the same lines. "Don't worry, I'll think of something."

"I was afraid you'd say that."

"Are you sure you know where you're going?" Stone asked me a while after we'd turned off Thirty-Six Highway on to the gravel farm road, just outside Chillicothe. "We've already wound around this back road for several miles."

"Yes, he lives at the end of this road. The road dead-ends in a cul-de-sac just past his driveway."

Stone continued driving my Jeep another mile or so before we came up on the Sneeds' mobile home. When we pulled up, Chuck was in his yard, gutting a deer with a large buck knife. He was so engrossed in slicing the deer up its belly, he didn't even look up. I averted my eyes to avoid watching the deer's entrails spill out onto the ground. I had a real affinity for wildlife, and watching them being dissected was not something I enjoyed.

Chuck never looked up as we got out of the Jeep and walked over to him. He had on blood-splattered jeans, with an empty knife sheath hanging from his belt. A green wool cap and a faded camouflaged sweatshirt completed his ensemble. A half-empty beer bottle was propped up against the deer's antlers.

"Whadda ya want?" he asked. He finally looked up, clearly impatient and aggravated at being distracted from his task of cleaning the buck.

"Remember me, Mr. Sneed?" I asked. "We met before. I'm the lady from the flower shop, and this gentleman with me is my partner."

"Yeah, yeah, so whadda you want this time?"

"Our customer service department has sent me out to do a survey. They like to ensure our customers were satisfied with the flower arrangements we provided for their loved one's funeral services. I just need to ask you a few questions. I won't take but a minute of your time."

"Your little flower place in Rockdale has a customer service department?" Chuck asked. Okay, so this guy was smarter than I'd given him credit for. I looked over at Stone, who was rolling his eyes. The real flower shop in town had an owner, who was the official florist, and one clerk.

"Well, uh, yes, we do. We are very customer-oriented, you understand."

"Whatever," he said. "I ain't got nothing to do with no flowers. I wasn't even there to see them anyhow. You need to talk to my sister, Sheila, like I told you before. I'm busy here."

"You didn't go to your brother's funeral services?" I asked, with disapproval in my voice. "Why ever not?"

"I went to that hog-tying contest on Tuesday, like I told ya last time you was here."

"What about the funeral on Wednesday night? Couldn't you have made it to that, at least? Surely the hog-tying contest wasn't a two-day affair," I said. I noticed Stone was examining his fingernails. He wanted no part of this conversation. I could tell he was second-guessing his decision to bring me out here, and thought my fictitious excuse for visiting Chuck sounded as lame as it possibly could. I turned my attention back to Chuck, who looked more than a little pissed off.

"Wednesday night I was in a pool tournament at the Blue Dog Saloon, not that it's any business of yours. Took second place, too. Won myself a hundred clams, first place was two-fifty," Chuck stated, proudly

"Oh, I see. This pool tournament was more important than your brother," I said, with even more disapproval. "That's just unbelievable."

Chuck instantly got to his feet. He pointed his buck knife at me, and said, "Now, listen here, lady. Like I done said, it ain't no business of yours what I do. You wanna know about flowers, go talk to my sister, Sheila. I got more important things to do, if you can't see that for yourself. I don't need no lecture by the likes of you."

Stone stepped in front of me, the knife blade just inches from his nose. "Take it easy, Mr. Sneed. The lady is just doing her job. No need to get upset. She didn't mean anything by what she said. You know how women can be. You get back to your work now, and we'll get on out of here and leave you be."

"Sorry, lady," Chuck said. He obviously felt a little contrite for pointing his knife at me. "Didn't mean to scare ya. And it wasn't just a pool tournament, ya see. On Wednesdays at the Blue Dog, they have happy hour all day long. They got fourteen types of beer on tap, and ever' draw is a buck off till closing time. It weren't just the hundred dollars I was after."

Oh, well, that explained it then. Why didn't he tell me before that he could get cheap beer on Wednesdays? Then I would have understood his plight. How could a brother's wake compete with that? God, what a piece of work this guy was.

"Let's go, Stone," I said. "Thanks, anyway, Chuck. I'll go ask Sheila about the quality of the flowers we delivered."

Back in the Jeep, I said to Stone, "That guy's a horse's ass, but he's got nothing to do with his brother's death."

"What makes you say that? I didn't come to that deduction at all."

"Chuck Sneed isn't smart enough to pull it off. You'd have to be at least a little bit clever to sneak in to the inn, chloroform Walter, inject him with insulin, and then sneak back out without being detected. And first of all, you'd have to have the wherewithal to know you could kill a person by making their blood sugar plunge to a fatal level. That's not Chuck's style at all, don't you see?"

"Yeah, I guess you're right."

"Chuck would have stabbed him with his buck knife, shot him with that twelve-gauge in the gun rack of his truck, or just cracked him over the head with a beer bottle. Then he would have dragged Walter off into the woods and left him to die and be picked clean by buzzards like a road-killed 'possum. Now, if that had been the M.O. of the killer, then I could believe Chuck might be responsible."

"I see your point," Stone said. "Chuck isn't the cunning, scheming type at all. He's the stick his knife right in your face type."

Nineteen

After supper we watched the Thursday night football game on television with the Dudleys. They told us their family reunion would be held Saturday afternoon at the American Legion Hall in Rockdale. Eleanor said it was to be a potluck affair, and asked if I knew where she could buy some decent potato salad.

I told her I made a mean mustard potato salad, and I'd be happy to prepare a large bowl of it for her to take to the reunion. It was going the extra mile like this that helped give us an excellent reputation with our guests. Word of mouth advertising had proven to be very effective in producing new customers. Stone thought I sometimes went too far in my quest to please the guests, but I would do whatever it took to help his business be successful. And Eleanor had assured me she'd reimburse me for the salad's ingredients, so I wouldn't be responsible for the expenses.

I fixed a bowl of popcorn for each of us during halftime. While I was in the kitchen, the phone rang, and I answered it. Wendy was on the line.

"Mom?"

"Yeah, babe? Is something wrong?" I asked.

"My car started acting up at a little club in St. Joseph. We decided to go there for a couple of drinks after dinner, and now the car is really running rough. Andy thinks it probably needs a new fuel pump. He noticed an excessive amount of exhaust fumes earlier, and he said it might also have a cylinder going bad," Wendy said. "Andy said we could take it to Boney's in the morning so they can have a look at it."

"You know about Boney's Garage?" I asked. The first time I'd been aware of its existence was when Audrey told me Walter's best friend, Joey, worked there.

"Sure. They just changed the oil in my car a couple of days ago."

"Did Joey Cox do the work?" I asked.

"Yeah," she said. "Do you know Joey?"

"No, but I was told he was Walter's best friend."

"Oh, I didn't know that, but I only met him the one time. He told me he'd just started his job there a few days earlier. Anyway, Andy wanted me to let you know we'd be late getting home. We're about halfway home now. Don't wait up for us, and don't worry."

"Okay. Thanks for letting us know. If the car breaks down completely, call back," I said before hanging up. Talking with Wendy about Boney's Garage gave me an idea. The oil in my Jeep had just been changed three weeks ago, in Shawnee, in mid-October. Even though I'd probably racked up 300 miles since then, the oil obviously didn't need to be changed. But I decided to take the Jeep in to Joey Cox anyway, right after my nail appointment. I could visit Joey while he worked on my car. I was sure Joey would be impressed with how clean my oil was, not knowing I'd just had it changed recently.

Wendy and Andy were up early, eating toasted bagels in the kitchen, when I came downstairs. The coffee was already made. I'd heard them come in just after eleven, about thirty minutes after we went to bed. I couldn't sleep until I knew they were home, safe and sound. No matter how old your child gets, you never get over that habit.

They told me they wanted to be at Boney's the minute they

opened for business at eight. They'd promised Tom Olsen they'd be back out at the ranch in the morning, and they didn't know how long the repair on Wendy's car would take. They would surely be on the way to T-n-T Ranch before I was finished at the nail salon, and headed over to Boney's for an oil change.

Stone came down a few minutes later and enjoyed a cup of coffee with everyone before Wendy and Andy left for the garage, and he headed out to work on his lawnmower. His new part had arrived in the mail on Thursday. It was a small rubber gasket that didn't look to me like it could make a hill of beans worth of difference in how the lawnmower ran. But Stone assured me it was crucial for optimal performance of the mower, and he was anxious to see if it fit properly.

After I prepared breakfast for the Dudleys, triple-egg omelets with onion, mushrooms, and cheese, I'd go to the grocery store to pick up the ingredients I needed for Eleanor's potato salad. Once I was back, and had them stashed away in the pantry, I'd head over to the nail salon for my three o'clock appointment. After that, I'd take the Jeep to Boney's, and hope the kids were well on their way to the ranch, so I didn't have to explain my sudden need for an oil change. Later in the afternoon I would fix the potato salad, so it'd be ready Saturday morning for the Dudley family reunion. I had everything planned perfectly for the day.

I hadn't thought to ask Eleanor how many people were expected at the reunion, or how much potato salad I should make. I bought enough ingredients to feed an army, just to be on the safe side. If Stone was available when I started on the salad, I'd get him to help me peel potatoes. Peeling potatoes was one job that really didn't appeal to me. It ranked right below vacuuming, probably wedged right between cleaning toilets and ironing.

For someone who really didn't enjoy housework, I was doing

a lot of it these days at the inn. I'd be glad when spring arrived and we hired a gal to do the housekeeping and cooking again. It wasn't easy to find good help when they knew the job would be seasonal.

Back home, I was putting all the groceries away when my cell phone rang. It was Wendy. She was calling from Boney's Garage.

"Hey, Mom?"

"Yes, honey?"

"Can Andy and I borrow your Jeep today? We promised the Olsens we'd be out today, so Andy can help move the cattle, and learn more about the ranch and the livestock," Wendy said.

"Won't they be able to fix your car?"

"Yes, but not until early afternoon," she replied. "Joey said they'd have to special order the fuel pump because they can't keep fuel pumps on hand for all the different vehicles made. He could order it this morning and have it on the delivery truck first thing this afternoon, he said. So we'll leave the car with him and pick it up later on this evening."

"Just out of curiosity, are they open on Saturdays?"

"Yes. They're only closed on Sundays, Joey told us."

"Well, sure, you can use the Jeep," I said. "I can take Stone's car to get my nails done, and I'm just planning to spend the afternoon fixing some potato salad for the Dudleys, for the family reunion they're attending tomorrow."

"Mmmmm, I love your potato salad, Mom. Can you make an extra batch for us to have with our supper tonight?"

"Sure, babe. Eleanor is paying for the salad, but I don't think she'd mind. You can come pick up the Jeep whenever you want to."

There went my plans to have Joey change my oil this afternoon. But I could go to the garage tomorrow instead. I was still plenty sore from being hit by the SUV, so a little rest in the afternoon was probably in order. I had a box of old photographs

I wanted to arrange in an album, I had the potato salad to prepare, and I hadn't had time to watch Oprah in days.

Stone peeled potatoes for me while I rounded up the other ingredients I needed for the salad. I diced a dozen boiled eggs, chopped some celery, and stirred in two large jars of mayonnaise, and a smaller jar of mustard. I was making a huge batch, most of it for the family reunion, and a smaller amount for supper tonight. It would just be the four of us here for supper, because the Dudleys were dining at a friend's house in Overland Park, Kansas.

The Dudleys would be leaving on Sunday morning, and I was ready for them to go. I had run out of ideas for meatless suppers. I was about ready to plop a bowl of macaroni and cheese down on the table in front of Eleanor, and heat up a porkless TV dinner for Steve. I'm sure they'd be impressed. But knowing them, they wouldn't complain. They really were a fine couple. I wish all of our guests were so easy to please.

Our next scheduled guests didn't arrive for a week. Honeymooners from South Carolina would be here for a long weekend. My mind was already racing with ideas to make their stay special. I'd start with rose petals on their bed when they arrived, and a bottle of champagne on ice in their room. Naturally, they'd get the nicest suite, one nobody had died in. Stone gave me free reign in handling the guests. He even occasionally had great ideas of his own to contribute.

I was washing my hands in the sink when the phone rang. Stone answered the telephone, and handed it over to me. I dried my hands on a towel and took the phone. I figured it would be my daughter because she was about the only person who called me at the inn. Most of my friends rang me on my cell phone.

"Hey, Mom!" Wendy sounded anxious, worried about

something. I could always tell when something was bothering her by the tone of her voice.

"Hi, Wendy! How's your day going out at the T-n-T Ranch?"

"Good. Andy's learning a lot, and I'm enjoying myself too."

"Did they get your car fixed at Boney's?" I asked.

"Yeah, I called Joey, and he said it's running fine now," she said. "Andy's out in the barn with Tom, and I'm walking around the big pond with Sallie. She's really a sweet dog. But that's not why I called you. I wanted to tell you about something strange that happened to us this morning, on the way out here to the ranch."

"What happened, dear?" Stone had been on his way out of the kitchen, but stopped and stepped back in. My last question had caught his attention. He waited to see what I'd find out from Wendy.

"Well, didn't you say the vehicle that struck you in the hospital parking lot was a dark-colored SUV?"

"Yes, I did. Why?" I asked.

"There was one fitting that description that followed us all the way from Rockdale out to the ranch. I think it started tailing us from right by the Alexandria Inn, almost like it was waiting for us to leave there this morning."

"Was the SUV navy blue, by any chance?" I asked.

"We couldn't tell for sure, only that it was a darker color."

"Could you see the driver?"

"No, the car never got close enough to us to even detect if it was a male or female driver, but the SUV turned every time we turned, even though it stayed quite a bit back. I'm surprised we even noticed it was following us. In fact, we weren't sure it was actually tailing us until it pulled down the gravel road the ranch is on," Wendy explained.

"It followed you all the way to the ranch?"

"Yes, but when we pulled into the Olsens' driveway, the car

kept going, driving right on past the ranch. The driveway is too long to see much, you know, like the exact color of the car or the gender of the driver."

"Did you happen to notice if the left front headlight was broken out? If so, I'd be almost positive it was the same car that ran me down," I said.

"Andy said he thought the headlight casing was intact, but he could have been mistaken. And it could have been repaired already. The driver would surely be aware the police were watching for a dark SUV with a broken headlight, and gotten it repaired as quickly as possible."

"That's true," I agreed. "But why would someone follow you and Andy? You really aren't involved with the case, except for Walter's autopsy. It doesn't make any sense to me."

"Think about it, Mom," Wendy said. "If the car never got close enough for us to identify the driver, then the driver couldn't identify who was driving the Jeep either. I'm sure he thought he was following you. Your yellow Jeep is easy to spot. I think someone is targeting you, and I'm very concerned about it. Stone will be too. I don't like the idea you're being stalked. There's no telling what this guy has in mind."

"I can't honestly say I like the idea of being stalked, either," I said. "Maybe it was just a coincidence. There are a zillion dark SUVs on the road, as Sheldon Wright will tell you. Perhaps this particular one was just going in the same direction as you two were."

"Mom, the gravel road the ranch is on dead-ends about a quarter mile past the T-n-T Ranch. After we pulled up to the farmhouse, we just sat in the Jeep and watched, and sure enough, it crossed back in front of the ranch not more than a couple of minutes later. It doesn't sound like a coincidence to me."

"I see your point," I said. "Well, you two don't need to worry about it. Enjoy your day out at the ranch and I will talk to Stone and Wyatt about the SUV."

"Promise?"

"Yes. Stone is standing right here with me," I assured her. I hung up the phone and thought to myself for a moment. It unnerved me to think Andy and Wendy were convinced I was being stalked. The very idea sent a shiver up my spine.

Wow! I'd never had a stalker before. This was a whole new thing for me, and like Wendy, it concerned me. I kind of wished now I'd never gotten involved in the case, and had just let the authorities handle it, as Stone and Wyatt had recommended. All I could hope for was that the case was solved soon, before this stalker caught up with me again. I might not be as lucky next time as I was the last. And, as Wendy had said, there was no telling what he planned to do to me.

Most likely my stalker was the same person who killed Walter. On the one hand, I wanted to stay hidden away in the inn with Stone at my side until the investigating team made an arrest. If I kept completely out of the public eye, I'd probably be safe. On the other hand, he or she had walked directly into the inn to kill Walter, so what was to keep the perpetrator from doing it again? This was obviously a bold, reckless, and determined individual. This stalker had already, most likely, killed one person and had nothing to lose by committing another murder.

I wasn't keen on letting this stalker intimidate me. I was being haunted by Walter's innocent, young face in my dreams. I wouldn't rest easy until Walter's killer was convicted and justice was meted out. I also didn't like being confined to the inn. Perhaps I could split the difference by making sure I was never out in public alone or at the inn by myself. I would try to keep myself immersed in a crowd. There was safety in numbers.

"What did she say?" Stone asked me. "From this end, it sounded like someone followed the Jeep out to the ranch, and the kids think someone is stalking you."

I explained what Wendy had said, and Stone was all for my first idea of staying put inside the inn, with him never leaving my side.

"But I have a nail appointment at three," I said.

"Cancel it."

"I'd be right on Main Street, in a busy little salon. There's no way he could come in and harm me in any way. No stalker would be that brazen, would he?"

"Whoever killed Walter was brazen enough to come into the inn even though you and Wendy were here. There's no telling how far this person will go if he's worried and determined enough. I'll tell you what," Stone said. "I have nothing going on this afternoon, so I'll drive you to your nail appointment, and I'll wait in the car for you. I'll watch everyone who walks into the salon and come in myself if I feel it's necessary. If there's anywhere you need to go, until the killer is caught, I'll drive you. You need to be alert at all times, aware of everything going on around you. In the meantime, I'm going to talk to Wyatt and relate everything Wendy told you to him. He needs to know what's going on. How does this plan of action sound to you?"

I was happy with Stone's suggestions. My nails were an absolute mess. How did this kind of thing not bother me before I started dating Stone? There was a time when ragged, unpainted nails didn't faze me in the slightest, and now they were intolerable. It's funny how a person's perspective could change when love entered the picture.

Together Stone and I finished preparing the potato salad, and I made a bread pudding with vanilla sauce to serve for dessert that night. I knew it was one of Andy's favorites, and he would be flying home tomorrow afternoon. Wendy was planning on taking him to the airport, now that the fuel pump had been replaced in her car.

After the cooking was done, I took a long soak in the tub. The bruising on my hip and leg hadn't abated any, but the soreness was gradually working its way out of my body. Long soaks and plenty of Bengay seemed to be doing the trick.

"Are you convinced now it's in your best interest to put all this investigating nonsense behind you?" Stone asked me later that evening. "You've stirred someone up, and this person is a known killer. Remember, I want you to let me know if you need to go out somewhere. And I also want you to ensure the doors on the inn are always locked, even when we're in the house. Okay?"

"Okay, I will." I stopped just short of promising Stone I'd no longer pursue my quest to help identify the killer. I knew I couldn't be trusted to fulfill that particular promise. When push came to shove, I couldn't prevent myself from stepping right into the middle of things.

TWENTY

"I'll wait right here," Stone said, parking just to the right of the front door of the nail salon. He couldn't see directly into the salon, but the two parking spaces in front of the door were taken. Still, he could see anybody leaving or entering the business, and we were both satisfied with that. "If I see anyone enter the salon, I'll be right behind them until I'm satisfied they aren't coming in to harm you in any way."

"Okay, Stone. Thanks for bringing me. I shouldn't be long. The owner told me she set me up with their new girl, who is very efficient," I said.

Stone gave me a kiss and I climbed out of the Corvette. I'd only had my nails done here once before, and I'd been assigned to a young Vietnamese gal who had done a fantastic job. I'd hoped I'd get her again, but no such luck.

The owner greeted me when I entered the salon. She was also Asian, a tiny, quiet woman in her early forties. She pointed back toward a woman in the rear of the shop, a younger lady with her back to me. She was hanging up her jacket, as if she'd just reported for work. When she turned to face me, I nearly lost my balance. It was Roxie Kane, Walter's one-time date, the gal I'd gotten kicked out of the anatomy class. Something told me she wouldn't be pleased to see me, and I was correct.

She walked up to the front of the shop, and said, "You again? What do you want now? I told you I have nothing more to say to you."

"I'm just here to have my nails done, Roxie." I held out my hands to show her my nails, just to demonstrate to her how badly they needed to be manicured and polished. She didn't even look down at my hands, but kept staring at me instead. I considered turning around and walking out of the salon. I wasn't sure I trusted my nails to this woman, who already had an axe to grind with me. I had to remember to tip her well, just to make up for the first time we met.

"How did you know I just started working here? Are you stalking me now?" Roxie asked. How did I explain to Roxie I wasn't a stalker, but rather a stalkee? Maybe she was my stalker, for what little I knew.

"I had no idea you worked here, Roxie. I promise, it's just a stroke of luck."

"Whose luck, mine or yours?" She asked. "Because mine's not running so good. I had to go in this morning to do some extra credit work to make up for the test I flunked because of you. If I hadn't convinced Mrs. Herron, the professor, it was you, not me, who was interrupting the class, I would have had to take the entire course over."

"I'm so sorry, Roxie," I said. I meant it too. "I really had no intention of getting you kicked out of class. I was afraid it would be my only opportunity to speak with you. Little did I know you'd be doing my nails today."

"Hmmph!" She clearly had not accepted my apology as readily as I'd expected. Her petite Asian boss was pointing Roxie back toward her station. She wasn't about to let our petty little differences allow cold hard cash to walk out her salon's door.

"Come on," Roxie said, after an exasperated sigh. "I'm in the last station, back in the back."

I didn't say much at first, while she worked on my left hand. She had removed what little polish remained on my fingernails.

Finally, I thought it wouldn't hurt to chat with her about the murder investigation. If she was the person who was stalking me, and I really didn't think she could be, she'd have to kill me with a fingernail file, because it was the closest thing she had to a weapon at her station.

"I was surprised I didn't run into you at Walter's wake or funeral," I said.

"You didn't run into me because I wasn't there."

"You weren't?"

"No. Why would I be? I had one lousy date with Walter. It's not like we were long, lost friends or lovers. He spent the entire evening talking about Sidney," Roxie said. "Even at the time, he had no intention of making any kind of connection with me. I was just a pawn in his game, in his desire to get Sidney to take him back."

"Didn't that kind of tick you off?"

"Well, sure, at the time. I was angry with him for using me. But now I've got a new boyfriend, and he's fantastic. He's everything Walter wasn't. I really had no reason to want to see Walter dead. I wouldn't risk my entire future just to get back at him. I only stopped by the inn the other day to let him know it was wrong to use women the way he used me, which was just to make his girlfriend jealous. I heard he had another date with a girl named Audrey. I'm sure he was just using her in the same fashion. He was a jerk. That's all there is to it," she said. "And I felt obligated to tell him he was a jerk."

It didn't sound to me as if Roxie had any real motive to kill Walter. One unromantic date would not cause a woman to want to see the fellow dead. She might have disliked Walter, but she didn't hate him enough to kill him. She had no animosity against Sidney either. I got the impression they hadn't even known each other well.

"Do you know Sidney?" I asked.

"No, not personally, I only know she'd dated Walter for a long time," she replied. "Once they broke up I figured he was fair game, so I accepted his offer to go out on a date. It was a mistake, but I didn't know it at the time I agreed to go."

"I understand," I said, as I watched Roxie remove the old polish from my nails, which was about gone before I arrived. I had applied it myself, many days ago.

"We went to eat at the Longhorn Steakhouse and then went on to the Legends Theatre for a movie. But I knew five minutes into dinner the relationship would never amount to anything. Walter talked about nothing but Sidney. It was very irritating. In fact, I asked him to take me home after we ate because it was obvious to me he would much rather be with Sidney. He apologized, but said he had promised me a movie and he was determined to take me to see one. I figured what the heck, since it was a movie I'd wanted to see. I don't think we said one word to each other the entire time we were at the theater."

"I don't suppose you're a diabetic, are you?" I asked.

"No, sorry. I'm happy to say I'm perfectly healthy."

It didn't sound to me like she had any real reason to kill Walter, or to hurt Sidney in any way either. I'd come to a dead end with Roxie Kane. I sat silently while she buffed the nails on my right hand. I picked out a pale pink color for the polish. Once she had finished trimming and buffing the nails on my left hand, I excused myself to use the restroom. I'd had too much coffee, as usual, to wait much longer, and I knew it would take a while for the polish to dry once it was applied. I decided I'd best use the restroom while I could.

After I flushed the toilet, I washed my hands, and ran a comb through my hair before returning to Roxie's station. She started polishing the nails on my right hand, saying very little to me. I think she was still seething at me from getting her kicked out of her anatomy class.

"Hey!" I heard the owner yell. "What's going on back there?"

I looked over at her, and she was pointing under the door of the restroom, where water was running out at a steady pace. It was pooling up in the rear of the salon, soaking into cardboard boxes on the floor, which were probably full of nail polishes, files, clippers, and other essential items for the salon.

"What did you do in there?" the diminutive Asian lady asked me.

"Nothing," I answered. "I just used the bathroom, flushed the toilet, and washed my hands. That's all I did."

She flung the door opened, and said, "The toilet is running over. If we don't get it stopped and the floor mopped up quickly, we will have to close the salon down until the mess is cleaned up and the toilet is repaired. Otherwise, it would be a code violation, and also it's hard to work around."

Both the owner and Roxie scowled at me, as if I were personally responsible for the faulty toilet. I hadn't reached down into the tank and ripped out the guts of the toilet. Why were they glaring at me?

"What have you done now?" Roxie asked me.

"Nothing, Roxie. I swear I didn't do anything but flush the toilet. It shouldn't be clogged. I didn't use an excessive amount of toilet paper or anything." I blew on my fingernails as I got up and walked back toward the bathroom. I could at least turn the water off to the toilet, something the owner had yet to think about doing.

Tiptoeing through the water, I reached inside the bathroom and flipped on the light switch. *Zap!* The bulb in the light fixture sparked, and then the electricity to the entire salon went out. The only windows were in the front of the salon, and it was very dark in the rear of the large room.

"What have you done now?" the owner asked. "Now I'm most definitely going to have to shut the salon down."

"I didn't do anything but turn the light on," I said. "There must be something wrong with your wiring and your plumbing. Have you got a flashlight so I can turn the water off to the toilet?"

The owner walked quickly up to the front off the store to retrieve a flashlight. I blew furiously on my nails, hoping to dry them out before I fiddled with the shut-off water valve. Roxie wouldn't appreciate having to start over on polishing my nails. In the meantime, the water continued to pour over the top of the toilet bowl.

"What are you trying to do to me?" Roxie asked. "I can't afford to go home early. I need this money to put gas in my car, just to get to my classes this week. What have you got against me? Why are you trying to sabotage my workplace now?"

"I'm not, Roxie. I have nothing against you at all. Nothing, Roxie, I promise," I said. "I haven't intentionally done anything to sabotage the salon. Listen, my boyfriend is out in the car. He's very handy. I know he can fix the toilet and get the electricity back on. It's probably nothing but a blown circuit breaker and something equally simple on the toilet."

"Please don't do anything else to try to help us, ma'am. You've done enough already," the owner said to me. I figured it was time for me to go. I could remove the nail polish from my right hand when I got home and have my nails done somewhere else at a later time. I headed toward the exit, but before I got there, the door opened, and a large, stern-looking gentleman walked in. Stone was right on the man's heels.

"I'm from the Missouri Board of Cosmetology. There's been a recent report of unsanitary conditions at this salon. I'm here to do a thorough inspection, and also to check for valid state licenses," he said. He looked toward the back of the room where all the chaos was taking place. "What in the hell is going on here?"

"You!" The owner pointed at me, fury clearly etched across her brow. She stood in a pool of water, holding a flashlight in one hand and a mop in the other, and looking totally bewildered. She pointed the handle of the mop at me, and hollered, "Get out of my establishment, lady! Right now!"

I knew at this point there was no convincing them I hadn't called in the report of unsanitary conditions. Obviously, it'd been called in on a previous date. Until the toilet had spilled over, the salon had looked perfectly sanitary to me. Stone was staring at me as if I'd grown horns. I grabbed my coat off the coat rack, dropped a twenty-dollar bill on the front counter, and headed out the door. I didn't look directly at Stone, or glance back at Roxie, the owner, the inspector, or the other customers and employees in the salon. I jumped into Stone's Corvette, like it was a getaway car, and said, "Let's go!"

Wendy and Andy arrived back at the inn just in time for supper. They were both wound up and rattling on about their day at the ranch. Andy had decided he was going to put in an offer on the place. He could line up things in Myrtle Beach and take possession of the ranch in early spring. He already had an experienced pilot interested in buying his charter flight business and he was living in a rental house, so moving out of it would pose no problem.

"I'm delighted," I said. Stone nodded in agreement.

"I'd go ahead and close on the ranch now, though," he said. "That way the Olsens can get moved into their assisted-living facility. I'll try to fly back for a few days each month to get some work done on the farmhouse. And I'll hire someone to take care of the livestock in the interim," Andy said. "Uncle Stone, could you drive out and look over the place now and then?"

"Of course," Stone replied. "I'd be happy to keep an eye on

the ranch for you."

After much more discussion about the T-n-T Ranch, the subject of my stalker came back up. Both Wendy and Andy were pleased to hear Stone was now my new personal chauffeur, so I wouldn't be out and about alone. I didn't tell them about my disastrous visit to the nail salon.

Supper consisted of barbeque pork ribs, potato salad, baked beans, and dinner rolls. The Dudleys were eating with friends tonight so pork was allowed on the menu. Most of the conversation centered on the T-n-T Ranch, and my presumed stalker. Wendy had invited Detective Wyatt Johnston to join us for dinner, and he agreed with Stone on the necessity of me having company on any outing, and also about keeping the inn locked up at all times.

Wyatt seemed a bit discouraged by the progress the investigating team was making in the murder case. There were potential suspects with possible motives and questionable alibis, but not enough evidence to press charges against anyone. The interviews were ongoing, but the investigation had almost come to a standstill.

The footprints had matched Roxie Kane's boots, as had the single strand of hair found on the victim, but no reasonable motive could be attributed to her. A reward fund had been established for anyone who reported a tip leading to the apprehension and arrest of a suspect. So far, however, very few tips had come in, and all those had lead to dead ends.

The rest of the evening's conversation centered around the T-n-T Ranch, and Andy's decision to put in an offer on it. Wyatt offered to help Andy in any way he could. He had friends in the Atchison Police Department, who could make extra trips out to drive by the property until Andy got moved in to the house.

After supper, Wyatt went home, and Andy and Wendy went to a movie in St. Joseph. Stone and I watched an old classic John Wayne movie on the television. The Dudleys returned to the inn just as the old western concluded, and I locked the inn up behind them. Stone and I went to bed early. I finally fell sleep after I heard the kids come home from the movie.

TWENTY-ONE

I woke up early on Saturday morning. I would be making three-egg spinach and mozzarella cheese omelets for breakfast, along with hash browns and English muffins. The potato salad was ready to go with the Dudleys to the family reunion. And I'd made an appointment for an oil change, at two o'clock at Boney's Garage. I'd been assured Joey would be performing the service on my Jeep.

I didn't think any stalker in their right mind would be up and about at six in the morning, so I sat out on the back porch with a cup of coffee and the newspaper. The front-page news no longer centered on the death of the young college boy. The city council was feuding over whether or not the fountain in the city park needed to be replaced or merely refurbished. Funds were always tight in the small town of Rockdale. Apparently, emotions ran high on both sides of the issue.

After I finished reading the paper and refilled my coffee cup, I sat on the porch reflecting on the list of suspects in my little notebook. Several I'd dismissed either because they had a strong alibi or because they lacked strong motives and had no passionate desire for retribution. I was still a wee bit suspicious of Walter's half-brother, Chuck Sneed. There was more to his story than met the eye, but I knew there was no way I'd get Stone to take me back out to his house. And there was no way I'd even consider going out there alone. He seemed very "stalkerish" to me.

I would have liked the opportunity to speak with Sidney Hobbs, but only to see if she had information on any of Walter's enemies or acquaintances who might have a reason to want him dead. She was entirely too emotionally distraught to have committed the murder herself.

I had never even considered any of the customers touring the haunted house the day of the murder as suspects. They were mostly harmless young ladies, with no connection to Walter, and small children. There was nothing remotely suspicious about any of them.

I had removed Walter's father, Clarence, from my list, because of a lack of any real motive for him to kill his own son. He had nothing to gain and seemed sincerely anxious to have his son take over his heating and cooling business.

Walter's mother, Melba, was another story. She seemed just crazy enough to do something completely bizarre and out of character, and then not remember doing it an hour later. She could have mistaken her son for someone who was out to get her, someone who wanted to hurt her in some way. But was she competent enough to come up with a plan of action like injecting insulin into someone to cause a low sugar reaction? I didn't really think so. I felt it would be giving Melba more credit for intelligence and cunning than she was worthy of.

Roxie Kane had been checked off my suspect list for having a near non-existent relationship with the deceased, even though she had been with him just minutes before his death. Her one date was a "been there, done that, and moved on" type of thing. True, she'd been extremely upset with Walter, and she'd felt humiliated and used by him, but she really had nothing to gain by Walter's death. She didn't know Sidney well enough to crave any retribution against her either.

Walter's relationship with his sister, Sheila Talley, was still questionable to me. She obviously had differences with him, particularly regarding their mother's will and power-of-attorney status. Money could be a motive for her, and having Walter become Melba's sole heir could well be a bitter bone of contention for her. But, yet, Sheila had been sincerely moved by sorrow at the loss of her brother, and I couldn't quite visualize her carrying out such a devious and deadly deed. I guess I was still on the fence with Sheila.

Audrey McCoy remained on my list. She might have wanted to exact revenge on Walter for using her to make Sidney jealous, knowing she was Sidney's "archenemy." She had substantial differences with both Walter and Sidney, and wasn't afraid to voice her opinion of both in public. She made no secret of her disdain for Walter, or her dislike of Sidney.

My main suspect at this point, however, was Melba's attorney, Sheldon Wright, of Hocraffer, Zumbrunn, Kobialka, and Wright. He had a financial motive, the crafty intelligence necessary, and the conniving personality to pull off such an act. He was far too interested in the family's financial situation, and incredibly impatient to get her paperwork done. In Melba's condition, she could be persuaded to change anything he wanted her to change. And I still couldn't fathom how anyone but Sheldon Wright could be responsible for running me down in the parking lot with his navy blue SUV. It seemed probable it was the same dark SUV that had followed Andy and Wendy to the T-n-T Ranch.

I still wanted to talk to Walter's best friend, Joey, today at Boney's Garage while he changed my oil. Joey wasn't even on my suspect list, but I surmised if anyone knew of any enemies Walter might have had, it would be Joey. I felt both the investigating team and I could be overlooking someone as a suspect entirely.

For example, Walter could have beaten someone out for a starting position on the college basketball team, and that person might have desperately wanted the position. It didn't seem to me to be worth killing someone over, but people had died for lesser reasons than a starting position on a basketball team. I'd heard of young men being killed for their tennis shoes, or jacket, or even the twenty-dollar bill in their pocket.

But since I still believed Wright was the one who was currently stalking me, I wanted to pressure the authorities to delve further into his alibi and motives. If he was evil enough to try to harm me, he was evil enough to kill Walter, too. Had the investigators interviewed him thoroughly? Had they possibly even cleared him? Wyatt hadn't mentioned him at supper, and I'd yet to hear of any alibi he might have had for the day Walter was murdered. There wasn't anyone who could verify he was home alone at the time of Walter's death.

Sheldon Wright was the one suspect I wanted to concentrate on, but I couldn't track him down alone, and I knew I wouldn't fare well in trying to get Stone to help me. Maybe I could talk Wyatt into interrogating him further, if he could do so without jeopardizing his job. He could question him a little more about my accident in the parking lot and about the possibility of him stalking me. We already knew he owned a navy blue SUV, which fit the description of the vehicle that had struck me.

It was about seven-fifteen when Stone joined me on the back porch with his own cup of coffee. He made it clear he wasn't happy about me sitting out on the porch alone. I sat quietly while he read through the newspaper. When I heard other people moving around inside the inn, I went in to start preparing breakfast. Eleanor Dudley was pouring two cups of coffee, one for herself, and one for her husband, Steve.

"Good Morning. How was dinner with your friends last night?" I asked her.

"Very good. She served a delicious pasta with Alfredo sauce. We had a very nice visit with them. We hadn't seen them in quite a few years."

Damn, I thought. Why hadn't I thought of serving pasta for the strict vegetarian? I made a decent Pasta Primavera. I used rigatoni and lots of fresh vegetables. Sometimes, when I wasn't cooking for vegetarians, I added chicken or shrimp to the dish. Oh well. She had survived on my casseroles all week. I smiled at her and said, "Good. I'm so glad you had a nice evening with your friends. The mustard potato salad is all ready for you to take to the Dudley family reunion this morning."

"Thanks Lexie. I really appreciate you making it for us. And, by the way, it's the McCoy family reunion. My side of the family, not Steve's," she said.

"McCoy? Did you say McCoy?" I asked. "McCoy is your maiden name?"

"Yes, I grew up in Kansas City, and my aunt and uncle have always lived right here in Rockdale. They're the ones who organized the reunion."

"I guess I just assumed it was the Dudley family holding the reunion. Do you know an Audrey McCoy?"

"Sure. Audrey is my niece. She's my sister Norma's only child," she replied.

"What kind of girl is Audrey? I met her the other day at a funeral, but only had the opportunity to talk briefly with her," I said.

"She's a nice gal, but very driven and determined to have her own way," Eleanor said. "Unfortunately, she takes after her father instead of my sister. My sister is very laid back and mellow, but her husband is extremely temperamental and more than a little overbearing. It doesn't take much to set him off, and Audrey is the same way. I just mark it down to her being a little spoiled by being an only child."

Audrey was one of the people on my list I wanted to speak with again, if for no other reason than to convince myself she couldn't have had anything to do with Walter's death. She seemed considerably pleased to have him dead, and also pleased about how badly his death had devastated Sidney. How could I use this family reunion coincidence to my advantage? I had to give it some thought while I worked around the inn.

After I served breakfast and then cleaned up the kitchen, I performed some housekeeping chores. I dusted, vacuumed, and cleaned mirrors and windows. Once I was finished I took a coffee break in the kitchen, instead of on the porch, so as not to upset Stone again. At about nine-thirty, Eleanor came in to retrieve the potato salad.

"Well, I better pick up the salad and get going, so Steve and I can get to the American Legion Hall by ten," she said. "That's the time the reunion begins."

"Oh, no!" I said, with mock concern on my face. "I just thought of something. What time is lunch at the reunion?"

"We're eating at noon. Why?"

"I just remembered a critical ingredient I forgot to add to the potato salad," I told her.

"What's that?"

"Uh, er, well, um, you see, I forgot the mustard," I stammered.

"You forgot the mustard in your mustard potato salad? That's odd. What a strange ingredient to forget. How long will it take to stir it in?" she asked.

"Well, actually, I need to go get some at the store. I meant to do it last night and forgot. But I am going out today anyway, so why don't I just drop the salad off at the American Legion Hall at eleven-thirty. That would be much better, anyway. It will still be fresh and cool that way. Much tastier than to let it warm up to room temperature, don't you think?" I asked. "And no chance for bacteria to set in, either."

"I imagine you're right. Are you sure it's no trouble for you?"

Eleanor asked.

"No trouble at all," I assured her. With any luck, I'd run into Audrey at the reunion and get a minute or two to speak to her. I felt safe in approaching her in a crowded public place such as the American Legion Hall would be today, with the family reunion taking place there.

I wanted to ask Audrey what kind of car she drove and see what her reaction was. If she were stalking me, she would realize I was aware I was being stalked, and I was also aware that she was my stalker. It might make her think twice about continuing along that line. I could also check out the parking lot for a dark SUV with a busted-out headlamp in case she lied to me, which she was sure to do if she was guilty of first-degree murder and possibly attempted vehicular homicide. I really had no idea if the two events were connected, but thought it was likely and wanted to ask Audrey about her vehicle just in case the two incidents were related. Usually a person's reaction to an unexpected question will give them away if they lied. I was pretty adept at reading people's body language.

Stone would never consent to me driving to the American Legion Hall by myself, but I could tell him the same story I told Eleanor, other than the part about forgetting to put mustard in my mustard potato salad. It really wouldn't be a lie, because potato salad really was best when it was cool and fresh. Stone would surely prefer to wait out in the parking lot while I took the potato salad inside. He was still under the impression it was a reunion for Steve's side of the family and not the Mc-Coys, and there was no pressing reason to tell him otherwise.

Mrs. Dudley agreed with my plan to drop the potato salad off right before lunch and needed to get on her way. I told her she looked terrific, and I meant it. I was glad to see she was wearing a black pantsuit that didn't emphasize her large posterior. She had gone easy on the makeup, and she was wearing black flats, not sequined high heels. She'd even had her hair styled, and she looked very elegant.

I told Eleanor to have a good time and went to find Stone. He said he'd be happy to drive me to the American Legion Hall to drop off the Dudleys' potato salad. I hadn't mentioned the appointment at Boney's Garage, because Stone knew I'd just recently had the oil changed in my Jeep. I'd have to play this one by ear and hope it didn't land me in any trouble. However, my luck in that regard had not been good lately, and I doubted it would change any time soon.

As I took clean sheets out of the dryer in the laundry room at about eleven, I looked outside and was surprised to see large snowflakes coming down. I knew a strong cold front had come through early in the morning, but I hadn't expected snow this early in the season. Snow in early November in Missouri was rare, but certainly not unheard of.

By eleven-fifteen, as I was stepping into Stone's car with the big bowl of potato salad, the snow was coming down at an even brisker rate. It was still melting on contact with the pavement, but was beginning to stick on the grassy areas.

"Was this predicted?" I asked Stone.

"Yes," he said. "The weatherman on the morning news said several inches of snow was possible, with an accumulation of an inch or so. Most of it will melt on contact with the warmer ground temperatures, but the melting snow will be turning to ice as the temperatures drop. He said to watch for slick roadways this afternoon. By tomorrow the roads should be clear, he said, as it is expected to warm up again. Wendy will need to be careful driving Andy to the airport."

Stone drove carefully to the American Legion Hall. He let me out at the front door before pulling around to park the Corvette in the parking lot. As I walked into the large meeting room, I glanced around quickly. I spotted Eleanor on the other side of the room in the midst of a large crowd of people. They were all standing directly in front of the table full of food. She was engaged in a lively conversation with a younger couple.

I needed to find Audrey before I went over to place the potato salad on the table, because Eleanor would see me and naturally expect me to leave right after setting the bowl down. Just as I was beginning to give up hope on finding Audrey, I saw her walk out of the ladies' restroom. I rushed over to her.

"Hi, Audrey. It's nice to see you again," I said.

"What are you doing here?" she asked. "You surely aren't a member of the McCoy family, are you?"

"No, no, of course I'm not. Your Aunt Eleanor and Uncle Steve have been staying at my partner's bed and breakfast this last week. I made this mustard potato salad for her, and I was just dropping it off when I saw you. I thought I should say hello before I left. I'm afraid I might have offended you in some way at the wake the other night. I certainly didn't intend to."

"Well, hello then," she said. She sat down in a fold-up chair, and turned away from me. It was obvious she had nothing else to say to me and was dismissing me. I would have to get right to the point.

"Isn't that your vehicle in the parking lot with the flat tire? I think it was a dark-colored Chevy Suburban, or maybe some other make of SUV."

"No, it's not mine. I rode here with my parents," she replied. Her answer was non-committal, so I still didn't know if she drove a dark-colored SUV.

"Oh, I see. You left your SUV at home?" I said, trying to sound as if I was just making polite conversation.

"I didn't drive my car," Audrey said. Why was she being so evasive? Did she not want me to know what kind of vehicle she drove? It was at this moment I looked up and saw Eleanor waving me over to the food table. I told Audrey good-bye and headed toward Eleanor.

I wasn't going to get to ask Audrey any more questions. Then it hit me that this really would be the last opportunity I'd probably have to speak with her, and I needed to pin her down on what kind of vehicle she drove. So I turned around to go back and ask her why she'd been following me. Hopefully I'd be able to judge by her reaction to my off-the-wall question if it was she who was stalking me. I had nothing to lose at this point.

I gave Eleanor an "I'll be there in a second" gesture and rushed back toward Audrey. Just as I drew near her chair, I stumbled over a tear in the carpet. My body pitched forward, and I instinctively reached out with my arms to catch myself. The large bowl of potato salad flew out of my arms and landed upside down in Audrey's lap, all over her cream-colored sweater and her nicely creased tan slacks.

"You idiot!" She cried out, jumping up off the chair. "What's wrong with you, anyway?"

"I'm so sorry—"

"There's mustard in that salad, isn't there? I can smell it. Do you know how hard it is to get mustard stains out of clothing? This is my brand new chiffon sweater, and it cost me a small fortune. I bought it specifically for this reunion and now it's ruined. I expect to be reimbursed for this, lady!"

"Oh, certainly, Audrey," I said. "It was my fault, and I fully intend to buy you a new sweater to replace the one I just accidentally damaged. I'll also pay for having your slacks professionally cleaned. I really am sorry, but it was truly just an accident."

"I'll bet," she said. By now, Eleanor was standing right beside me. Her hand was over her mouth, which was hanging open in astonishment. She could see how angry her niece was and how flustered I was. After a moment of silence, Eleanor stepped between us.

"Audrey, dear," Eleanor said, "I'm sure Lexie didn't mean to dump the salad in your lap. This torn carpet is very dangerous. We're just lucky she didn't get injured when she tripped. I'll be happy to drive you to your house to change clothes."

"Thank you, Eleanor," I said. "I'm so sorry about the potato salad. I certainly don't expect you to repay me for the salad ingredients. And I apologize to you again, too, Audrey. Please send me the receipts for the sweater and for the cleaning of your slacks, and I will reimburse you."

"Don't worry about the potato salad, Lexie. There's enough food over there to feed an army, and the McCoy family is only a platoon. We'll get along just fine without potato salad. There are several other kinds of salad over there as it is." Eleanor helped me clean up the mess before she went away with Audrey, and I left to go back outside to the car. I was sure Stone was wondering what was keeping me. I had to explain the tripping accident to him since I was carrying an empty salad bowl, which had somehow not broken. I almost wished it had shattered, so I could have just tossed the broken shards of glass into the nearest trash can and not had to explain why it was now empty and the reunion had only just begun. The new mustard-stained chiffon sweater I was going to replace must have cushioned the bowl's fall.

I didn't mention my conversation with Audrey to Stone, just said I had approached her to say hello, when I accidentally tripped on a tear in the carpet. Stone just shook his head as if nothing I could ever say would surprise him. He made no comment about the empty salad bowl on the way home. I was content to discuss the snow, which was beginning to stick to the road.

Back at the inn, I washed the large salad bowl and placed it back in its place in the cabinet. It occurred to me that not only was I making very little headway into this murder investigation, I was also making very few new friends. So far I'd angered nearly everybody I'd spoken with about the case. What did that say about me? I must really be a very aggravating, annoying kind of person. What in the world did Stone see in me? Sometimes, recently, I could barely even stand myself.

While fixing everyone ham and cheese sandwiches for lunch, Stone spoke with Andy and Wendy about the weather. The roads were getting slick and icy. He was concerned about Wendy driving to the airport on them. He asked her if she'd mind if he rode along with them. He'd even drive her car if she felt more comfortable not driving it herself. Wendy was glad to have him tag along. I knew she had no reservations about driving in inclement weather; she had done it many, many times before. But I also knew she enjoyed Stone's concern about her welfare. She missed having a father figure in her life. Stone had filled that gap nicely, treating her as if she were his own daughter. Since his wife had been unable to bear children, Wendy filled a gap in his life, as well.

Andy's flight left at three o'clock, and he had to be there an hour in advance, so the three of them were going to leave the house by one-thirty, which meant they couldn't waste a lot of time over lunch.

I contemplated calling Boney's Garage and canceling my two o'clock appointment. The mere thought of being out in public alone frightened me. But would a stalker go out in this kind of weather? I didn't really think so. If I drove straight to the garage, what harm could come to me? The more I contemplated it, the more convinced I felt I could make it to Boney's and back with no problems.

Chances were Stone would never even realize I'd gone and had my oil changed—again. And if somehow he did get word of it, I would blame it on a moment of poor judgment. Then it came to me that Stone was getting accustomed to moments like that.

As Andy was loading his suitcase into the trunk of Wendy's car, I wished him good luck on getting all his affairs taken care of in Myrtle Beach, and told him I looked forward to him moving back to the Midwest. I hugged him and then kissed all three of them before they pulled out of the driveway.

I fully expected to be home, safe and sound, busily preparing a fruit salad for dessert later in the evening, by the time I saw Stone and Wendy pulling back down the driveway.

TWENTY-TWO

"Are you Joey?" I asked the young man in a grease-stained, blue striped shirt, and old tattered blue jeans. He had a ball cap on that had "Valvoline" stitched across it. I was surprised to see he was the young man in the photo, printed in the newspaper who'd been staring at me during the sermon at the gravesite.

"Yes, ma'am. I'm Joey. May I help you?"

"I'm here for my two o'clock appointment for an oil change. I was told you were going to do it," I said.

"Yeah, that's right. I'll be right with you after I finish with this tire rotation. Do you mind waiting in the office?" he asked.

"No, that'd be fine." He'd been conversing with an older gentleman, probably the owner of the Honda Civic he was rotating tires on. Once the gentleman and his car were gone I'd be able to speak with Joey while he changed my oil. I was relieved I had driven here without being obviously tailed by another vehicle. There were relatively few vehicles out on the road, other than four-wheel-drive trucks with snowplows mounted on the fronts of them. The amount of snow coming down and accumulating on the roadways was even surprising the local meteorologist, according to the news station I'd been listening to on the radio. Four to five inches of snow already covered the ground. It was a very unusual early season occurrence in this region.

There was a dingy-looking coffee pot in the office, full of what looked like week-old coffee. The carafe was so stained you could barely see the thick, black coffee inside it. As bad as it looked, I poured myself a cup of it to sip on while I waited. The small Styrofoam cup on top of the stack had a greasy fingerprint on the outside, so I tossed it in the trash, and used the next one down. The coffee was as strong and bitter as I expected it to be, but not bad enough to discard and go without.

I was sitting there, sipping coffee and gazing at the falling snow, when my cell phone rang inside my purse. The caller ID indicated it was Stone. My first thought was that they'd run into trouble on the road.

"Hello?"

"Hi, Lexie," Stone said, cheerfully. "I called you on the house phone and you didn't answer."

"I guess I didn't hear it," I said. That wasn't a lie. It's hard to hear a telephone ring when you are many blocks away from it.

"Well, I just wanted to let you know we got to the airport all right, and Wendy and I are just waiting here with Andy until his flight is called. I didn't want you to worry about us."

"Thanks, Stone. I was kind of concerned. I know Wendy is a good driver, but you never know what the other guy is going to do."

"That's true. How is everything at the inn?" he asked.

"Everything at the inn is fine. The Dudleys aren't expected to arrive home until five or five-thirty. I'm just sitting here, watching it snow and enjoying a cup of coffee." Again, I wasn't lying. And I was quite sure there was nothing amiss at the inn. Everything had been just fine when I'd left there a mere fifteen minutes prior to Stone's call.

"Well, good. I'm glad to know you're relaxing. You've had a rough week. After the Dudleys leave tomorrow, you will have some time to get some rest, and hopefully your soreness and bruising will go away."

"I'm looking forward to it," I said. "The soreness is already starting to diminish, but the bruising will probably hang around a bit longer."

"I'm ready for you to pull your Jeep in, Ms. Starr," I heard Joey say. I hurriedly put my hand over the bottom of my phone and nodded my head. After Joey exited the office, I went back to the phone, afraid Stone had heard Joey speaking to me. Apparently he hadn't; he was talking about Andy's plans once he returned home. I listened for another thirty or forty seconds.

"Listen, Stone," I said. "Why don't you visit with Andy while you still have a chance, and you can tell me all about it when you get home."

Stone agreed and hung up. I went outside to drive my car into the open bay where Joey could lift the car up over his head, on the racks, to drain the oil.

"How are you today, Ms. Starr?" he asked.

"I'm fine, and you?"

"Not bad, even though they've got me working on a Saturday. I had another gal named Starr in here yesterday for some repairs, and also a couple days ago getting an oil change," Joey said.

"That was my daughter, Wendy. She's the one who told me about you." She and Audrey McCoy, that is. I didn't want to let on I was only getting my oil changed so I could grill the young mechanic about any knowledge he might have about who would want to murder his dear friend.

"Oh, that's nice. Didn't I see you at Walter Sneed's funeral?" he asked. "I can't get over how much you look like my Aunt Yvonne."

So, maybe that explained why he was staring at me in the photo taken at the gravesite. I was happy he mentioned Walter. Now I didn't have to find some clever way to segue into that topic of conversation.

"Yes, I was there. I thought you looked familiar too, Joey.

Were you a friend of Walter's?" I asked.

"Yeah, Walter was my best friend. Had been since we were in junior high. I still can't get over the shock of his death. I almost called in sick today, because I truly do feel ill over the whole thing."

"I'm sure it will take a great deal of time to accept it and deal with it. No one ever expects to lose someone so young and healthy. I can't imagine anyone would want to kill him. Can you?" I asked

"No, he was a great guy."

"Did he have any enemies?"

"No. None that I can think of, anyway," Joey said.

"Was there anyone jealous of his athletic accomplishments?"

"Sure, there were a few guys I suppose. He beat out quite a number of guys for the starting point guard position on the basketball team at the community college. But I can't see how any of them could be jealous enough to kill him," Joey said. "Basketball is just a game, after all."

I watched him work for a few minutes before he said, "You know what? There is this one guy, named Caleb, who got in a fistfight with Walter a couple weeks ago. Caleb had the hots for Sidney, you see."

"Really? Where does this Caleb guy live? Here in Rockdale?" I asked.

"I have no idea. I don't really know him," Joey replied. "I can hardly believe the guy would go to such an extent though. Killing Walter over some girl would be insane."

"He has a motive, I suppose," I said. "I wonder if he has an alibi."

"I don't know. A couple of detectives from St. Joseph talked to me a few days ago, but I didn't think to tell them about Caleb. I wonder if I should contact them. What do you think?" Joey asked.

"Detective Wyatt Johnston with the Rockdale Police Department is a good friend of mine. I'll talk to him and suggest he question this Caleb fellow. Do you know his last name?"

"Davis, I think. Or maybe David, or maybe even Davies."

"That's probably close enough to track him down. Is he a student at the community college?" I asked.

"Yes. I think Walter told me he is in the Army Reserves, too," Joey said. Hmm, I wondered, is Caleb a friend of Roxie Kane's, by chance? Is there any kind of connection there?

Joey had drained the oil and put in a new oil filter. He was now lowering the car to add the new oil. As he wiped his hands off with a greasy blue rag he looked at me with an odd expression.

"You know, your oil was very, very clean. Whatever kind of oil you used last time, I would use the same kind again. Do you remember what kind it was?" Joey asked.

I looked up at Joey's ball cap. "Valvoline," I said. My mind was already on something else. How would I tell Wyatt, without telling Stone, about this guy, Caleb, who had fought physically with Walter, not all that long ago? How would I indicate where I'd heard about Caleb? Oh, what a web of lies I could weave.

"Hmmm. It's a good oil, but still . . ." Joey looked puzzled before changing tack and getting back on line with our previous conversation. "Sidney sure is devastated by Walter's death. I feel so sorry for her. She was a mess at the wake, and her dad wouldn't even let her attend his funeral."

"Yeah, I know. I can't believe he wouldn't let her attend her boyfriend's funeral. I think he is being much too protective of her," I said, to make conversation more than anything else. I had taken out my notebook and written "Caleb Davis, David, or Davies" in it.

"Well, when her dad was in here the other day to get a new headlight put in his Ford Explorer, he said Sidney was too distraught to attend the funeral. Mr. Hobbs told me he was worried about how attending it would affect her health," Joey said, as he poured the third quart of Valvoline into the oil reservoir.

"What? What did you say?" I asked. My attention was now riveted on Joey. "Sidney's dad had a new headlight put in an SUV recently? In his Explorer? What happened to the broken headlight?"

"Yeah, I think it was late Tuesday. He was lucky we had the right one in stock so I didn't have to special order one. He said he clipped his mailbox and needed it fixed right away."

Of course he did! More likely he clipped me—in the hospital parking lot a couple of days ago. And he definitely needed it fixed right away, before the authorities spotted it. Was he acting on behalf of his daughter? Was he now stalking me to protect her? Or was he the killer and my stalker? Was there some reason he wanted Walter dead?

"What color is Mr. Hobbs' car, Joey?"

"Well, it's like a dark forest green. Why do you ask?"

"Just curious."

Oh, my God, I couldn't believe what I'd just heard. I couldn't wait to pay for my oil change and get back into my Jeep so I could call Wyatt. Suddenly I saw no reason to even mention Caleb to Wyatt. I had narrowed down my list of suspects to just two—Sidney and her father.

I thanked Joey and handed him twenty-five bucks. Then I nearly backed over him in my haste to exit the service bay. The road was really slick now. The temperature had dropped, and the melting snow on the pavement had turned to ice. As dangerous as it was, I drove the Jeep with my left knee while I dialed Wyatt on my cell phone. I was sure he'd tell Stone about the phone call, but at this point I felt I had no choice but to report to him what I'd just discovered. I would deal with the ramifications of this phone call later.

Wyatt answered on the third ring. He was directing traffic at an intersection on the western edge of Rockdale, he said. A conversion van had rear-ended a FedEx truck.

I told him all about my conversation with Joey at Boney's Garage, even mentioning Walter's fight with Caleb in passing. He thanked me for the information and promised to drive over to the Hobbs house as soon as the wreck was cleared up.

As I pulled away from the red light on Main Street, I looked up into my rearview mirror and noticed a big white car approaching me from behind. As it got closer I could see it was a Lincoln Continental, and a man was driving the vehicle. I didn't think much about it at the time.

I turned on to Maple from Main Street to take the shortcut back to the inn. The Continental turned behind me. When I turned onto Fifth Street, the Continental turned behind me again. I looked at the driver in my rearview mirror. I noticed he had a jacket on, with the hood over his head, but I was almost certain it was Mr. Hobbs. It stood to reason he and his wife had two vehicles, so maybe he was driving her car. He probably wanted to keep his car out of sight as much as possible so no one would connect the dark SUV to the murder case and hit-and-run accident in the hospital parking lot. Was he really following me? I wondered.

Just to check, I turned right at the next crossroads at the last second, instead of pulling straight through the intersection. The Lincoln turned right behind me. I nearly froze in place, terrified now. I was convinced I was being tailed. Mr. Hobbs must have seen me pull out of Boney's Garage, or maybe he'd been lying in wait for me to come back out on the road.

I turned left down the next street. He turned left. I drove two blocks and turned right. He turned right. We were now driving through a residential area of town. Not one person was in sight.

Everybody was staying inside because of the weather conditions. How could I lose him? I couldn't drive fast enough on the icy roads to put any distance between us.

I made my way back to the highway, hoping the more heavily traveled roads were in better condition. They were, but just barely. I was able to gain a little speed as I drove, but the Lincoln behind me kept right on my rear bumper. There was no one at the inn. Driving there might be the worst thing I could do in this situation. It was a little isolated and sat back from the road quite a distance.

I made a sudden U-turn in the middle of the highway. The Lincoln did the same thing right behind me. There was absolutely no doubt now my stalker was following me, and he had evil intentions where I was concerned. I looked down at my dash and was instantly relieved to discover Stone had filled up my gas tank. I wouldn't run out of gas any time soon, at least. Maybe I could keep driving until I was certain Stone would be home, and then return to the inn.

It suddenly occurred to me to call Wyatt back. All I had to do was hit "Send, Send," on my phone, and it would ring through to him. I could tell him my location and have him send patrol cars out to rescue me. I reached into my purse and pulled my cell phone out just as the Lincoln behind me tapped the rear bumper of my Jeep. It jarred me just enough for me to drop the phone on the floor of the passenger side. Now I couldn't reach the phone, and I couldn't pull the Jeep over to pick the phone up off the floorboard either.

I pushed down on the accelerator, picking up as much speed as I safely could without losing control of the Jeep. Still, I couldn't lose the Lincoln Continental. I decided then, if I couldn't call Wyatt, I would drive back to him. If I pulled up to him at the scene of the accident in downtown Rockdale, there wasn't much Mr. Hobbs could do to me. If Wyatt had already left the scene, I would drive straight to the police station. I would pull into their parking lot and run into the building as fast as I could.

I felt a little bit of relief, now that I had a workable plan. I had to turn around and head back toward Rockdale. I couldn't drive through the median because the Transportation Department had recently installed a cable down the center of it to help prevent head-on collisions.

So, instead, I pulled off onto the next exit ramp. This turned out to be a bad decision. As I reached the road at the end of the ramp, the rear end of my Jeep was tapped again. This time the hit was harder and more violent than the time before. I was unfamiliar with the area, and I didn't know where the road I was on led, but there was no place to turn around to get back up on the highway. Surely, if I turned at the next intersection, I would end up back in town eventually. At least the road I currently traveled on was paved. I sped up a little, as did the Lincoln. He was now tapping the rear bumper of my car repeatedly.

Between the incessant tapping and the icy pavement, my Jeep was swerving from one side of the road to the other. The road had not been treated with salt or sand, and there was no one else on the road. I was driving on black ice now, barely able to keep the Jeep on the pavement even without being pounded from behind.

I drove past a closed gas station, and a couple of vacant buildings. I saw no other human being, except for the angry face in my rearview mirror. He no longer tried to hide his face under the hood of his coat, as if he didn't care if I recognized him at this point. Mr. Hobbs was getting impatient with me. He was now trying to spin me out by ramming one side of my rear bumper and then the other. Before I realized it, the pavement ended, and I found myself driving down an icy gravel road. We were out in the middle of nowhere now.

My heart was pounding in my chest, and I was breathing harder and harder, gasping in pure terror. I didn't know how I was going to get back to town from my current location. I didn't know where this road went, or even if it was leading to a dead end. If it was, it might very well be a dead end for me too. Now that Mr. Hobbs probably knew for sure I recognized him, he had almost no choice but to kill me. He had killed before and would not hesitate to do so again, I was certain.

What could I possibly do? It was hard to think while trying to maintain control of the vehicle. I looked up into my rearview mirror again and was surprised not to see the white Lincoln. Then I heard it pull up beside me on the driver's side. He veered his car to the right and steadily pushed my lighter car over to the edge of the road. There was a deep ditch running along beside the gravel road.

I heard a sickening crunch on my left front quarter panel, and felt the Jeep turning over on its side into the ditch. I felt blood trickling down the side of my face where I'd hit the driver's side window, which had shattered in the rollover. Before I could unbuckle my seatbelt, crawl out of the window, and make a run for it, Mr. Hobbs had me by the arms and was pulling me out of the Jeep.

"Couldn't leave things well enough alone, could you, Ms. Reed?" he asked, thinking I was Rhonda Reed, investigative reporter. He was a big man, even more menacing now than he had looked in my mirror. He pulled my arms behind my back, as I screamed in vain. He pulled a roll of duct tape out of his coat pocket, and began wrapping it tightly around my wrists. I was surprised he didn't just kill me and get it over with. My Jeep and body probably wouldn't be located for hours. Apparently, he had other plans for me.

I was kicking at him with my legs now, hitting him in the

shins over and over again. He let out several yelps and was getting angrier and angrier. He called me a few obscene names and shoved me down to the ground. I inhaled fresh snow as I gasped for air. I found I couldn't stand back up with my arms tied behind my back. I continued to kick at him as he tried to tie my ankles together. Eventually he succeeded, being larger and much stronger than I was.

He unlocked his trunk now, and picked me up to drop me into it. I was relieved he hadn't killed me yet. I wasn't sure what he had in mind for me, but I was certain things were going to get worse before they got better. I was still screaming when he started to close the trunk of the Lincoln, even though there was no one nearby to hear me. He opened it back up and put a piece of duct tape across my mouth to silence me.

I heard the driver's door open and close, and felt him turn the car around and head back in the direction from which we had come. I could tell when we left the crunchy gravel road and were back up on the pavement. I was writhing around, trying to see if there was a release in the trunk of the car, but I couldn't quite get turned just right. Knowing it was probably a futile attempt, I wrestled my arms around as much as I could. If I could somehow get my arms loose, I might be able to pull up the carpet and look for the trunk release cable. I knew they were usually located on the driver's side of the trunk.

I fought and fought to loosen the tape around my wrists but was having no luck. My eyes were beginning to adjust to the darkness. I could see a toolbox off to the left of my head. If only I could regain use of my hands, maybe I could find something in the toolbox to pry the door latch open. I twisted and twisted my arms, hoping to cause the tape to wear and begin to rip. I knew my time might be running out, and I had never been this scared before in my entire life.

I had to assume Mr. Hobbs was taking me off somewhere in

the woods, away from civilization. Once he got me out there he'd no doubt kill me and bury or hide my body out amongst the trees, where it would take authorities even longer to find it. I hadn't been able to see if he had any dents or scratches on his car he'd have to account for or have repaired, probably in some neighboring town. I was sure the Lincoln had to have sustained some kind of body damage, as hard as he'd battered my car with it. I hoped this would eventually lead to his arrest for the murder of Walter and me.

I could hear other vehicles now and knew we were traveling along in traffic. Not heavy traffic, by any means, but other cars were passing us from time to time. As I continued to try to free my hands, I felt the Lincoln slowing to a stop. Off in the distance I heard a train whistle. This gave me an idea.

We were obviously waiting for a train to pass at a railroad crossing. As the train got nearer, the sound of it rolling along the rails got louder. I turned my body around so that my taped legs were facing the rear of the car. As the train closed in on the crossing, the engineer began to blow the train's whistle. At the same time, I began kicking frantically at the right taillight assembly from inside the trunk. I hoped the sound of the train whistle would mask the sound of me kicking at the taillights. It was hard to kick with my ankles taped together, but I could tell I was making progress when I heard cracking noises.

Just before the train cleared the crossing, I felt the taillight break free. I pushed at it with the heel of my shoes until most of it fell out onto the pavement. I had hoped there was another vehicle parked behind the Lincoln, but I could see through the opening now, and there were no cars behind us. As we drove over the tracks and began to pick up speed, I tried to push my shoe through the opening, but the opening was not as wide as my shoe, and it was hard to do with my ankles tied together. Using the heel of my left shoe, I pressed it down against the floor of the trunk and pulled. I did this several times before I felt my shoe slip off.

If I remembered right, I had on red socks, the same color as the taillight assembly. This might make my sock harder to detect, but it was the only hope I had at this point. I pushed the toes of my left foot into the opening I'd made by busting out the taillight assembly. It was a tight fit, but I was able to get them to protrude beyond the hole where the taillight assembly had been.

This put me in an awkward and uncomfortable position, but I felt there was at least a slim chance someone would notice if they pulled up behind the Lincoln. I began wiggling my toes as much as I could, and continued doing so until my foot began severely cramping. I had read that this was the thing to do if ever locked in the trunk of a car. At the time I would never have imagined that this would one day apply to me.

After resting my foot for just a few seconds I began wiggling my toes again. I kept this up as we traveled along a busier road. The speed of the Lincoln had picked up significantly, so I figured we were most likely back up on the highway. It felt to me as if we were heading toward Rockdale. The good thing was there was more traffic on the road and, therefore, more drivers to notice my toes sticking out of the taillight opening. The bad thing was that at this speed, and with the current road conditions, the other vehicles would be farther behind us, making my toes more difficult to detect.

I was beginning to think this idea was not going to provide a satisfying conclusion. I felt bad that I had gone against Stone's wishes for me to never leave the inn alone. I was terrified, and there were tears running down my cheeks. Why hadn't I just left well enough alone, as Mr. Hobbs had suggested? How was this going to help the reputation of the Alexandria Inn? My death would just stir up more news that would shed an even worse light on the establishment. Stone had moved to the Midwest to be closer to me, and now I was probably going to be out of the picture.

I continued to wiggle my toes, even though my toes were bitterly cold, and there was an intense aching in the arch of my foot. I was about to give up hope and pull my toes back into the interior of the trunk, when I heard the sound of a siren in the distance. It was closing in on the Lincoln rapidly. The sound of the siren nearly enveloped me in joy.

I felt the speed of the Lincoln kick up a notch or two and continue to move faster and faster. We were passing other cars at an alarming rate now. I was wiggling my toes like crazy. The siren continued to get louder.

Suddenly the Lincoln left the highway, careening down an exit ramp. It turned to the right, and then quickly back to the left. We were moving fast, sliding about on the icy road beneath us. I heard more sirens now, coming from the opposite direction. By the time we turned again, the sirens were right on our tail. I thought the siren was coming from the vehicle directly behind us. I swished my toes back and forth as erratically as I could, hoping to draw attention to them, although I was beginning to feel confident it was Mr. Hobbs they were chasing, and I would be out of this predicament soon.

Suddenly I felt the car begin to spin around, doing about three complete rotations before it slammed headfirst into something that stopped us in our tracks. I heard glass breaking and the squealing of metal being torn apart. I felt something like a tire iron strike the side of my head as I was flung about in the trunk of the car. Then I heard the sirens being turned off and car doors slamming. I heard a voice call out, "Step out of the vehicle with your hands up!"

I heard sounds of a scuffle, and finally I heard the blessed sound of a pair of handcuffs being ratcheted down. It was the nicest sound I'd ever heard in my entire life.

Only seconds later, the trunk of the car opened, and I was staring up at Detective Wyatt Johnston. I thought he had never looked so wonderful as he did at this moment. He reached out and gently removed the tape from across my mouth.

"Lexie, are you okay?" he asked. I told him I was okay as he pulled out a pocketknife and began cutting away the duct tape on my wrists and ankles. "I'm so glad you called me when you did."

"How did you find us?" I asked.

"After you called, I got worried, so I summoned another officer to take my place directing traffic, and I headed over to the Hobbs residence. Mrs. Hobbs was home but she told me her husband, Jeffrey Hobbs, was gone. I asked her if he drove a dark-colored SUV, and she said, 'Yes. He drives a Ford Explorer. Why?' " Wyatt told me. "I told her I needed to speak with him, and she told me Jeffrey had taken her Lincoln Continental into town. She said she had expected him to be home already."

"Go on," I said.

"Well, I got suspicious. When asked, she told me her Lincoln was white. I tried to call you back on your cell phone and you didn't answer, which worried me even more."

"The cell phone was still in the Jeep, which is turned over in a ditch off a gravel road west of town," I said. "Not that I could have answered it anyway, with my hands tied together."

"So, I drove to Boney's and asked Joey about you. He told me you had left about an hour earlier. I tried you on the phone once again, and then called Stone on his phone. He thought you were at the inn. He said he was almost there. He and Wendy were just arriving back from the airport. I told him I had talked to you on your phone right after you had left Boney's Garage."

"Was he upset?" I asked Wyatt. I knew this was an idiotic question.

"Of course he was. He was extremely worried and scared half to death. Anyway, Stone called me back a minute or two later, and by then he was frantic. He told me you weren't at the inn, so I sent out an APB on a white Lincoln Continental. The entire police force was out looking. Then we got a nine-one-one call from a driver who said he saw toes sticking out of the broken taillight of a white Lincoln heading west on the highway out of Rockdale. He gave his location, and we all turned around and headed in this direction, converging on Mr. Hobbs so he'd have no way to escape. Knowing you were confined in the trunk, we had hoped to avoid wrecking him, but obviously, it was not to be. Thank God you're okay, other than the little cut by your ear. Anyway, once he plowed into the light pole, it was all over but the cuffing and stuffing."

Wyatt grinned from ear to ear. I could tell this car chase, which had spoiled an abduction, had made his day. He handed me his phone and asked me to call Stone. He wanted me to let Stone know I was okay as soon as possible, to ease his mind. "We've got the ambulance coming to take Hobbs to the hospital. He is bleeding pretty profusely from a large gash on his forehead, and a smaller one on his arm. I think his left wrist might be broken, as well."

"I hope so," I said.

"Tell Stone I will get you home as soon as you are debriefed, and have given your statement at the police station. If he'd like, he can meet us there."

Stone was incredibly relieved when I called to tell him what had happened. He told me if he wasn't so happy to hear I was okay, and to know my stalker had been apprehended, he'd be angry at me for sneaking out of the inn on my own. I apologized and came really close to promising I'd never get involved in something like this again. "Never say never" was my motto. At the time, getting involved again was the last thing I ever wanted to do, but I knew time would ease those frightening memories, and the fear and apprehension would go away, but I'd always have my impulsive, and sometimes reckless, nature to contend with.

TWENTY-THREE

At the police station, I gave my statement and related everything I could remember from the time I left Boney's, until the time the Lincoln struck the light pole. Stone and Wendy had arrived at the police station before us, and they were waiting impatiently for us to get there. They both rushed up to hug and kiss me when I stepped into the station in front of Wyatt.

After making sure I was going to be okay, Wendy headed back to the inn. Before she left, she assured me my facial cut would heal sufficiently without stitches. Stone sat through the debriefing period with me, holding my hand tightly to give me moral support. My hands were still shaking slightly from the ordeal I'd just been through.

Halfway through the question and answer session, the chief of police stepped into the room and said someone had called in about finding a yellow Jeep upside down in a ditch out on County Road Thirteen. The chief had sent out a wrecker from Doug's Towing to bring the Jeep back to town. I knew it was going to need a great deal of bodywork before I drove it again.

The chief also told us Jeffrey Hobbs would be interrogated thoroughly, before being charged with, most likely, a number of crimes. It was doubtful he'd ever see the light of day again, he said, which pleased me immensely.

Once he was brought to the police station from the Wheatfield Hospital in St. Joseph, where his head wound was being stitched up, and a cast put on his wrist, he would be thoroughly interrogated, booked and arrested, and then held in the county jail while awaiting arraignment.

The chief expressed his relief that the murder suspect had been apprehended, and that the abduction had turned out the way it had. He thanked me for my part in the apprehension of Jeffrey Hobbs, and then asked me to never insert myself into a police matter of this nature again. Stone and Wyatt both nodded their heads in agreement with the chief. I just smiled, and agreed the apprehension of Mr. Hobbs was a great relief, and the abduction was resolved to my liking too. I made no promises about the future. Never say never, I thought to myself once again.

"You're not cooking tonight," Stone told me as he drove me back to the inn. "Wendy is at the inn, explaining today's activities to the Dudleys, who should have arrived home by now. I'm treating you, Wendy, and the Dudleys, to dinner out tonight. Then you are going to take a long, hot soak in the tub and relax by the fireplace while we watch TV."

"Well, you won't hear any arguments out of me. This has been the most distressing day of my life. I really didn't think I'd live to see you and Wendy again. It reminded me, once again, of just how much the two of you mean to me. I love you so much, Stone," I said.

"I love you more," he replied.

We had a very pleasant evening. The Dudleys were understanding of our failure to inform them about the recent murder in the inn. They'd known someone had died, but they hadn't realized the murder had taken place at the inn. It didn't seem to bother them too much. They were relieved the situation today had turned out in the fashion it had. They had thoroughly enjoyed their stay, and would be recommending our establishment to family and friends, and would no doubt be back again for future family events.

I fell asleep watching TV with my head on Stone's lap. The next thing I knew I was waking up to a bright, sunny day. The snow had all melted, and the sun was warming the air up. It looked promising for a beautiful autumn day. It was after eight, and Stone had fed the Dudleys cold cereal and toast. They were now packing up and getting ready to head home to Oregon.

I got dressed and came down to the kitchen for my first cup of coffee, just before Wyatt popped in the back door of the inn. He sat down at the kitchen island next to Stone. I poured him a cup of coffee, and offered him a tray of pastries. He selected a cinnamon roll and then asked me how I was doing.

"I feel fine today, Wyatt. I got a good night's sleep and my heart rate has finally gone back down to normal," I said. "Thank you for reacting to my phone call yesterday in the manner you did. Your quick wits probably saved my life."

"You're welcome. I'm glad you called when you did, and that you were smart enough to kick out the taillight in the Lincoln yesterday. We teach that in a self-defense class we give periodically at the college," Wyatt said. "Of course, having your arms and legs tied up made it more difficult for you, but thank God you found a way. You know, Lexie, with your impulsive nature, it wouldn't hurt you to enroll in the course the next time we offer it."

"After the events of yesterday, I'll certainly consider it. What did you find out in the interrogation of Jeffrey Hobbs?" I asked.

"Once he was backed into a corner, he admitted he killed Walter. He also owned up to ramming you with his car in the hospital parking lot. He had followed you there."

"Did he say why he killed Walter?" Stone asked.

"He knew Walter had asked his daughter to marry him, and Hobbs was dead set against it," Wyatt said. "Jeffrey was sure

Sidney would eventually agree to marry Walter. After all, they'd been together for the greater part of three years. Both he and his wife had tried to talk her out of the marriage, but she kept telling them she was old enough now to marry anyone she wanted to marry, and they couldn't stop her. He said he didn't have anything against Walter personally, but he was determined to see his only daughter married to someone who could provide well for her and their children. He didn't see how a man, working as a teacher, or worse yet, a missionary, could provide a very stable future for Sidney and her offspring. Jeffrey and his wife both also feared their daughter would marry Walter and move to Albuquerque with him so Walter could take over his father's heating and cooling business. To them, this was an even worse scenario, to be so far from their only daughter and future grandchildren."

"But killing Walter to prevent such a scenario? That seems awfully mercenary to me," I said. "I can't imagine anyone wanting their child to marry for money, as opposed to marrying for love."

"Mr. Hobbs also admitted to stalking you. For some reason, he thought your name was Rhonda Reed. He recognized your Jeep from seeing you in it in the college parking lot last Saturday, at the cheerleading practice," Wyatt said. "Why were you at cheerleading practice?"

Both Wyatt and Stone looked at me with questioning expressions. I merely shrugged.

"Jeffrey is an endocrinologist in St. Joseph," Wyatt continued. "He has a private practice there. That's why he knows about insulin and hypoglycemic coma, and also why he has access to insulin. He makes good money for his family, and they live in the upper-crust part of town here in Rockdale, in the new Walnut Ridge Estates subdivision."

"So Jeffrey—Dr. Hobbs, I should say—wanted his daughter

to marry a doctor like him?" I asked.

"Or a surgeon, a lawyer, or even the CEO of a large firm. He just wanted Sidney to be able to continue to live in the manner she was accustomed to," Wyatt said. "He said he felt desperate, knowing Sidney was in love with Walter, and not knowing how he could legally prevent her from marrying him. His biggest fear, he said, was that they'd run off and elope. He felt he had to do whatever he could to prevent Sidney from marrying Walter. He couldn't stand the thought of a common man in a blue-collar job being his son-in-law. The only certain way he could come up with to get rid of Walter was to kill him, in order to assure marriage to him was no longer an option for his daughter."

"I guess he accomplished his goal," I said. "Sidney will never marry Walter now. Instead she'll see her father spend the rest of his life in prison, and know it was he who killed the love of her life. What a sad story. She'll really be devastated now. She's lost both her boyfriend and her father. I assume she knew nothing about her dad killing Walter, did she?" I asked.

"Oh, no, and neither did his wife. She was as flabbergasted as Sidney was when the detectives went over to inform them of Jeffrey's arrest," Wyatt replied. "What a shame. It's so awful for the two of them."

"Yeah, it's such a shame," Stone said. "And Walter seemed like such a nice and thoughtful young man. I would have been proud to call him my son-in-law."

"He was a young man who wanted to spend his life helping others," I added. "I don't think he cared at all about having a lot of material things, and I seriously doubt Sidney did either, or she wouldn't have fallen in love with a man of his convictions."

"Speaking of helping others and getting married, Lexie, have you considered my suggestion from the other day?" Stone asked.

I didn't know if he was proposing marriage, or just asking me to move in with him full-time at the inn, but either way, I told him I would be thrilled to make the Alexandria Inn my new home. I could no longer imagine my life without Stone in it. I would put my house in Shawnee on the market in the near future and begin selling and/or transferring all my belongings. I knew Wendy would also be relieved to see me become a permanent resident at the Alexandria Inn.

"Oh, well, it's about time. I'm thrilled for the two of you," Wyatt said. "And, Lexie, I probably don't even have to tell you this, but a newspaper reporter was interviewing the chief when I left the police station yesterday, and your name will be all over the front page of the *Rockdale Gazette,* and probably multiple other newspapers tomorrow morning. Kind of like it was last year after you helped solve the murder case involving Veronica's father."

"I was afraid of that," I said.

"Me too," Stone agreed. "But something tells me it is something I better get used to."

RECIPES

FRIGHTENING FINGERS AND BLOOD

2 cups brain matter (or substitute with shredded white cheddar
   cheese at room temperature)
1/2 cup butter (room temperature)
1 1/2 cups all-purpose flour
1 teaspoon salt
1/4 teaspoon cayenne pepper (can use more if you want spicier)
1 jar of purchased salsa or roasted red pepper dip

Preheat the oven to 325 degrees F.

Pulse in your food processor butter, cheese, flour, salt, and
cayenne until it comes together and forms a soft dough. Remove
the dough from the food processor and put in the refrigerator
for about 30 minutes. Once removed from the refrigerator,
scoop out mixture with a medium cookie scoop or a couple of
tablespoons. Take each scoop and hand roll into the shape of a
finger and make sure to use a fork to lightly score the knuckles.
Bake for approximately 10 to 12 minutes or until lightly brown.
If any of the fingers break they are still yummy finger pieces so
don't waste them. Cool and enjoy. Tray these fingers with a big
bowl of salsa or roasted red pepper dip (blood) in the center of
the tray for dipping.

RED-DEVILED EYE OF NEWT

1 dozen eyes of newt (or substitute with hard-boiled, shelled eggs)
1/2 cup mayonnaise
1 tablespoon relish
1/4 teaspoon salt
2 tablespoons sweet pickle juice
Small jar green olives with pimentos
1 tablespoon red food coloring
1 cup white vinegar
1/2 cup warm water

Slice eggs in half so that that each egg piece is round and not oval. Scoop out the yellow to mix in a separate bowl and flake the yoke with a fork and add in the mayo, relish, salt, and pickle juice. Stir and refrigerate mixture until the eggs are ready to fill.

To dye the egg whites, first cut a small piece of the rounded bottom of each egg to make a flat part so the egg will sit flat and not roll. Next mix 1 cup vinegar, 1 tablespoon red food coloring, and 1/2 cup warm water, and pour in a shallow pie plate. Place egg halves down into the mixture with the flat base side of the eggs not getting in the dye if you can help it. Let this sit for about 10 minutes and then using gloves, take the red egg eyes out of the mixture and dry right side up resting the flat base side on paper towels until ready to fill.

Using a pastry bag, fill each red egg side with the chilled eye mixture and top each egg with a green olive with pimento pushed slightly inside the filling for stability.

Chill until ready to serve.

CHOCOLATE TARANTULA SPIDERS

1 (6-ounce) package dark chocolate chips or semisweet chocolate chips

1/4 cup Red Hots (or other small red candies for the eyes)
2 cups hair of the dog (or substitute with crispy chow mein noodles)

Place the chocolate chips in a glass bowl and melt in the microwave on high for approximately 1 minute. Stir and melt more if the chocolate isn't smooth. Then add in the chow mein noodles until they are all coated, being careful not to crush the noodles.

Drop heaping tablespoons of the mixture onto rolled-out waxed paper into small mounds. Leave a few noodles in the bowl for the legs. Next add these noodles with your fingers to create spider legs off the sides of each mound. Press in the Red Hot candies or other red candies to create eyes.

Refrigerate for 20 to 30 minutes and enjoy.

BLEEDING HEART FUDGE

1 cup sugar
2/3 cup (5-ounce can) evaporated milk
2 tablespoons butter
1/2 teaspoon salt
2 cups miniature marshmallows
1 package cinnamon baking chips (10 ounces)
1 bag cinnamon imperial candy (9 ounces)
1/2 teaspoon warlock blood or cinnamon oil
1 teaspoon vanilla extract

Line an 8-inch square baking pan with waxed paper. Combine sugar, evaporated milk, all but 1/4 cup of cinnamon imperials, butter, and salt in medium, heavy-duty saucepan. Bring to a full rolling boil over medium heat, stirring constantly until cinnamon imperials are melted and mixture is smooth.

Stir in cinnamon chips, vanilla, cinnamon oil, and marshmallows and mix thoroughly. Pour into prepared baking pan and sprinkle with remaining 1/4 cup of cinnamon imperials. Refrigerate for 2 hours or until firm. Lift from pan and remove wax paper. Cut into pieces.

ABOUT THE AUTHOR

Jeanne Glidewell, and her husband, Robert, live in the small town of Bonner Springs, Kansas. Besides writing, Jeanne also enjoys fishing, traveling, and wildlife photography. As a 2006 pancreas and kidney transplant recipient, Jeanne volunteers as a mentor for the Gift of Life program in Kansas City, mentoring future transplant recipients as a way of giving back. Promoting organ donation is an important endeavor for her.

Jeanne's had many magazine articles published, as well as the romance/suspense novel, *Soul Survivor,* and the first two novels in the Lexie Starr series, *Leave No Stone Unturned* and *The Extinguished Guest.* Jeanne is a member of Sisters-in-Crime and Mystery Writers of America and is currently writing the fifth book of the series. You can contact her through her website, http://www.jeanneglidewell.com.